BEYOND THE PAST

Jo Huddleston

Book #2 in the Caney Creek Series

ISBN 13: 978-1-9392191-1-4

Published by Sword of the Spirit Publishing
www.swordofspirit.net

DEDICATION

To the memory of my cousin, an avid reader.

ACKNOWLEDGMENTS

Thanks go to

My publisher and editor, Donald J. Parker, who saw merit in this series and, with his writing expertise, made it better. I thank him for his patience with me throughout this publishing process.
Members of American Christian Fiction Writers for their support, especially Ane, Bonnie, and Jim, for allowing me to ask my questions to which they responded.
Those who gave their endorsement and support of this novel.
My ancestors who told me their beautiful stories.
My family's support.

Questions for Reflection and Discussion
For individual or group use
Beyond the Past by Jo Huddleston
Please see Jo's website, www.johuddleston.com

Praise for *That Summer*
Book #1 in The Caney Creek Series

"Sweeping from the early days of the Great Depression to the 1950s, Jo Huddleston's debut novel is a memorable story of the heartbreak and happiness one man encounters as he struggles to find the true meaning of faith and family."
AMANDA CABOT, author of *Waiting for Spring*

"As surely as Caney Creek runs through the town, the story of *That Summer* swept me back to the pre-depression era, a time of hope and opportunity. Following Jim's ambitions, this book examines the effects of following self versus following God and the sometimes maddening, sometimes inspiring results."
CHRISTINA BERRY, award-winning author of *The Familiar Stranger*

"A compelling and poignant tale with characters destined to capture your heart."
LAURIE ALICE EAKES, author of *Choices of the Heart*

"That Summer is a wonderful romance set in the Southern Appalachians during the Great Depression. Jo Huddleston understands the people of that time and place so well she pulled me right into the story and didn't let me go until the end. Highly recommended!"
CARA LYNN JAMES, author of *Love on a Dime* and *A Path Toward Love*

~ ~ ~

"Casting all your care upon him,
for he careth for you."
1 Peter 5:7

Chapter 1

January 1, 1951
Atlanta, Georgia

Emmajean bolted upright in bed, her heart hammering against her chest, and eyes searching the darkness. What had awakened her? She glanced at the clock. Two o'clock in the morning. She'd only been in bed a scant thirty minutes. She had worked with Barry till after the New Year's Eve celebrations settled down.

She eased aside the shade at her bedside window that overlooked the street to see what awoke her. Three cars parked beneath the street light and four men huddled on the sidewalk. Two of the cars were police cars, one was not. Two of the men wore uniforms, the other two had on suits. They approached the house and hurried to get up the steps to the front porch. When they knocked on the door, Emmajean scrambled from her tangled covers, searching for her house slippers. She jerked her housecoat from across the foot of the bed and pushed her arms into it. As she cinched the belt around her waist, she stepped across the room and opened her bedroom door. At the same moment, Barry opened his bedroom door directly across the living room from hers, buckling the belt in his pants. When he saw Emmajean he put a finger against his lips and motioned with his other hand, palm forward, for her not to come out of her room.

Another knock came through the door and a gravelly voice said, "Open up. Atlanta police."

Barry went toward the door, again motioning for Emmajean to stay put. He opened the door a small crack and backed up as the four men pushed through.

An overweight man in a brown suit stained with mustard looked at Barry. "Are you Barry Wagner?" Then he swung his gaze toward Emmajean, still standing in her doorway. She saw his degrading smile and tugged the cotton housecoat closer beneath her neck.

"Yeah, I'm Barry."

"Is that your car parked in the driveway?"

"Yeah. What are you doing here?"

The man exchanged glances with his partner who smirked toward Barry. Brown Suit turned his attention to Emmajean. He unbuttoned his suit coat, which strained against his girth. "Young lady, are you Emmajean Callaway?"

Wondering how he knew her name, she answered, "Yes, sir."

The heavy man walked farther into the room and motioned for Barry to sit on the sofa. The two men took chairs across from the sofa. The uniformed policemen stood near the door.

The designated speaker for the men cleared his smoker's throat. "I'm Detective Hamilton. We have a few questions for you. Where were you this evening for the last three hours?"

"Right here. Both of us."

"Is that right, Miss? Were you here all evening with this man?"

Emmajean knew they had not been home all evening, but Barry gave her a slight nod of his head. "Yes, sir."

"Come on out here and join us." Hamilton waved Emmajean to the sofa.

Emmajean eased across the living room and settled next to Barry on the lumpy sofa. What was going on? Were they in some kind of trouble?

"What are you doing here?" Sweat dotted across Barry's brow. "You must be at the wrong house."

"Nah, we're not at the wrong house. We have witnesses who say you've not been home this evening. They say you were seen in your car north of town at a drive-in, and this pretty little redhead here went to different cars delivering some kind of goods."

"Now you leave her out of this."

"Out of what?"

Barry fell silent.

The detective pulled some papers from his inside coat pocket, snapped them open, and held it up for Barry and Emmajean to see. "This here's a search warrant. We've been watching you two for a while and we have cause to take a look around." His degrading sneer spread across his face. "Okay, boys. Get started. I doubt there's anything in the little lady's room, but look everywhere."

When one of the officers started toward Barry's bedroom, Barry jumped up from the sofa.

Detective Hamilton rose and moved in front of Barry. "I think you'd better just have a seat there. You can get up when we're finished looking around."

It didn't take the policemen long. "Looky here." One of them came out of Barry's bedroom holding up a small brown paper bag opened at the top resting on the palm of his hand. He carried several more bags bunched in his other arm and hand. The detective met the officer and peered into the bag.

"What do we have here?" The other detective joined him, reaching into the bag, checking its contents.

"And there's plenty more in the bedroom, sir."

"Okay, you two, let's go. Both of you get yourself dressed. We're going downtown."

"You can't take us anywhere."

"Oh, but I can, Mr. Wagner. You're under arrest for possession of and selling of a controlled substance. You know, drugs. Marijuana." He turned to the other detective and said, "Hank, read them their rights."

Turning to the two officers, Hamilton said, "Gather all that stuff up, and let's get it all to the station."

"No. You can't take any of my things."

"Well, yes, Barry, we can and we are. Now, get yourself and your little lady ready to go."

Emmajean had remained dumbfounded throughout the entire questioning. Why was Barry carrying on so? Why did the detective think they had any illegal drugs and what did that mean, anyway? When the two suits motioned her toward her bedroom, she complied and shut the door behind her.

She wondered how she could get out of this. She didn't want to go to the police station. What if her family found out? She whipped her gown off. After she donned her bra she stutter-stepped and yanked on a pair of blue jeans, pulled a Georgia Tech T shirt over her head and slid into a pair of Keds. She grabbed her purse from the chest and eased over to the window. She raised it inch by inch.

~ ~ ~

Barry returned to the living room from his bedroom. He had on a white T shirt, shoes, and held his jacket across one shoulder. He shifted his feet, waiting with the other four men for several minutes, all of them somewhat nervous in each other's company.

Detective Hamilton finally approached Emmajean's bedroom door and knocked lightly. When she didn't answer, he knocked more forcefully.

"Miss, are you ready? It's time we got going."

Barry wondered what Emmajean was trying to pull. She had ways of outsmarting folks. When she still didn't answer, Barry watched the detective as he motioned toward one of the officers. "Go outside and check that window on the front of the house. We don't want her slipping off."

Barry hoped she had left. He didn't mean for her to get involved with the police.

~ ~ ~

Emmajean raised the window just enough so she could slip through and drop to the ground, which was only a few feet below. Angela was right: she was too skinny. But that served her purpose tonight. She threw her purse out first and heard it splat on the ground. Hanging onto the window sill with both hands, she backed out as quickly as she could. With her six foot body suspended, she turned loose her grip on the window sill and dropped the remaining short distance to the ground.

"Going somewhere, Miss?"

She whirled around to find a policeman just behind her. He seized her upper arm as if with a vise and pulled her toward the front porch.

"Hey, what are you doin'? Let me get my pocketbook."

He kept his hold on her arm as she bent down and retrieved her purse. The officer led her to the front porch and hollered, "I got her, sir."

When the men came outside, they carried five large plastic trash bags. The police had handcuffed Barry's hands behind his back. He looked at the ground as they led him to one of the police cars. The policeman who held Emmajean's arm steered her toward the other police car, stuffed her into the back seat and shut the door.

Emmajean perched on the edge of the back seat. "Where are you takin' me? You can't just take me away from my house."

When the officer didn't respond, Emmajean tried to get his attention again. "Hey, talk to me. Where are we goin'? I want to go back to my house."

Finally, Emmajean gave up trying to engage the officer in conversation and slid back in the seat. That's when her tears began to track down her cheeks. Since she had left Newton after graduating from high school, nothing had gone right for her. Nothing. She came to Atlanta to get into the fashion world. That didn't work out, so she got a job at Mr. Baker's diner and moved into an apartment with Angela. She'd met Barry at the diner and soon began working for him delivering packages to guys who met them at a drive-in restaurant. She didn't know the packages held illegal drugs. She really didn't know. She had already realized she was country-come-to-town but was too proud to admit her failures and slink back to Newton. Now look at her!

Hustled into the police station, Emmajean looked up at the big round clock on the wall that said three o'clock. Three o'clock in the morning, and here she was in the downtown Atlanta police station.

The police fingerprinted Barry and Emmajean. Another officer took their pictures and booked them. Now an hour or so later, where was Barry? She hadn't seen him since they'd been fingerprinted. She sat alone in a small dingy room with only a metal table and two folding chairs. The wooden door swung open, banging into the wall. Detective Hamilton came in and stood across the table from her.

"Now, Miss, I want some answers and I want them straight. What were you doing with Barry Wagner earlier tonight?"

Emmajean didn't answer. She knew trouble when she saw it, and she was not going to volunteer any information. "I want my one telephone call." She had watched television since she'd arrived in Atlanta. She knew they had to give her one telephone call.

"Miss, I said I want some answers." He took a few steps toward her. "We've got your friend in another room. He's already spilled the beans, and now we want to hear your side."

She hesitated. Had Barry already told them what they were doing north of town tonight? Would Barry betray her, or was the detective lying to her, trying to trick her? She decided that surely the detective wouldn't lie to her. The police people were supposed to be folks you could trust. "We met some boys at the Dixie drive-in on the north side of town. Barry gave me small paper bags turned down at the top and told me which car to take them to. He said not to look inside, or I might be embarrassed. He said just deliver the paper bags and bring back the money they would give me."

"You never looked inside the bags?"

"No. Since Barry told me not to look I figured there must be man-stuff inside and I didn't want to pry into his business."

"You really didn't look in the bags?" He finally sat in the chair across from Emmajean. "You trying to tell me you didn't know what you were delivering?"

"That's right, I didn't."

"Are you that stupid? Your friend must not care much for you, asking you to help him deliver drugs." He ran his fingers through his thinning hair. "Where're you from?"

"Newton. That's north of Chattanooga."

"I know where it is. That explains it. You're not a city girl. You're a country girl."

"Well, yeah, we had a small farm. We didn't live in town." That fact embarrassed Emmajean. She had come to Atlanta to leave her humble lifestyle behind. She'd sure done a great job of getting a new lifestyle! She looked at the clock on the wall of the little room. Eight o'clock. They'd been there the rest of the night. "You have to let me use the telephone."

Hamilton asked her a few other questions but she fell silent. As he left the room, Emmajean shouted at his back, "Give me my telephone call."

A short while later a female clerk stepped into the room. "Okay, honey, you can make your telephone call. Follow me. When you're finished, off you go to a cell."

Emmajean stood at the telephone on the wall in the hall and had difficulty dialing the operator with shaking hands. Finally she placed her call—person to person, collect.

Jim looked up when he heard one tap on his office door. Peggy, his secretary, came in. "You have a collect call from someone calling herself Emmajean. Do you want to accept the call?"

"Yes! Put her on, please."

The intercom buzzed. Jim jabbed the button. "Yes?"

"I have Emmajean on the telephone."

"Thank you, Peggy."

Jim stabbed a button on the telephone. "Emmajean! What's wrong? Are you okay? Talk to me."

From the other end of the line he heard Emmajean's sobbing.

"Emmajean. I can tell something's wrong. Now, tell me about it."

"Jim, I'm in jail." More sobbing.

"Where are you? What have you done?"

She repeated her words. "Jim, I'm in jail. I need help. Can you please help me?"

"Yes, Emmajean, anything. Tell me what's going on."

While Emmajean told her story in chunks separated by crying, his brain ran about two steps ahead, thinking what in the world he could do. Emmajean was in Atlanta, and he was here in Newton. How could he help her?

"Emmajean, you hold on. I'll be there in a few hours. Listen to me. Stop crying, and listen to me! Don't say another word to anybody there. Nobody. Don't sign anything. Not anything. If I can get a lawyer to you before I get there, you can talk to him and no one else. Hear me?"

Emmajean swallowed so loud Jim could hear her over the telephone. "Yes, I hear you. Please hurry. I'm scared. But I won't say anythin' else."

"Tell me where you are."

Jim could hear his sister asking someone where she was. "I'm at Atlanta Precinct #312. Right down in the city."

"Can you hang on there a few hours?"

"Yes."

Jim could hear the doubt in her voice. "I'll see you in a while."

~ ~ ~

Jim no sooner cradled the telephone when he picked it up again and buzzed Peggy. "Get me the law offices of Chip Rawlings. And please do it now."

He tapped his pen on his desk and waited with his other hand on the telephone. What a way to start a Monday morning. As soon as Peggy buzzed him, he got on the telephone again.

"Hello. Chip?"

"No, sir. This is his receptionist. How can I help you?"

"This is Jim Callaway. I'd like to speak to him, please."

"Mr. Callaway, I'm sorry, Mr. Rawlings is in Chattanooga today on a case. He'll probably be there a few days. Can someone else help you?"

"Yes. Let me speak to his partner, please."

"Wait one moment, please, and I'll connect you with Mr. Claude Walton."

When Mr. Walton answered his telephone, Jim identified himself again.

"What can I do for you, Mr. Callaway?"

"Well, I wanted Mr. Rawlings to help me with something in Atlanta. My sister is being held there and I want to get someone to her as soon as I can."

"Mr. Callaway, none of us here can do law work in the state of Georgia. We can be present at an arraignment, but we can't actively take any part in it."

"Oh." Jim heard the defeat in his own voice.

"However, I know a lawyer down there we've used before. I could put in a call to him and ask him to visit your sister. His name is Bertrand Cox. Would that be okay with you?"

"Yes, it would."

"Fine. Now tell me where your sister is and her full name."

"Atlanta Police Precinct #312. Emmajean Callaway. But one more question. Do you have a lawyer in your office that could go down to Atlanta with me? I realize he can't do anything on the case, but I'd feel more comfortable with someone local down there overseeing things."

"Well, yes, I believe I can send one of our young lawyers with you. But don't be telling the folks down there that he is *overseeing* the case. That wouldn't go over too big. Let's see, we could let Terry Fields go with you."

"Fine. That's fine, Mr. Walton. Can he go today, right now?"

"Yes, I believe so."

"Please tell him I'll pick him up in a few minutes. You've been a great help. Thank you."

When Jim tried to put some papers into order on his desk, he reached again for the telephone. "Peggy, please get me the residence of Caroline Hensen in Knoxville, Tennessee." While he waited for the call to go through, Jim continued to move some things on his desk until Peggy buzzed him.

"Caroline, it's Jim. You okay today?"

He waited for her to finish some small talk. "Caroline, I wanted you to know I have to go down to Atlanta immediately. It's Emmajean. She just called me, frantic and crying. She's in some kind of trouble with the Atlanta police, along with a guy she must have been seeing. I don't know how long I'll be down there."

He nodded as he listened to her reply. "I've got to run. I'll call you when I get back. Bye."

On his way out of the office, he asked Peggy to please get word to his Chief Financial Officer Bob Allbright and tell him about Jim leaving. "I'll be in Atlanta to help my baby sister with something. For anything that comes up you can't handle, just talk to Bob. I'm thinking I'll be gone for a couple of days. I'll check in with you a time or two."

~ ~ ~

When Jim arrived at the lawyer's office, Terry Fields was waiting on him. "Mr. Fields, you probably should take a few clothes with you, maybe for two or three days."

Fields agreed. Jim took him to his apartment and then went home to grab a few things for himself.

They finally got on the road toward Atlanta. "Mr. Fields, thanks for coming with me. Mr. Walton told me you couldn't actually work on a case in Georgia, but I'm glad you'll be around."

"Sure, glad to help anyway I can. But please call me Terry."

"Sure. How long you been a lawyer?"

"I passed the bar four years ago soon after I finished law school at UT and been with this firm since then. I've been in several cases with the partners already, and I've learned a lot."

"Have you ever been in on a case involving drugs?"

Terry looked at Jim with questioning eyes.

For the next several miles as he drove, Jim explained what he knew of Emmajean's problem with the Atlanta police. "That's all I know, and that's not much. I told her not to talk to them or sign anything until the other lawyer or I got there."

"You gave her good advice."

"I just hope she follows it. She's scared."

"Being scared is natural even if you've just been pulled over for speeding."

~ ~ ~

Precinct #312 was certainly in the middle of Atlanta. Jim left his car in the closest parking lot he could find to the precinct. Their destination was one of many brick buildings crammed into small spaces.

The female at the front desk of the precinct didn't look especially friendly as Jim stepped up to speak to her. "I'm looking for Emmajean Callaway, please."

"She's with her lawyer now."

Jim looked at Terry who stepped to the counter. "We're part of her lawyer's team. We'd like to join them." He handed her his card. Jim didn't hesitate to hand her one of his cards.

The lady locked eyes with Jim. "You're no lawyer."

"No, ma'am. I'm her brother."

She kept their cards. "I'll be right back."

A few moments later the female reappeared, her countenance and body ramrod straight. "Follow me."

Jim and Terry fell in behind her and followed her to the far end of a long narrow hall. She stopped at the last door on the left, knocked once, and opened the door. Stepping aside she motioned them to enter the room. After one step inside, all Jim saw was a blur of motion speeding toward him.

Emmajean wrapped her arms around Jim's neck and sobbed onto his chest.

"There, there. Hang on, Emmajean. I'm here. I'm right here with you."

Her sobs shook her body for a few minutes until they subsided. Jim pushed her away and held her shoulders. "You going to be okay?"

Doubt shone in her eyes. "I'll be okay now that you're here. I'm sure glad to see you."

Bertrand Cox, the Atlanta lawyer, introduced himself and Jim and Terry did the same, exchanging business cards. Jim explained Terry's presence. A deep frown showed on Cox's face upon hearing of the young lawyer's involvement in the case.

"Mr. Cox, I'm only here as a support for Mr. Callaway. He wanted somebody from home to be with him. I assure you I will only observe. I won't move in on your case."

Cox looked Terry up and down before finally speaking. "I've been talking with Emmajean. It seems she unknowingly has gotten herself into a little mess." He told Jim and Terry the story as Emmajean had told him.

Jim waited for the lawyer to say more, but he didn't. "Mr. Cox, can you help her?"

"That's what I'm here for."

"Please give us a straight answer. Even Emmajean needs to know exactly where things stand."

Mr. Cox pushed back his chair and rose from the beat-up metal table. He paced the tiny windowless room before coming back to the table. "I've handled many cases involving drugs. I've usually won them. Now Emmajean's case here is a little different. She was a party to the drug selling, but had no knowledge that she was. That's the wrinkle in the case."

"You mean you can't be my sister's lawyer in this because she was innocent of what she was doing?"

Terry attentively stood to the side, not saying anything. Jim looked at him, and when he didn't speak, Jim remembered Terry was only supposed to be an observer. They would have to wait until they were away from the Atlanta lawyer before they could discuss any of this.

Mr. Cox returned to his chair facing Emmajean. "Yes, I think I can help your sister. I'm ready to give it a shot. That is, if you want to retain me."

"Yes, I do. Mr. Walton recommended you, and that's enough for me. What are you going to do? What's next?"

"First, there'll be a preliminary arraignment. It's scheduled for Thursday morning. At that time, I will plead the court for bond and release of your sister. The case will then be presented before a grand jury, but I don't have information on when that will be. With the charges what they are, I'm sure the grand jury will decide that the case needs to be bound over to a jury trial. A judge will set a date for trial to begin."

"Okay, she gets out on bond. What's next?"

"Emmajean must stay in the state, preferably in Atlanta."

"Will she be free to get out and about? Maybe get a job?"

"Yes, she will." Mr. Cox turned toward Emmajean. "But during that time, young lady, you must not get involved in any criminal activity whatsoever. Not even a parking ticket. Do you understand that?"

"Yes, sir." She shot a miserable glance toward Jim.

"Well, that about does it for now, y'all. I'll start right away working on Emmajean's defense. Are you boys going to stay or head back home?"

"We'll stay a while. May I telephone you if I have questions?"

Mr. Cox started toward the door. "Yes. Yes. You have my card there. Anytime."

As he disappeared through the door, Jim handed Emmajean his business card. "Emmajean, here's my card. You call me anytime. Collect. I wrote my home telephone number on the back side." He grabbed her in a bear hug, and she held on to him until the female warden came to take Emmajean to her cell.

~ ~ ~

"It tore me up to see them take Emmajean to a cell." Still in Atlanta, Jim and Terry had just finished supper.

"I'm sorry, Jim. We can probably see her again tomorrow. I feel certain that bail will be set at the arraignment on Thursday."

"Two more days in jail! For something she didn't know she was doing."

"That's right, Jim. But if I was Mr. Cox, I'd figure out a defense of Emmajean based on her not having knowledge of conducting a sale of illegal drugs. And even at that, she was just aiding her friend Barry."

"Some friend! I'm glad he didn't get her hooked on the drugs." They rose to leave. "Let's go get some rooms, stay the night and maybe go back to Newton sometime tomorrow. Then come back down here early Thursday morning. That okay with you?"

~ ~ ~

When Jim and Arthur met for lunch in Newton on Wednesday, Jim filled in his best friend on his trip to Atlanta. "Bones, I'm afraid for her. Down there in the jail cell. She was pretty shaky even when we were with her. I hate thinking about what kind of shape she's in all alone now."

"Jim, you still call me that nickname you've used since we were kids."

"Yeah, Bones, and you still look like a bunch of gawky bones walking around."

"Anyway, Jim, your sister has always been a feisty, determined kid. She'll do what she has to. You need to calm yourself down."

"Yeah, you're right. Everything going okay with you and the family?"

"Well, as a matter of fact, maybe not. That boy of ours is really pushin' his limits. He's messin' up in school. If he doesn't straighten up, he might not graduate with his class in June."

"What's happening?"

"We all know he's never liked school. He skips classes and sometimes a whole day. The school telephones so often you'd think they were our best friends. When he's not at school, we can't figure out where he is and he won't tell us."

"Has he still got that old car of yours?"

"Yeah, and with it he could be anywhere."

"How are his grades? I guess they're not too good."

"You got that right. Jim, I'm as scared for Art as you are for Emmajean. And his mother worries all the time about him."

"How is Callie?"

"Like I said, she worries a lot. Thank heavens, our girl is doin' well in school."

Jim studied his friend's face. Something else was bothering him. "Bones, what else are you not telling me?"

"Jim, I think Art is runnin' with some boys who're doin' some drinkin'. You know how that is, Art's liable to be drinkin' too."

"I sure hope he's not drinking and driving. If he got stopped for that he'd probably be in a jail cell like Emmajean."

~ ~ ~

Thursday morning at ten o'clock Judge Orr's gavel struck the block, sending an echo through the almost empty chambers.

The bailiff read the charges. "Case #176, Barry Wagner is charged with possession with intent to sell an illegal substance, a Class B felony and Emmajean Callaway is charged with aiding the act of possession with intent to sell an illegal substance, a misdemeanor." The judge gave a slight nod and the bailiff took a seat.

"Do the parties have legal representation present?

Mr. Cox and Barry's lawyer both stood. "Yes, Your Honor, they do."

"Is the prosecution present and ready to go?"

An assistant district attorney seated at a table to the right stood. "Yes, Your Honor." Then he sat.

"Very well, let's get this arraignment underway, gentlemen."

Mr. Cox rose. "Your Honor, I request bond be set for my client on her personal recognizance. Her release will not pose a real and present danger to others or to the public at large. The defendant has no prior criminal record. The charges against my client are aiding in the criminal act. The 8th Amendment to the United States Constitution provides, 'Excessive bails shall not be required nor excessive fines imposed, nor cruel and unusual punishments inflicted.'"

"Yes, I know what the 8th Amendment says." The judge growled and rubbed his chin, glaring at Emmajean. The prosecution didn't voice any objection to bonding out the female defendant.

"Bond set at $5,000." Judge Orr pounded his gavel on the block. "Mr. Cox you and your client may leave the courtroom."

After Jim paid the bond, the four of them left and pushed through the front doors of the courthouse. "Mr. Callaway, I'll keep you up to date. When the grand jury convenes and their verdict. If a jury trial is set, I'll let you know." He trotted down the courthouse steps and turned left.

Jim held Emmajean's elbow as they descended the front steps. Terry walked on the other side of Emmajean, taking in her every move.

"Let's get you checked into your room at the YWCA." Jim pointed to the right. "It's just down the street."

"Jim, you've already got me a place to live?" She turned to Terry. "See what a good big brother I have?"

He returned her smile. "I guess that's what big brothers are for."

"Jim, can you take me to Barry's house to get my things there?"

"No. You'll not have any more associations of any kind with Barry. Remember that. The folks that run the YWCA will watch out for your needs. You can have your meals at their cafeteria, and they have recreation and things. After we get you checked in, we're going shopping for any new things you want. Terry, you're going too aren't you?"

"Yeah. Sure. I like to watch people spend money. You'd better watch your billfold, Jim. This pretty girl looks like shopping excites her."

Emmajean smiled. "It does, it does. Let's hurry to the YWCA and then go shopping at Rich's."

After shopping, the guys were worn out, but Emmajean remained fresh and wanted to continue. "Emmajean, let's call it quits for today and go get some supper." Jim motioned her toward the sales clerk behind the counter.

Emmajean dumped all the garments she had selected onto the counter top. "Okay, Jim. This was a lot of fun." Then she sobered. "Big brother, thank you for takin' care of me today and for all these clothes. I didn't have anythin' but the clothes on my back, and you took care of me, again." She looped her arm through his as he paid for the garments, and the clerk placed them in a large sack.

Emmajean, reached to pick up the sack.

"Here, I'll get that for you."

She turned and saw that Terry had volunteered to carry her things. She took a good look at him and decided that he was cute. She loved his smile. She'd been so torn up and busy all day she hadn't paid much attention to him. "Sure, thanks, Terry."

After they returned to Emmajean's room with all her shopping bags, she spread the clothes one by one across her bed. "We did some shopping, didn't we?"

"Looks like it. If you need other things, write them down, and when I come back, we'll go shopping again."

"Jim, that's so sweet of you."

Jim exchanged a look with Terry. Jim knew what Terry had planned to do before they left Emmajean. "I'll be in the lobby, ready to go when you are, Terry."

He hugged his sister before leaving the room.

After Jim left, Emmajean shot a wary look toward Terry. "What's going on?"

Terry stepped toward the bed and laid his briefcase on it. He opened it and withdrew a package wrapped in brown paper and tied with twine. He turned toward Emmajean. "Jim knew what I planned to do. That's why he went on to the lobby. I wanted to give you this."

Puzzled, Emmajean took the package from his outstretched hand.

"What?"

"It's for you."

She pulled the twine, and it slipped away as the brown paper unfolded to reveal a Bible. It was a well-worn black Bible. She looked into Terry's brown eyes for an answer.

"This was my grandmother's Bible. Mother gave it to me a long time ago. I noticed you didn't have a Bible. I want you to have this one."

"Why?" Emmajean spoke in her no-nonsense, straightforward way.

"You didn't have one. Now you do. I thought you might like to have it."

"But it belonged to your grandmother."

"Yes, it did." He closed his briefcase. "Now it belongs to you. I hope you enjoy your time spent reading it. Maybe it will help you not to be lonely down here all by yourself."

"You're right, Terry." She started to step toward him but then changed her mind and stood still.

"I'd better get on out to the lobby. Jim will wonder what happened to me." He leaned toward Emmajean and placed a light kiss on her cheek. "I'll see you again before long."

After Terry had left the room, she closed the door and leaned back against it. Nobody outside her family had ever been kind to her. She clutched the Bible to her chest and smiled.

Chapter 2

Caroline Hensen lifted two paper grocery sacks from the back seat of her shiny new black Plymouth. She pushed the car door shut with one swing of her hip and started across the yard on the brick-laid sidewalk. She hitched the grocery sacks a little higher, climbed the steps and crossed the deep porch to the double doors. She set one bag of groceries on the porch swing. Using the key, which Jim has insisted she take, Caroline let herself into the Federal-style house. She retrieved the bag from the swing and made her way to the kitchen, pushing the front door shut with her foot. Her footsteps on the hallway floor echoed through the downstairs.

She set the groceries on the counter and dropped her pocketbook and keys beside them. After she draped her long coat across a dinette chair, Caroline raised the two small windows above the sink just a bit to help dissolve the mustiness of the little-used room. She looked out across the backyard and saw Caney Creek flowing on the back boundary of all properties on this east side of Newton. Snow still clung to the branches of pine trees lining the far side of the creek.

The creek's shallow water meandering across smooth stones had often lulled her asleep when this was her home. Before Jim. Before her parents had disowned her, their only child, when she became pregnant and ultimately refused to give the baby up for adoption. Before her parents' untimely deaths in a car crash. Before their wills had left the house and the hosiery mill to Jim.

Caroline shook her head to clear away the cobwebs of her past. She wasn't that second-year college girl in love with a seventeen-year-old boy from the mountains. She sang her favorite tunes, hoping to fill the emptiness in the seemingly vacant house. She hadn't heard a second echo of footsteps from the hallway. Pushing her strawberry blond hair behind her ear, Caroline began putting away the groceries she'd brought, her back facing the door to the hallway.

~ ~ ~

Jim paused in the kitchen doorway and marveled at how Caroline looked so at-home in his house. How her presence oozed into the room, bringing with it much needed freshness. He stood in the doorway for a few minutes enjoying her singing. Jim wanted to sneak up behind her and wrap his arms around her, but it was too soon for that. He cleared his throat.

~ ~ ~

Caroline spun around, letting out a soft squeal. And there Jim stood in the doorway. Jim. Her Jimmy. The sight of him still caused a catch in her breath and a tumble in her stomach, even now.

Twenty years ago they had their fateful summer of fun and loss when her daddy had exiled her to Knoxville to have her baby. That move severed all connections with family, hometown, and Jimmy. Then last month they had a surprise reunion through their children—James, Caroline and Jim's son, and Lynn, Jim's daughter with Louisa his deceased wife—both students at the University of Tennessee in Knoxville.

Now Jim stood in the kitchen doorway, leaning one shoulder against the door facing, his ankles crossed and arms folded in front of his chest. He gave Caroline that charming smile that touched her every nerve ending.

"Jimmy!" She placed her hand over her heart. "What are you doing here?!"

"I live here, remember?"

"You startled me. You're early. I planned to have dinner finished when you came home from the mill. I just got here."

"You know I do my best thinking on my feet and stood at my office window when I saw you drive by on four-eleven, headed this way."

No, she didn't know where he did his best thinking. So much to learn about him to fill the twenty-year span they'd been apart. "You didn't waste any time getting here, did you? Tell me about Emmajean. When have you talked to her?"

"I talk to her almost every day. She's okay but she's antsy, staying put at the YWCA. She would rather be out and about, stirring up some excitement. She's anxious to hear the grand jury decision, and we don't know when that will happen."

Jim pushed away from the doorframe and stepped into the kitchen. When he finally stood beside Caroline at the sink, he leaned down and gave her a brushing kiss on her cheek. "Caroline, how does anybody call back twenty lost years? Can it be done?"

"Jimmy, during the past twenty years we both experienced misery at times. But the years had their good too. I had James and he's been a joy to raise. You and Louisa had a good marriage, however shortened by her death. And you have your daughter Lynn from that union."

"You're right. I guess I'm looking more at the bad than the good."

"Jimmy, we can't forget the past but we can try to live for now, beyond the past." Her past had molded her into the mature woman standing in Jim's kitchen in her hometown of Newton, the county seat of Sanford County, Tennessee. She had chosen estrangement from her parents rather than give up her baby for adoption. She became a single mom, which no one accepted for a girl in the 1930s.

Caroline went to the refrigerator, got the milk, and put some into a tea kettle to boil for hot chocolate. She set the kettle on the stove and turned the burner on.

"Caroline, can we ever get our lives straightened out? And the lives of James and Lynn?"

"I think James and Lynn are adjusting well. Being twenty- and eighteen-year-olds helps, and they have school to keep their minds occupied."

Jim slid a chrome-trimmed dinette chair out and sat at the kitchen table.

"Jimmy, it's us we have to work on."

"Your home's in Knoxville, mine is here. My mill is here too. How long will it take to renew our relationship by long distance?"

Caroline placed two steaming mugs on the table and sat across from Jim. Just looking at his handsome face and meeting his dark eyes stirred memories of two young people, foolish and optimistic. But her family sought to extinguish their dreams long ago. Yet, a flicker still existed. Jim and Caroline were no longer young and foolish. Could they bring back what they had? Should they try?

"The kids will be here before long. One of them had a late class till four o'clock. I need to get dinner started, or it won't be ready by the time they get here." She pushed her chair away from the table, but before she could stand, Jim took hold of her hand.

"Sit with me just a few more minutes, please."

She saw the loneliness and fatigue shadow his eyes. "Of course. But, Jimmy, things really will be okay. With Emmajean. With us. With James and Lynn. We'll do everything we can for the kids and Emmajean. As for us, I imagine our abrupt parting happened a lot quicker than our drifting back toward each other."

Jim nodded, a slight smile finding its way into his eyes. "We'll take our time. Not rush into anything."

Caroline had just finished setting the dining table for four when she heard a commotion at the front entrance.

"Hello! We're here." Caroline heard her son's voice and started toward the foyer. Jim had been in the living room and beat her by a step or two.

"Hello, you two." Caroline hugged James and then Lynn. Jim shook James's hand after he'd hugged Lynn.

"Go on and put your coats in the closet and set your bags at the foot of the stairs." James helped Lynn off with her coat. "Come on into the living room by the fire and warm yourselves," Jim said.

"Daddy, it's like a heat wave here compared to Knoxville. We still have several inches of snow on the ground up there and y'all don't have much left."

Caroline watched their children. "James, did you make the drive without much trouble?"

"We did, Mom."

"How about that strip of construction south of Stinson?" Jim asked.

"Dad, it's about all cleared out now. So not much slow-down there."

Caroline glanced toward Jim when her son had called him Dad. They exchanged a knowing glance. James had taken the news of being Lynn's half brother in stride. He'd been raised by his mom with no other family. He showed delight when he learned that he did have some family—Lynn and her daddy. Without asking Jim's permission, he'd started calling him Dad.

~ ~ ~

"Lynn, what's going on with school?"

"Not much, Daddy, just studying, going to the library, that stuff."

Laughing, James held up his hand for a turn to speak. "In between all that stuff as she calls it, she has to watch out for all those boys lined up to ask her out."

Lynn looked at her hands in her lap. Nothing had been easy for her about finding out that James was her half brother. She thought that handsome James would be her boyfriend. They both held deep feelings for the other. Although James had taken the news with no trouble, Lynn had needed a lot of encouragement from her daddy and from James.

~ ~ ~

After a delicious meal, the four lingered at the table. The atmosphere had lost some of its tension they'd experienced when they ate together on New Year's Eve.

"I know y'all probably are used to having cornbread with your meals, but I don't know how to make it." Caroline had never had to do any cooking after she had moved in with her Aunt Martha before she had James. Her aunt had everyday help, and when she had died, Caroline inherited the home and the help.

"I'll teach you." Lynn practically jumped from her chair but stayed put, excitement in her eyes.

"And I know y'all like chicken and dumplings. I have no clue where to start to make that."

Lynn showed excitement again. "I'll show you how, Caroline."

Caroline had wondered what Lynn would call her. She didn't expect she would call her Mother because she'd had a mother. Caroline responded with compassion, indicating that Caroline would be fine for Lynn to use.

"Lynn, that's so kind of you. I'm sure there will be other things you can help me with."

"Yes, ma'am. Daddy's favorite supper is pot roast with potatoes and carrots. You must learn how to prepare that. Right, Daddy?"

"That's right."

~ ~ ~

Jim looked at his children. "I'm so proud of both of you. James, this is your junior year at UT—you have any feelers from places you've contacted about work after graduation?"

James glanced at his mom. They'd talked a little about this. She became so sad when she thought of James leaving. "No, sir, nothing yet."

"You've got time."

"Yes, sir."

After Caroline and Lynn had finished with the dishes, they carried a tray laden with mugs of hot chocolate and cookies into the living room.

"Anybody for hot chocolate?"

"Lynn taught me just how you like it," Caroline said.

"Looks like y'all did a good job. Here, let me take the tray." Jim set the tray on the coffee table and passed around the steaming mugs.

Caroline's thoughts wandered to last New Year's Eve when they'd done this same thing. That evening all four of them were stumbling through the newness of the relationship among them. Were they any farther along on their relationships than they were that night?

~ ~ ~

Caroline looked up at Jim from where she sat at the dressing table. "What if some people there recognize me?"

"It *is* impossible to disguise your beauty."

"No, really I'd prefer not to go this morning. Maybe later."

"Caroline, your son wants to go to church with Lynn."

"He can go. That's fine."

"You'll have to go some day."

"Jimmy, that someday is not today."

Jim paced the room and stopped at a window and stood, looking out."

"Jimmy?"

"What?"

"What are you thinking?"

He spun away from the widow and faced here. "What? You want to know what I'm thinking? What about this? *We* have children now. When I first saw Lynn I knew I was a goner. My world turned around her. Everywhere I went, I took her with me. I'm pretty sure you went through something like that with James."

Caroline nodded.

"The four of us are *family* now. It would mean a lot to James if you would go to church with us."

"Jimmy, more than likely some folks will be there who will recognize me."

"Like I tried to say—it's not about me, and it's not about you. Our lives have to be what's best for James and Lynn."

"I don't know, Jimmy."

"Caroline, what if someone *does* recognize you? If you wait six months to go to church here in Newton, they will still be there."

"I suppose you're right."

"Okay. Lynn and James are waiting to go. Hurry up and finish getting ready. We don't have much time before we need to leave."

Jim could see the dread—almost fear—in her sapphire eyes.

~ ~ ~

They barely got to church on time. People filled the back pews, just as every Baptist church she'd ever attended. Lynn and

James led them up the aisle dissecting the two sections of pews. They had to go about half way toward the pulpit to find room for four. Heads turned toward them and Caroline wanted to melt into her shoes and become invisible.

Lynn smiled toward those who looked their way. Finally seated, Jim helped Caroline off with her coat as did James for Lynn. Caroline compared this small gathering with her church in Knoxville. When the choir members entered to take their seats behind the pulpit, Caroline again compared her Knoxville church choir that almost outnumbered this Newton church's Sunday attendance. As the service began they stood with the congregation.

After church, they went to the Blanchard Hotel dining room for lunch.

"That was a nice service." Caroline shot a suspicious look at her son.

"It *was*, Mom. The pastor greeted us at the door as we left and everyone was friendly. And nobody asked who you were after Dad introduced me by name and you as my mom. I'm glad you went with us."

Lynn's laughter swept the table. "Probably tongues are wagging over a lot of lunches about now. 'Who was that beautiful lady with the Callaways?'"

"Thank you, Lynn. I appreciate your trying to lighten the mood for our lunch."

"Caroline, now that wasn't so bad, was it?"

She sent Jim a withering look. "Good for the three of you. Even James had been there once—Thanksgiving weekend last year. Today made me the stranger in the house. I was uncomfortable."

"Mom, what made you uncomfortable? The people there or your own mind?"

"My own mind? What are you inferring?"

"I just . . . ."

Jim waved his hands across the center of the table. "Time out here. It's never good to cast blame. So, we'll drop this discussion about church right here. Let's all settle down. Take a sip of your iced tea, and let's all cool off a little."

They did as Jim suggested and silence replaced the earlier combustive moments.

"Daddy, how are my cousins?"

Caroline smiled. "You have a bunch of them, don't you?"

~ ~ ~

In his office on Monday morning, Jim paced the floor remembering the weekend and pondering just where he and Caroline fit in the scheme of things, when Peggy buzzed him on the intercom.

He strode to his desk. "Yes, Peggy."

"The Atlanta lawyer Mr. Bertrand Cox is on the telephone."

"Thanks, Peggy. Put him on, please."

When the telephone rang, Jim picked up the receiver. "Mr. Cox?"

"Yes. How are you this morning, Jim?"

"Fine. What do you know about Emmajean?"

"I've received word from the court that the grand jury will be convened the middle of February. Not that we can do anything, but I wanted you to know how things were progressing. Neither Emmajean nor any of us can be there. The prosecution will present their case as strong as they can, hoping that the grand jury will agree with them that the case warrants a jury trial."

"So we're still in a waiting game. If it's sent to a jury trial, when will that take place?"

"Don't know. Can't even guess. But Emmajean will remain out on bail all through this. If it goes to a jury trial, then we'll all be there in the courtroom at that time. Well, that's all I know and wanted to keep you posted."

"Mr. Cox, I appreciate you calling. Thank you for keeping us informed and up to date."

Jim replaced the telephone in its cradle, turned his chair toward the window, and watched the traffic on four-eleven. Where had all the time gone? It seemed only yesterday that Emmajean had cried the morning he had left home and parted ways with his brothers and sisters at their three-room schoolhouse. And when he got the job at the hosiery mill, he got so full of himself, he almost ruined everything with everybody. If his friends and family hadn't been as loyal as they were to him, he'd never have made it. And that landlady he had—she sure pulled him back when he needed it. He'd received many a tongue-lashing from her in her jovial way.

He thought about Emmajean. She often telephoned him, calling collect as he had told her to do. He didn't want to wait for her next call. He pushed the button on his intercom. "Peggy, please put in a call to Emmajean on that number I gave you. You may have to wait a bit for them to find her, it's a community telephone used by all the girls."

Eventually Peggy announced to Jim that Emmajean was on the line. "Hey, little sister, did I catch you at a good time?"

"It's gettin' close to lunch, and I have to get to the cafeteria early, in a few minutes."

"Yeah? Why's that?"

"Jim, I'm workin' in the cafeteria now. I think my workin' at Mr. Baker's diner helped them pick me. I work here three meals a day and even get paid a little."

"That's great. Do you need to go shopping again?" Jim imagined the smile on her face.

"Shoppin'? Of course, when are you comin' down?"

"I thought this coming Saturday. Can you get away for the afternoon?"

"I'm pretty sure I can. I'll check, and if you don't hear from me, you'll know I can get away for a while on Saturday."

"Fine. I look forward to seeing you and taking you shopping. If you can arrange it, maybe we can have lunch. Check on that."

"I will. Uh, Jim, do you think Terry could come with you? I'd like to see him again."

"I don't think lawyers work on Saturday, but I'll mention it to him."

"Okay, thanks."

"You don't want to be late for lunch work in the cafeteria so I'll let you go. Are you well?"

"Yes, Jim. I'm glad you called. Bye."

"Bye." He placed the telephone in its cradle and continued in thought . . . Enough of this woolgathering, I've got a mill to run.

Chapter 3

The number of patients increased after the holidays when people had gathered with family and friends. They put off getting treated for what ailed them. Today Shirley Ann worked the ER and in mid-day it was fairly quiet. Then Shirley Ann heard the sirens before she got word from the ER doctor. A car wreck.

As the two ambulance workers rolled their gurney inside, they began giving vital signs to the doctor. "Pulse 120, BP 150 over 90, respiration 13, temp 100. Injuries from car wreck. Appears to be some internal damage and bleeding, broken arm. In and out of consciousness. He's got alcohol on his breath."

When the gurney passed by Shirley Ann she gasped. It was Art, Arthur and Callie's son. She went directly to the counter and telephoned Callie. When no one answered, she telephoned Arthur at work.

"Arthur, this is Shirley Ann. I'm at the hospital. It's Art."

"Art? At the hospital? What happened?"

"He's just been brought in by ambulance. Appears to have been a car wreck. He's got a broken arm and some internal damages."

"I'll be right there. Callie's not home. Can you try to find her for me?"

"Yes, Arthur, I'll try. Bye."

Instead of bye, all she heard was the slamming of a telephone. How was she going to find Callie? Since it was Wednesday, she'd try the church to see if she was at Bible study. First she'd call her big brother, Jim. Arthur would need some support.

When Arthur parked at the hospital and got out of his car, he saw Jim drive into the lot. They walked into the hospital together.

"Arthur, do you know what happened?"

"Not exactly. Except it's obvious he wasn't in school like he was supposed to be."

They waited till the doctor came toward them, and at the same time Callie pushed open the outside door and came to stand in the lobby by Arthur.

"You two the parents of Art?"

"Yes. Tell us, how is he?"

"Your son is pretty banged up. I understand the car was demolished. Art's in surgery now getting that broken arm back in place. And we're X-raying to check for internal damage. We know he's got some bleeding, but right now we don't know from where."

Callie stepped closer to the doctor. "Did he say anything before he went to surgery?"

"Not much. Just some mumbling. He's in and out of it. We'll know more before long and I'll let you know." The doctor turned and went back up the hall.

"Arthur, do you know any more than what the doctor said?"

"No, Callie, I don't." He put his arm around her shoulder and hugged her close.

"Anything I can do, Bones?" Jim felt he might be in the way but he offered.

"I reckon not. We just have to wait. Maybe you could check with the police . . ."

Just then two policemen entered the lobby. "Are you Art Gray's parents?"

"Yes. What can you tell us?" Arthur squeezed Callie's shoulder tighter

"Your son had a wreck up on the Old Knoxville Highway. He didn't make a curve and left the road without leaving tire marks." Callie gave him a questioning look. "No tire marks means he didn't put on his brakes. Witnesses in other cars said he just sailed off the road at a high speed. Nobody else was in the car. Art had been drinking. He's lucky to be alive."

Callie began to cry. "Arthur, what did we do wrong? Why did this happen?"

Arthur tried to comfort her and led her to a chair to sit.

Jim followed them. He put a hand on Arthur's shoulder.

"Jim, we talked about Art not long ago. Callie and me are at the end of our rope with him. Now look, he's really fixed it now. And drinkin' just tops it off."

A few hours later the doctor moved Art to a room.

Standing outside his door, they listened to the doctor. "The internal bleeding was coming from his spleen. It was badly bruised, and we removed it. Recovery from that will be quick. We all can live without a spleen. It's the arm that'll take longer to heal. We reset it and put in a couple of pins. The cast will be on his arm for at least six weeks. Then we'll X-ray again to see if it's healing right. Y'all have any questions?"

Arthur clenched and unclenched his fists. "I guess not. Can we see him now? Is he conscious?"

"Yes, you can go in. He's a little groggy, but he's conscious. I wouldn't stay too long. He needs his rest."

Jim waited outside in the hall and Arthur and Callie stepped inside.

~ ~ ~

Someone touched his arm.

Jim turned. "Shirley Ann, thanks for calling me. Does it look bad, you think?"

"I think his body will heal fine. It's the fact that he was drinkin' that will cause trouble."

"Yeah. I figured that. What did he think he was doing?"

"Just skippin' class and showin' off, I guess."

Jim rubbed the back of his neck. "Bones and Callie have tried everything with that boy to get him on the straight and narrow. Nothing works. Now his sister Jennifer is a sweetheart, goes to school, she's a good girl. How can parents raise two kids the same way and them turn out to be completely different? Wow. I'm glad I just had one—well *we* had just one. Y'all helped me raise Lynn. Y'all and my landlady."

Shirley Ann looked at her brother. "How is Lynn doin'?"

"Good. Good. She's about over the shock of finding out that James is her half brother. She was certainly infatuated with him and thought he'd be her boyfriend. She and James came home for the weekend recently."

"And Caroline? Did she come down?"

Jim saw nothing but caring in Shirley Ann's expression. She'd been nothing but kind to Jim even though he was seeing Caroline every now and then. She knew the whole story. All the family did. They all could have turned their back on Jim and rightly so, figuring he wasn't being loyal to Louisa, his deceased wife and mother of Lynn. Even Callie, Louisa's sister, seemed to hold no ill will against Jim.

"Yes, Caroline was here for the same weekend the kids were."

"It was good for y'all to have time together. Y'all and the kids."

"Thank you, sis. You and Callie have been onto me to remarry so I wouldn't be alone. Who would have thought that

Caroline would turn up like this and with my child. I don't know if we can work out anything permanent, but it's necessary for us to be cordial because of the kids. We'll build a relationship for that, if nothing else."

~ ~ ~

Caroline watched as Mildred prepared dinner. With each dish Caroline peppered her with questions.

"Mrs. Hensen, why do you want to know how to cook? I'll always be here, you know. I've been cooking and keeping house for you since James was a baby and your aunt was still living here. What's got into you? Could it be you're wanting to impress James's daddy?"

Caroline could feel heat rise to her face. She started to deny Mildred's last question but decided that she already knew they had visited several times. "I guess you're pretty observing. I do want to be able to prepare some meals for him when James and I go down for a visit."

Mildred smiled. She'd been urging Caroline for a long time to get out, date some.

But Caroline hadn't dated anybody since she and Jim had been separated twenty years ago by her father. She didn't want to think about that now. The past was past. She was ready for the future, whatever it held.

She heard voices in the living room. James and Lynn had come on their break from classes. Caroline had become accustomed to their brief visits during the day.

She left the kitchen and made her way to the front of the house. "I thought I heard voices in here. Are you between classes?"

"Yes, ma'am." Lynn unloaded her books onto the sofa.

"Hey, Mom. We had a couple of hours and decided to spend it here. It's still cold out there but doesn't look like snow today."

"Y'all make yourselves at home. I'll heat some milk for hot chocolate." Caroline backed away from the living room as the two kids talked. Watching them brought her pleasure. She'd often wondered if she should get Jim's opinion on asking Lynn to move out of the dorm and into her home. She had plenty of bedrooms and more room than she and James would ever need. Maybe she'd get around to asking him the next time she saw him.

"It's always more relaxing when we come here than staying someplace on campus."

"Lynn, you're always welcome. I hope you feel like this is your home also."

Lynn looked at James and remembered how excited she'd been to think about having James as a boyfriend. They'd spent every free moment they had together. Then when Lynn found out James was her half brother, she'd almost fallen apart.

"What? Do I have something on my face?" James said.

"No, I was just watching you and thinking back. Everything's fine."

"Yeah, it sure is. I got a ready-made family for New Year's. It's going to be a great year. And many more years to come." James reached across the sofa, lightly squeezed her hand, and smiled.

Caroline entered the room carrying a tray laden with steaming hot chocolate and some cookies Mildred had made that morning. She set the tray on the coffee table. "Maybe this will help to warm you up." She went to the fireplace and poked around on the wood, sending sparks up the chimney. "Maybe this will also help. Let me know when you leave, so I can say good-bye."

Mildred stepped into the living room. "Mrs. Hensen, telephone."

She hurried to the telephone. "Hello."

"Hey." It was Jimmy. "What're you doing?"

"As a matter of fact, just talking with Lynn and James."

"No kidding?"

"Yes, they come to the house sometimes when they have a block of free time. I fixed them some hot chocolate, and they're quiet now. They study when they come by."

"Wish you could have fixed me a cup of that hot chocolate. When are we getting the four of us together again?"

The four of us. Will it ever be the two of us? "Any time you want to make a weekend of it. The kids won't have a break till Easter. Will we get together there or here?"

"The three of you came here the last time, so guess it's my turn to do the traveling this time. This coming weekend I'm going down to see Emmajean. Would the next weekend be okay with you?"

"Sure. I'll plan on it. How is Emmajean?"

"She's hanging in there I think. That's why I try to go down every now and then to help keep her perked up and not so lonely. She's got a little job there at the YWCA. That will probably help some to keep her mind off her troubles."

"Jimmy, you are so good to Emmajean."

"I wouldn't want it any other way. She's my baby sister and she needs me to support her in this predicament she's got herself into. I'd like to wring that guy's neck for getting her to help him do his drug selling for him. But, of course, I can't."

"Let's hope the court sees him for what he is, and he is punished for his deeds."

Chapter 4

Emmajean bounded down the stairs to the lobby where Jim and Terry waited. They both hugged her, Terry's just a slight one.

"I am so glad to see y'all. Thanks for comin' down. I'm off work for lunch *and* supper, so what do we do first?"

"How about we get a quick lunch and then go shopping again?"

"Jim, you make me feel like it's Christmas every time you come down here. On the other hand, we had some very lean Christmas times when we were kids, didn't we?"

"We did at that. How about you, Terry, we don't know much about you. Did your family have big Christmas celebrations?"

"We did. Mother saw to that. She liked to entertain and have folks in all through the holidays. I don't want to say I was spoiled, but looking back I guess I was. I've got my head on a little straighter where things like that are concerned. I'm a pretty down to earth guy now."

Emmajean hung on his every word. She linked arms with both of them and pulled them toward the outside door. She felt her legal problems lighten when Jim and Terry were around.

As they were finishing their lunch, Jim excused himself, leaving Terry and Emmajean alone, sitting across from one another. Emmajean searched Terry's eyes, and they exchanged a smile.

"When Jim told me you wanted me to come down this time with him, I was excited that you wanted to see me again."

She swatted the air. "Did Jim tell you I wanted him to bring you?"

"Yep."

"I didn't tell him not to say anythin' to you, but he should have known not to mention it. Oh, boy, wait till I get my hands on him. But I am glad to see you, Terry."

He reached across the table and placed his hand over hers. "I don't know a better way to spend a Saturday than to be with you."

Emmajean didn't move her hand. The warmth from his hand rushed through her body, and she felt heat creep up her neck to her face. "You mean that?"

"Sure." He lightly squeezed her hand.

"Why?" Nobody but family had ever paid any attention to her in a nice way. Especially since coming to Atlanta. Being a gofer in the fashion business, she was just a fly on the wall. Nobody paid her any attention.

"Why what?"

"Why would you want to spend time with me? Terry, I'm a nobody in trouble with the law."

"Emmajean you're in trouble with the law because your *friend* Barry led you astray. It's not your fault. And let me tell you that you're not a nobody." He reached with both hands to take hold of hers. "You're a somebody and don't let anyone tell you any different. I'll admit that you're headstrong but beautiful with your auburn hair and sparkling blue eyes."

Jim returned to the table. Emmajean saw him glance at her hands enveloped in Terry's. A half smile crossed his face briefly, but he said nothing.

With her hands back in her lap, Emmajean thought of what she should say. "Jim, where'd you go? Anythin' wrong?"

"No, I was just checking in with Bones. Art's still in the hospital, but he's doing better."

Since Jim knew she had asked for Terry to come to Atlanta, Emmajean wondered if he had left the table to give them some brief privacy.

"Everybody finished eating? Ready to go shopping?" Emmajean asked.

Terry let out a mocking moan and smiled at Emmajean."Yeah. Let's get started. Rich's first?"

~ ~ ~

The next day Jim headed over to the hospital.

"Jim, what are you doin' here?"

"Hey, Shirley Ann, just came by to see about Bones's kid. How's he doing?"

"The doctor released him yesterday while you were in Atlanta. He'll have to take it easy for a few days to let the incision heal where they went in to see where the bleedin' was coming from. After a follow-up visit to the doctor, he'll probably be allowed to return to school. His arm will be in a cast a few more weeks."

"I bet Art was glad to hear he could go back to school." Jim smiled. "Not being at school caused his wreck in the first place. How are Bones and Callie?"

"As good as can be expected, I guess."

"Shirley Ann, the cops were here questioning Art after the wreck. Where does all that go from here?"

"I really don't know. We've never had any trouble of this kind with our three girls. Juvenile court comes to mind. Art's just seventeen."

"I guess we'll find out. Wasn't being nosy, just concerned."

~ ~ ~

During the next work week Jim sometimes thought of two relationships—his with Caroline and Emmajean's with Terry. Emmajean seemed to Jim to feel inferior, but Terry had brought a light to her eyes. And he saw the way they had smiled at one another Saturday at lunch as he'd approached the table. Maybe something good was about to come her way. Sure would help her during the months ahead with the possible trial coming up.

When his thoughts turned to Caroline, his heart thudded a little faster and he wanted to smile. He'd have to wait till Saturday to see her again. Where was all this going with the four of them? The kids seemed to be adapting to the circumstances their parents had set in place for them twenty years ago. In the midst of everything, could he and Caroline ever bring back what they'd had? Should he even think about that happening? He supposed long distance relationships were difficult to sustain and wondered if he and Caroline should even consider that. Probably should just enjoy the time when the four of them were together.

He leaned both elbows on his desk then put his face in his hands. He heard one tap on the door, and it opened.

When he finally looked up, the door was closed again. He pressed fingers into his temples as if to force the frustration away. He pushed the intercom and heard "Yes, sir."

"Peggy did you need to see me?"

"Yes, just a moment, please." Jim's telephone rang.

"Hello."

"Mr. Callaway, I didn't want your visitor to hear your response. I wanted to know if you wanted to see the police chief."

"Peggy, do you know what he wants to see me about?"

"No sir, but he said he would wait till you could see him. He's just sitting out here."

"Well, now. Okay I guess you can show him in."

Jim motioned the police chief to a chair opposite his desk. "What can I do for you, sir?"

"I'm George Rosen." They shook hands. Rosen took a small writing pad from his shirt pocket. "I worked the car wreck that sent Art Gray to the hospital. I saw you there with the family members. Mind if I ask you some questions?"

"I certainly don't mind but I doubt I can help you. I didn't witness the wreck and haven't talked to the boy."

"But you *know* Art Gray, right?"

"Yes, I do. Why are you here?" Jim's patience had been tried to its breaking point, and he didn't want this conversation to continue.

"I wanted to ask you about the boy."

Jim felt like he was back in the courtroom in Atlanta.

The police chief continued. "Can you tell me a bit about him? What kind of kid he is? What kind of student?"

Jim glared at Rosen. All Jim knew was what Bones had told him and he wasn't telling this man any of that. "No, I can't."

"Why's that, Mr. Callaway?"

"Well, he's not my boy. He's my friend's boy. I guess you need to talk to his parents instead of me."

"I see. You don't want to cooperate." Jim saw Rosen's impatience growing.

"It's not that I don't want to cooperate, sir. I think you're maybe meddling a little, and you want me to help you. I don't stick my nose into other people's business."

The police chief folded his writing pad and returned it to his pocket. "I'm sorry you won't work with me here."

"I would if I could. But you best talk to his parents."

"If that's the way you feel." He rose from his chair and offered his hand. "Thank you for your time."

Jim didn't get up from his desk. He watched the man go through the door and close it behind him. Jim still sat in deep thought when he heard a tap on the door and Peggy stepped in. "Mr. Callaway, are you all right? You're not in some trouble with the police are you? Is there anything you need for me to do?"

"No, Peggy, I'm not in any trouble with the police, thank goodness. Now I know better how Emmajean feels down there in Atlanta. I almost let that man make me feel guilty because I wouldn't answer his questions." He saw the questioned look Peggy gave him. "He wanted me to talk to him about Art Gray. I wasn't about to do that. He asked me questions that he should be asking Art's parents. I don't think he liked me very much."

"He didn't look too happy when he left."

"Peggy, please don't say anything about his visit here or what I just told you."

"I won't, sir."

"Thank you."

Peggy left the office and Jim pushed on his temples again, this time even harder. But the helplessness he felt didn't leave. Caroline, the kids, Emmajean, and now Art. What will happen next?

Jim turned his chair to face toward the window.

Have you forgotten me?

Jim swiveled his chair around toward the door so fast he made himself a little dizzy. No one was in the room but he was certain he had heard someone speak. He started moving the papers around on his desk to decide which one needed his attention first.

You haven't talked to me in a while.

Jim raised his head but, again, no one else was in the room. His brow creased and he remembered the day Caroline's parents had told him she had returned to Agnes Scott early and didn't leave him a note. As he had returned to his room he heard a voice say, *Come unto me, all ye that labour and are heavy laden, and I will give you rest.*

Why did he think he could solve everybody's problems as well as his own all by himself? He bowed his head. *God, I guess I haven't talked to you in a while. I should have been praying about all I'm concerned with. I need the rest You offer. I need Your help to get me through the problems I'm carrying. Please give me comfort and direction for my steps. Forgive me for leaving You out of my daily life. Amen.*

~ ~ ~

Jim thought Saturday would never get here. Problems at the mill were up and down all week. And he still couldn't shake the police chief's visit. But now driving north on four-eleven, Jim felt a sense of release of aggravations and irritations. He smiled and hummed a tune. Headed to Knoxville, there would be no blatant annoyances, only some undertones of concern about Caroline and him he carried everywhere he went. He continued to smile the closer he got to her home.

It was mid-morning when he arrived. He'd left home early, not wanting to waste much of the weekend on the road. The front door opened before he could knock. Caroline's smile radiated happiness toward him. He stepped inside and closed the door behind them, looked around to see if they were alone, and hugged her close. When he released her, he planted a soft kiss on her lips.

"Mercy me! Jimmy, I've missed seeing you so much."

"Me too."

She tilted her head up, and he gave her another quick kiss. "Are the kids here? How about Mildred?"

"I gave Mildred the day off. The kids are out and about. I told them you'd be here by lunch."

Jim looked at his watch. "We have a little time to ourselves then."

Caroline nodded and grinned.

~ ~ ~

Jim watched Caroline set the dining room table for four. She had put something in the oven that Mildred probably fixed and frozen yesterday.

"Can I help?" Jim moved toward the kitchen sink.

"Can you make a salad?"

"Sure. I've been feeding Lynn and me for many years." He went to the refrigerator and pulled out the salad fixings.

When he finished, he turned to Caroline who worked with food at the stove. "Do I toss the dressing now?"

"We can do that just before we eat."

Jim saw the brightness in her cobalt blue eyes. Happiness seemed to shroud her. She was in her element in her home with everyone who meant so much to her.

"Do we have everything about done? Can we sit for a moment?"

"Almost, Jimmy." Caroline busied herself making last minute arrangements in the kitchen and dining room. When she finished, she took Jim by the hand and led him to the living room. They both sat on the sofa. Their shoulders touched.

Caroline turned to Jim. "Have you solved all our problems?"

"I sure have been thinking about our situation. Long distance relationships—"

"Daddy!" Lynn set her overnight bag in the hall and ran to Jim who stood and took her in his arms for a bear hug.

"Dad. Glad you made the trip safely." James shook Jim's hand. "Hey, Mom, something sure smells good. Is lunch about ready?"

"Yes, it is." She chanced a glance toward Jim and gave a slight shrug of her shoulders. He noticed the shrug and knew her meaning. He followed them into the dining room, still wondering if they could maintain a long distance relationship or even a friendship.

Jim faced Caroline as they sat at the long gleaming dining table. James sat to his mom's right and Lynn sat on Jim's right. Jim offered a short prayer of thanks before they ate. After they finished the delicious lunch and loaded the dishes in the dishwasher, they all moved to the living room for conversation. The kids were bubbly, and Caroline talked with them.

Was he going to just have to get used to having two kids around each time he saw Caroline? Was there a solution to all this? Could he be satisfied to have a friendship with Caroline? The first time he saw her after twenty years apart refueled old memories and sparks moved between them.

"It's getting late. Maybe we should all go to bed and be rested for tomorrow. Everyone going to church?"

Jim looked at his watch, not realizing the lateness of the evening. "I plan to. I've got to get my luggage out of the car."

Jim went outside and returned in a few minutes. He and Caroline checked the locks and turned out the lights before following the kids up the stairs.

Jim watched Caroline get the kids settled in their rooms and then waited for her to come his way. After he went into his bedroom and put his suitcase on the bench at the foot of the bed, he turned to close his door. Caroline still stood in the doorway, the hall lights behind her casting a shadow across her face.

She stepped into his room. Reminded him of the Caroline of twenty years ago. Sassy and not afraid to show her feelings. She walked up to him and put her hands around his neck. "A good night kiss?"

Jim looked toward the door. No one was there. He gripped her shoulders, holding her at arm's length and bent down to kiss her good night. He planned to give her a slight brush of a kiss, but she wouldn't settle for that. She leaned back and looked at Jim then leaned forward again, her lips parted. When their lips met this time, she made the kiss last longer and deeper. Jim finally gently pushed her back, smiling. "Not now, Caroline. We haven't decided if ever. And the kids are just down the hall. I'll be up for church in the morning. Good night. Sleep well."

Caroline stroked his face with the palm of her hand and traced his lips with a finger. His stomach tumbled and warmth filled him. Jim turned her around and guided her to the bedroom door. She turned before leaving. "Good night, Jimmy."

After church and lunch at the house, Lynn and James watched television in the back of the house. Jim's luggage sat by the front door. He and Caroline sat on the sofa, their thighs touching.

"I'd better get started home." Jim started to leave the sofa.

Caroline grabbed his hand and tugged him back to sit beside her. "Jimmy, we haven't talked about the future. Can you take a few more minutes before you leave?"

"Yeah." He leaned forward, putting his forearms on his knees. "You're right, we haven't talked about the future. But, Caroline, we don't know if there *is* a future for you and me. We don't know if we can retrieve the Us we once were."

"Oh, Jimmy, I know we can."

"How?"

"We could make it work this way." She scooted up to the edge of the sofa so she could look into his face. "I could live in Newton and the kids could both live in this house. That way we wouldn't be trying to work this out long distance."

"How in the world do you think that would work?"

"There are no romantic feelings between them. They act like sister and brother, which they are. Lynn could move from the dorm and be a lot safer here with James to look after her."

"And where would you stay in Newton? Have you thought about that?"

When she looked at him her smile widened.

"No, Caroline, you can't be thinking you'll move into my house with me. No, that will not happen." He left the sofa and paced in front of it.

"Jimmy, I could. I'd be good." She gave him that smile again.

Jim stopped his pacing. "Winter quarter for the kids will be over before long. Then let's see how things go through spring quarter and then summer. We'll get together when we can. I'm thinking Emmajean's trial will start soon and I'll be knee-deep in that, supporting her. You and I should see our lives a lot clearer by the start of school next fall."

Jim waited for Caroline's objections. She opened her mouth and then shut it. She stood, taking his hands into hers. "That sounds like a good plan. It will take a lot of patience on my part, but I'll agree with you. Till Fall, then." She planted a kiss on his lips and held him around the waist. He shared the hug but not the kiss.

Jim pushed Caroline away and looked toward the back of the house. He enjoyed her kisses, and under more favorable conditions he'd kiss her back. But the kids were only a few feet away watching television. "I'll go tell the kids I'm leaving." He turned Caroline loose and immediately felt the emptiness of his arms.

He went toward the back, then the three of them returned. Jim had his arm across Lynn's shoulders. "Okay, till next time then. We'll all get together soon."

Jim shook James's hand and gave him a loving pat on the back. "Dad, this visit has been brief but I sure enjoyed being with you. We'll watch after Lynn until we get together again."

Jim saw Caroline send an *I told you so* smile his way. James would watch after Lynn, like Caroline had said when she'd explained her plan.

Lynn grabbed her daddy around the neck and gave him a big hug. "I hate to see you go but I know you have the mill you have to run. I hope Aunt Emmajean's troubles get straightened out soon. Tell her hello for me."

"I will." He stepped through the door, and they all followed him onto the porch.

James reached for Jim's suitcase. "Here, Dad, I'll carry that to the car for you."

"Thanks, James."

They all waved bye to him as he drove down the driveway. Caroline's smile had disappeared, which tore a part of his heart away. He smiled anyway and the kids did the same. Then he turned onto the street and he could no longer see them.

~ ~ ~

The next day, Jim couldn't settle down enough to tackle the usual Monday morning stuff on his desk. He had too much on his mind and no solutions to any of them. He left his desk and walked out to Peggy's desk. "I'm going to walk around the mill for a little while. I shouldn't be gone long."

"Mr. Callaway, is something bothering you?"

Peggy had worked with Jim long enough to know that when he went into the mill, he usually had something on his mind that he had to work through. "Yeah, a few things. I just need some pondering time."

Walking across the production floor, the rhythmic sounds of the machinery didn't crowd his mind. The room's noise gave Jim a comforting background that allowed him to mull over several situations and decide whether he really had any choices in any of them.

In Bones's case with his son, Art, in some juvenile trouble, Jim came to the conclusion that he had no choices to make there. With Emmajean's trial looming, the only choice he had was to support her and to wait. Then when he thought of the impasse he had with Caroline, everything else fled from his mind. Caroline had a plan. He didn't. But would her plan work? No, of course it wouldn't work unless they were married. *Married*? Where did that word come from? He stopped walking to think about that. When he stopped, the noises of the mill seized him. He looked around, not remembering coming into the vast area of beehive activity.

The mill workers were accustomed to seeing the mill owner come around so they paid little attention when he stopped still. Startled, Jim recognized he was closer to the loading dock than he was to his office and he rushed toward it. Once outside, the cold air jolted him back to a small piece of normality.

Jim stood on the loading dock, amid the activity of men loading boxes onto a truck backed in and parked against the dock. He moved over to the opposite end of the platform. He remembered the guys he'd worked with on the loading dock many years ago, and then stared out across the parking lot. Filled with cars now that the mill had grown in number of employees, Jim only saw the little two-toned Buick that Caroline had driven. He rammed his hands into his pants pockets, and his mind's eye saw her drive around the corner of the building and park directly in front of the loading dock. He and all the other guys couldn't help but notice her, but she had eyes only for Jim. He was just off the farm then, and didn't know what had hit him. Her attentions made him proud. And, he remembered, he let it all go to his head.

So how was he going to handle her attentions this time? In this situation he did have some choices. She still caused his heart to gallop whenever they were in the same room. His stomach still flipped when she came near enough to touch. What could he do? He scuffed a chipped place in the concrete with the toe of his shoe. He turned, left the loading dock, and returned to his office.

When he walked into the office, Peggy handed him a slip of paper. "Mr. Bertrand Cox called. He wants you to call him back."

Jim looked at the piece of paper he held. "Probably about Emmajean. Please get him on the telephone, Peggy." He handed the paper back to her and walked toward the door to his office. "Thank you, Peggy."

"You're welcome, ..." but his door had already closed.

Jim stood behind his desk looking out the window at the traffic on four-eleven when his intercom buzzed. "Yes, Peggy."

"I have Mr. Cox on the telephone."

"Thank you. Please put him through."

Jim put his hand on the receiver waiting for it to ring. He lifted the telephone to his ear. "Hello. Mr. Cox?"

"Good morning, Jim. Or do you hate Mondays as much as I do? Anyway, wanted to tell you that the grand jury has examined the formal written accusations of drug selling against Emmajean and her friend. They think the evidence submitted by the prosecution warrants charges and Emmajean's case has been handed up to the court for trial." Jim tried to interrupt the attorney with a question but Mr. Cox went on talking as if he didn't hear Jim. "Now, the grand jury doesn't decide guilt or innocence, but only whether there is probable cause to believe that they did commit the crime. So the next step is for the court to set a date for the trial. Even when that date is set, the prosecutors and lawyers will have to strike a jury, that is, we'll pick people from a group of folks to be on the jury. That sometimes takes a few days. Then the actual trial will start."

Jim felt like he'd just received a lecture in Lawyer 101. "Has the trial been set?"

"It's set for June 11, that's when we'll start picking the jury."

Jim felt like he'd been hit below the belt. He turned his chair toward the window. He was speechless. A big part of the waiting was over. "Does Emmajean know all this?"

"I wanted to ask you whether you wanted to tell her or wanted me to go over to where she's living and tell her. What do you think?"

Jim stood, looked out the window and thought for a minute. He sat back in his chair and turned it toward his desk. "I'll see if I can shuffle my schedule and get down there tomorrow. If you don't hear anything from me, you'll know I'm going to tell her. I think I can explain it to her the way you just did to me."

"I'm sure you can, Jim. You just give me a call if you need me."

"Yes, I will. Thank you for calling and staying on top of this for us."

Jim hung up the telephone and sat in silence. He was limp in body and soul. His biggest challenge to support his baby sister stared him down.

He'd been with Emmajean when their parents died of pneumonia, and took her to live with him and Louisa just after they'd married. When she hit high school he'd moved out of Mrs. Hall's where he was boarding, and rented a little house for him, Lynn, and Emmajean. Those were awful years after Louisa had died. He had responsibility for his toddler, Lynn. He'd hired a young lady to keep her while he was at work on the highway between Newton and Chattanooga, and to be there when Emmajean came home from school. Thinking on all that made him think how hard it must have been on Caroline raising James by herself, with her aunt's help.

Then immediately after she'd graduated from high school, Emmajean used the money she'd been saving from some part-time jobs, bought a bus ticket to Atlanta, and was gone.

He would shuffle his schedule and he *would* go to Atlanta tomorrow to tell Emmajean what the attorney had just told him. He didn't want to do this alone. He buzzed the intercom for Peggy. "Peggy, please get Terry Fields on the telephone for me."

When the telephone rang, he snatched it up. "Terry?"

"Yeah, Jim, what's up?"

"Mr. Cox called me from Atlanta. The grand jury has handed her case up to the court for a jury trial." He heard Terry breathing hard. "Terry, did you hear me?"

"I heard you. Wow. I was so hoping it wouldn't come to this. If she was in this alone, and not been coupled with her friend I don't think it would have gone to trial. But they really couldn't just let him go."

"Are you free for a trip to Atlanta tomorrow?"

"Tomorrow? Let me see." Jim could hear him moving paper around. "I can go with you tomorrow, Jim. I know you're not taking me just so I can see Emmajean so thanks for including me."

"I'd like to leave early. Can I pick you up at your office about eight thirty?"

"That's fine."

"We'll be back tomorrow night."

"Okay. I'll see you in the morning."

After Jim talked with Terry, he had Peggy get Mr. Walton from Terry's law firm on the telephone. "Mr. Walton, may I have a few minutes of your time?'

"Of course, what can I help you with?"

"My sister's trial in Atlanta will start June 11. I wonder if you would let me use Terry Fields on a retainer so he can be present for the entire trial, including striking the jury. Could you do that?"

"Hmmm. Does Terry agree to this?"

"I wanted to talk to you first before I mentioned it to him. He's going down to Atlanta with me tomorrow to help me tell my sister that her trial has been scheduled."

"Hmmph. I suppose that would work. You already have our firm on retainer for the mill, and doing so personally with Terry for her trial would be fine and strictly legal. Thank you, Mr. Callaway, for your confidence in our firm and in Terry. He's a fine young lawyer."

"I have high respect for Terry. Thank you, Mr. Walton."

The next morning at eight thirty on the dot, Jim pulled his Pontiac up to the curb in front of Rawlings & Walton law firm office. Terry opened the door and jumped into the passenger seat. "Morning, Jim."

"Good morning, Terry. Thanks again for going with me. Emmajean doesn't know I'm visiting her today. And you being with me will be a plus for her." Terry squirmed in his seat and Jim glanced at the blush that crept up his neck.

Jim told Terry what the Atlanta lawyer had told him on the telephone. When Terry corrected him a time or two on his use of lawyer terms, Jim knew he was in trouble if he tried to explain everything to Emmajean. "Terry, how about when we see Emmajean you tell her this whole thing. That way I won't get it all mixed up and cause her any more stress than she has already."

"Sure. I can do that."

"Terry, after I talked with you yesterday, I telephoned Mr. Walton, and asked him if I could put you on retainer for Emmajean's entire trial, including striking the jury. Just to be with me. Emmajean and me. Legal support and moral support. I'm not sure I can hold it together for her if you're not down there with us. Mr. Walton said that would be fine and strictly legal."

"I'm honored that you want me with you, and I'll certainly be there for the whole trial. I'm logging in my hours spent with you on the firm's books. Since you have the firm on retainer already, I don't know if they'll bill you for my hours so far."

"That's acceptable with me. Whatever way they want to do it."

For the remainder of their trip to Atlanta, Terry answered Jim's questions about what was going on with his sister. Having Terry's presence all arranged lifted a nagging weight off his shoulders. If only the trial would go away that easily. But it wouldn't, and that made Jim doubly glad for having Terry around.

Later that day, after Terry explained the grand jury decision and the trial date to Emmajean, Jim watched as her bubbly personality began to sag like a tire slowly losing air. He could see the unshed tears rimming her eyes. Terry appeared to sense this also.

"Emmajean, the trial doesn't begin till June 11, and then it'll start with picking of the jury. You've got a few months to wait and in the meantime Mr. Cox will be preparing his defense of you.

Emmajean, I'll be with you every step of the way. I can't sit at your table during the trial, but Jim and I will be in the first row right behind you."

"You will?" She looked from Terry to Jim and back. "Why would you do that if you can't help with my case?"

"I can help *you* as the case proceeds. If you want me to."

"Yes. Yes, please be here. If it weren't for you *and* Jim bein' down here with me, I guess I would have already tried to escape this awful town."

Terry didn't say anything. Jim tried to fill the gap. "Emmajean, Atlanta is not so awful. There are awful people everywhere, and you just met up with one who looked okay on the outside but was mean on the inside. We're both going to be here while you go through all this. You can count on it."

Emmajean thought a moment, still looking at both men. "Thank you. That's all I can say, and I know that's not enough. All my life I've done most everythin' I've set out to do. But I couldn't do what's facin' me without you two."

~ ~ ~

The next morning, Jim had Peggy to get Bob Allbright, his Chief Financial Officer of the mill, to come see him right after lunch. When Bob entered Jim's office they shook hands.

"What can I do for you, Jim?"

"Bob, you know a little about the problems my sister, Emmajean, is going through in Atlanta. Her trial starts June 11. I have no idea how long it will last but I need to be down there with her. While I'm away I'm putting you in overall charge of the mill. Use my office or run it from yours. I hope you'll help me on this."

"Absolutely, Jim. I'll help anyway I can. I guess you'll get to come home on the weekends."

"Probably."

"If anything turns up during the week that I feel I haven't handled properly we can put our heads together and work it out."

"And, Bob, I'll call you along just to see how things are going. We have some months to wait for the trial to begin. During that time we should spend more time together, and I'll share some of the things that go on from this office."

"That'd be good."

"How about you shadow me every day as much as you can, and still do your job? And get someone in your office ready to step in and take up some of the slack you'll leave behind when you take my place. How does that sound?"

"Jim, you're a good man. You care for the workers here, and you run the mill like you love it. I'll try to do the same while you're away. I appreciate your confidence in me."

They shook hands again. "Okay, Bob, between now and June we'll get a system set up, and when I leave you won't even miss me, you'll be able to step right in without skipping a beat."

Bob turned to leave Jim's office. "Bob, uh, I sure do thank you for being so willing to help me out." Bob nodded and left the office.

After Bob left, Jim answered his intercom. "Mr. Callaway, Arthur Gray is on the telephone."

"Thanks, Peggy, please put him through."

Jim answered his telephone. "Bones, what's going on with you?"

"Jim." Jim heard the somber voice of his friend. "We've got trouble with Art. Do you know anything about Juvenile Court?"

"No, not much. Why?"

"Since Art was drinkin' when he had his car wreck, the officials are involved. The police have turned the case over to Juvenile Court with Judge Franklin. He's assigned a social worker from social services to work with us. She's telephoned Callie and set up an appointment for both of us to go to her office. Tomorrow."

Jim and Bones remained silent a few moments.

"Bones, how can I help?"

"I don't know. I really don't know. I guess I'll know more after our appointment with the lady tomorrow. Her name is Ethel Jernigan. Do you know her?"

"No. Don't believe I've heard that name. Bones, let me know something after your meeting. And if you think of anything I can do, just let me know."

"Sure will. Thanks, Jim. Bye"

"Bye, Bones." Jim held onto the telephone a little longer but heard only the dial tone. He rested the telephone in its cradle and turned his chair to look out his window. Doggone it, what in the world's happening? He had too much on his mind.

Chapter 5

Arthur and Callie walked into the offices of the county Social Services.

The girl at the front desk looked up at them. "May I help you?"

Arthur spoke for him and Callie. "We have an appointment to see Ethel Jernigan. I'm Arthur Gray and this is my wife, Callie."

"One moment, Mr. Gray." She picked up her telephone and spoke a few words. "Mr. Gray, y'all have a seat and Miss Jernigan will be right out."

Callie and Arthur sat on a small sofa. Arthur watched Callie cross and uncross her ankles, holding her hands tightly in her lap. His nerves were stretched to the breaking point. All of Art's shenanigans had caused them to be there in that office. He and Callie had just about talked themselves out, and still they had no solutions. Arthur hoped their meeting today would calm their worries.

"Mr. and Mrs. Gray, hello. I'm Ethel Jernigan." She offered her hand, which they both shook gently. "Come with me to my office."

Following her, Callie looked to Arthur for support. He took her hand and squeezed hard, telling her everything would be okay. His smile said hang in there.

After the three of them had taken a seat, Callie and Arthur remained quiet.

"Of course, y'all know why we asked you to come in today." She looked from one of them to the other. Callie and Arthur nodded. "When a youngster like your son, Art, breaks the law, the police call us in on the case. This time we were called in because your son had a wreck while drinking at his age. You understand that, don't you? He was underage and drinking, and that added to the severity of the car crash."

Again, Arthur and Callie nodded.

"What can you tell me about your son?"

Callie began. "He's a good boy. He's not perfect, just as none of us are."

"Has Art given you any trouble—about obeying your rules?"

Arthur spoke. "No, he does pretty good obeyin' us. He's a teenager, though."

"Yes, I know. But we can't just push this problem we have here to the fact that he's a teenager. Do you allow him to drive the family car? Did he have your permission to drive your car the morning he had the wreck?"

"Well, no, he drives an old car of ours. That's what he was drivin' when he had the wreck. He has our permission to drive that car."

"Did either of you see him leave in the car to go to school?"

Callie tried to help Arthur. "I work part-time at the church, and that morning I had already left the house before time for him to leave for school. And Arthur has to go in early to open up the hardware store."

"So you're saying you were both gone, and left Art to get to school?"

"Yes." Arthur felt his irritation mounting. "He's a senior in high school. You'd think he could at least get himself ready to go to school on time."

"But he didn't. Does this happen often?"

"No, it doesn't." Callie didn't know how much she should say, so she stopped.

"I've checked with the school about his attendance records. He's often absent, and even when he attends he's usually tardy and sometimes skips class and returns before school lets out."

"Miss Jernigan, what are you gettin' at here? What is it you want from us?" Arthur worked to tamp down his aggravation at this young woman who didn't look too much older than his son, Art.

"Number one, I want your cooperation." She straightened in her chair and clipped her words. "Number two, I want the three of us to work together for Art's good. I want us to make the best of a bad situation."

Callie leaned forward in her chair. "Miss Jernigan, can you tell us how bad this 'bad situation' you speak of is?"

She shuffled some papers on her desk but didn't pick up one. "Your son is recuperating from a broken arm, I understand. And is he back in school yet?"

Callie looked at Miss Jernigan. "No. He has a follow up visit with the doctor who will tell Art when he can go back to school."

"I see. And Art's not supervised during this time he's staying at home?"

"Not all the time." Arthur looked at Callie.

"Well, this bad situation you asked about—with your son unsupervised at home is not good."

"Ma'am, you told my wife you wanted us both here for this appointment. We couldn't much be at two places at once."

Miss Jernigan sat straighter in her chair. "Let's look at the seriousness of what your son did. Adolescent drinking can cause any number of health problems, all serious. Drinking under the age of twenty-one is illegal of course. Drinking alcohol at your son's age can do major damage to him." She looked down at the papers on her desk. "Drinking before age twenty-one can cause brain development damage, early liver damage, overall body deterioration that may interfere with normal development of the body, and loss of self-control, which is obviously what happened to your son when he had his car accident. And if he's with a group, say at a party, binge drinking may cause life threatening alcohol poisoning."

Arthur sat dumbstruck. "What's binge drinkin'?"

"Binge drinking is heavy consumption of alcohol over a short period of time, such as having five or more drinks on one occasion—like at a party. Do you know if Art has been going to any parties where they serve alcohol?"

Callie and Arthur shook their heads no, then Arthur spoke. "Miss Jernigan, Art is a hard kid to pin down. We ask him where he was when the school calls to tell us he wasn't at school that day. We can't get any information from Art. He just sloughs us off. Sometimes we just don't know …" Callie touched his arm and he stopped talking.

"Mr. and Mrs. Gray, you have just described Art as an irresponsible, happy-go-lucky boy. Even if you strictly monitored his actions, it appears he would do whatever he wanted to when you think he's at school. Is that right?"

Arthur looked at Callie and saw a warning on her face. "Miss Jernigan, it seems to me you're gettin' into some deep water here. You're not the police but you sure do sound accusin' when you talk about our son."

"As the social worker assigned by the authorities to Art's case, I'll be monitoring your family's lifestyle and his. Art's case goes to Judge Franklin, and I'll be sending him copies of my notes from our meeting and my meeting with Art."

Startled, Arthur questioned the woman. "Do we need a lawyer?"

"That's up to you, Mr. Gray. Art's entitled to be represented by an attorney in the courtroom. Some parents are a little more comfortable when their child is in Judge Franklin's court if they have an attorney there."

~ ~ ~

"Yes, Peggy."

"Mr. Callaway, Mr. Gray is on the telephone."

"Thanks. Please put him through."

When his telephone rang, Jim reached for it before it could ring the second time. "Bones, how did the meeting with the social worker go?"

Jim heard defeat in his friend's voice. "Jim, good and bad, I guess."

"How's that?"

Arthur described the meeting to Jim. "Good gracious, Bones. Are you going to get a lawyer?"

"I've never used one. I don't know any. Can you recommend somebody to me?"

Jim didn't have to think about that long. "I've got this lawyer helping me with Emmajean's case down in Atlanta. He's from here but he goes with me when I go down there. We've got an Atlanta lawyer doing her case, but it makes me feel better to know I've got somebody local to explain things to me."

"What's his name? Do you think he would help us out with Art?"

"I'll give him a call for you, and find out if you want me to."

"Jim, that'll be great. See if he can help us and if he can, tell him I'll be in touch with him."

~ ~ ~

"What did the lawyer say?"

"Callie, he sure sounded nice and accommodatin'. He said he'd be glad to help us out. Said Jim had called him, told him what was goin' on. He asked me to keep him up to date when anythin' happens with Art's case."

"Arthur, I can breathe easier now. What he's going to charge?"

"I didn't even ask. It has to be done. He did say he wanted to be here when Miss Jernigan has her talk with Art. He said Art shouldn't be alone for that."

"That's good news. I don't believe that social worker was going to let either one of us be with Art when she comes over."

The telephone rang, and they both looked at it. Art was in the house so it wasn't a call about him getting hurt again. Arthur picked up the receiver. "Hello."

Arthur paused, listening to the other person. "Yes, Miss Jernigan, Art will be here all week. We expect him to start back to school next week."

Callie understood who the call was from, and thought it might not be good news.

"Sure, Thursday afternoon at 2 o'clock would probably be fine. I'll tell Art...Okay, bye." He returned the telephone to its cradle. They exchanged looks. Why were they so tense about seeing Miss Jernigan? Because this woman held a better part of their son's future in her hands.

~ ~ ~

"Terry, I guess we'll stay until Miss Jernigan gets here."

Terry watched Arthur pace across the living room again. "I'll call y'all at Jim's house when she leaves."

"There's coffee in the kitchen. Just help yourself." Callie tried to calm her jitters. Coffee wouldn't help with that.

"Mr. and Mrs. Gray, Art and I will be fine with the lady. Don't worry. I think it would be best if you both settled down a little. You both look like you're guilty of something. That's not the impression we want to give to the social worker."

"Yeah, I guess you're right, Terry." Arthur took a seat and breathed a sigh.

"And Terry, you can call us Arthur and I'm Callie."

"Thanks, I will. Now, where is Art?"

"Here I am." Art slouched into the living room.

Terry stood and offered his hand, then saw that Art's right arm was in a cast. "Glad to meet you, Art. I'm Terry Fields. I'm a lawyer. I'll be with you during the social worker's visit today. She'll be talking to you, but I'll be here just in case she gets into a topic that I think you shouldn't talk to her about. Understand?"

Art, sullen and silent sprawled into a chair. "Yeah. But I won't need you. I can handle myself."

Jim and the Grays had told him about Art's overall behavior and attitude. They sure did an accurate job of that. Terry tried again to engage the teenager in conversation. "When you meet the social worker, Art, you need to make a good impression on her. She will report to Judge Franklin everything she sees and everything you say today. You need to straighten yourself up."

Art looked daggers at Terry. When he looked at his parents, he saw the same stern expression on their faces. He scooted up in his chair to sit straighter. "Y'all trying to scare me into being a good little boy?"

"No, Art." Terry stared him down. When Art looked away from Terry, he began again. "I would think your car wreck would have done that. I'm here to help, but if you don't want me here, just say the word."

Art shifted in his chair and sat even straighter. "Nah, you can stay."

Callie smiled but Art didn't pay her any attention.

The door bell rang.

"Art, she's here. You only speak when spoken to by her. You can answer her questions but be as brief as you can. Do you know how to say yes, ma'am and no, ma'am?'

"Yeah."

As Arthur went to open the door, Terry spoke again to Art. "Then I suggest you try using those words. You'll even have to use similar words when you get to court with the judge."

Miss Jernigan followed Arthur into the living room. Terry stood, and gave a nod to Art to do the same, which he did.

"Miss Jernigan, this is our son, Art, and this is Mr. Fields, our lawyer."

She offered her hand to Terry. He took a step toward her and shook her hand. She turned to Art, and considering his injured arm, she nodded.

"Please have a seat, Miss Jernigan. We, uh, we'll be goin' now." Arthur backed out of the living room, holding Callie's arm.

When she heard the front door close, Miss Jernigan sat to open her small briefcase, and pulled some papers out. Terry watched as she appraised Art with beady eyes. Art squirmed in his chair. Maybe nobody had ever been stern enough with Art to make him behave. But many people have tried unsuccessfully—his parents, teachers, even Jim has tried a little.

Miss Jernigan began. "Art, what grade in school are you?"

"You know . . ."

Terry cleared his throat. Art glanced his way in time to see Terry shoot him a slight shake of his head.

"Uh, I'm a senior."

"Do you like school?"

". . . uh, no . . . ma'am."

"Is there anything or anybody you like at school?"

"The only thing I like about school is my buddies."

"Thank you, Art, for telling me the truth. Now, let's talk about the day you had the car wreck. Did you go to school that day?"

"Yes, ma'am."

"How long did you stay?"

"Well, I just drove to school, I didn't go in."

"I see. Why did you drive to school if you didn't go in?"

Art glanced at Terry. Terry didn't offer him any help.

"Well, I just went by school to catch up with my buddies in the parking lot."

"Where do you park when you go to school?"

"In area B. It's around back between the school and the gym."

"Did any of your teachers see you that morning?"

"No. They don't ever come back there."

"So, how long did you spend with your buddies?"

"Aw, we just talked a while. When the bell rang, and they went into class, I left."

"Did they give you anything that morning?"

"What do you mean?"

"I mean, did your buddies give you anything that morning before you left?"

Art fidgeted and didn't look at Miss Jernigan.

"Art, please answer my question."

"Yes, ma'am, they did give me something."

"What did they give you?"

Art looked at Terry. Terry nodded at Art to answer the question.

"Well, they gave me a quart bottle of beer."

"Who gave you the beer?"

"Well . . ."

"Miss Jernigan, as Art's attorney, I don't think he should answer that question. He is not required to implicate anyone else. He'll be glad to answer your questions, but only if they apply to him and him only.

"Very well. So, Art, did you go into the school that morning?"

"No, ma'am."

"What did you do?"

"I left school and drove around."

"Where did you drive around?"

"Anywhere, everywhere, I guess."

"Did you eat breakfast that day?"

"No, ma'am."

Terry groaned inwardly. He saw where this line of questions was going.

"When did you drink the quart of beer *someone* gave you?"

"I started on it as soon as I was off school property."

"So you had no breakfast, and you drank your beer on an empty stomach?"

"Yes, ma'am." Art gave Miss Jernigan a questioning look.

"Art, where did you have your car wreck?"

"On the old Knoxville highway."

"Did your wreck occur where the road was straight?"

"No, ma'am. That's not a straight road, has some curves."

"So, then, what caused your wreck."

"I guess I tried to straighten out a curve." Art smirked.

"Tell me what happened."

"Well, I left the road, sailed actually. There was air between me and the ground. When the car landed it rolled over and sat on its top."

"Were you able to get out?"

"No. I crawled around over the inside of the roof. I wanted to get out through a window but with my broken arm I couldn't get around too good. And I couldn't roll the window down."

"How long did you stay in the car before someone helped you?"

"I'm not sure. I guess somebody in another car saw what happened, and went to tell the police. They came, and got me out. I don't remember how long it took them to get to me."

"Art, you're seventeen. You're underage for drinking." She glanced at Terry. "Wherever you got the beer, you drank it and you drove your car. That's the problem here: underage drinking and driving. That's why the court called me in. I'll be giving the judge notes about our meeting today. You'll hear from his office soon to set up a time for you to appear in court."

Art sat up, more alert. "Appear in court? I didn't hurt anybody."

"I just told you that you broke the law. That's why you have to appear in court. The judge will determine what's next for you." She stacked her papers, all corners aligned, returned them to her briefcase, and stood.

Terry walked her to the door. She didn't say another word.

When Terry returned to the living room, Art had left. Terry went to the telephone and called Jim's home number. Waiting as the telephone rang, Terry finally said "Hello. She's gone. Y'all can come back home now"

"How did it go?"

"Art, we'll talk about it when you get here."

"Will you be there until we get home?"

"Yes, I'll stay. Bye"

Chapter 6

All three of them came together in one car this time—Caroline, James, and Lynn. "Here we are. Looks like nobody's home."

"No problem, I have a key." Lynn dangled her keys for them to see.

Lynn didn't know Jim had forced Caroline to take a key to his home, "just in case," he'd said.

They piled out of the car gathering their things, and made it across the porch. Lynn used her key to unlock the door, and they set their suitcases in the foyer. James took the groceries they'd stopped for into the kitchen.

"Thank you, James." Caroline smiled at her son.

"Finals are over and one more quarter down." James screamed out.

"I'll second that." Lynn had collapsed onto the sofa.

"Let's all get our things on upstairs before Jimmy gets here and stumbles over them. He's not used to having a family move in with him while he's at work."

They each grabbed their stuff, and headed up to their usual bedrooms.

James called out from his bedroom. "I'm going to rest on the bed a while. If I go to sleep, wake me when Dad gets here."

~ ~ ~

Caroline and Lynn busied themselves in the kitchen, putting away the groceries they'd brought.

"Daddy will be surprised when he comes home and smells the roast we're doing for supper. I'll supervise, and you'll do it all."

"Wow, Lynn, you really mean for me to do all the work?"

"I might help some."

Lynn explained the steps toward a roast beef dinner. She helped by peeling the potatoes while watching Caroline as she worked through each step.

"You didn't have to wake me. I got a whiff of the great smells coming from down here. What're y'all making?"

"Lynn is showing me how to fix a roast with potatoes and carrots. I'm anxious to see how it turns out—that's Jimmy's favorite meal."

"Y'all must be doing everything okay. I'll be in the television room."

When they had assembled everything and the large pot simmered on the stove, they set the dining room table. Caroline looked around at the house she grew up in, surprised she still felt like she was at home when they visited Jimmy. She walked through the house, touching pieces of furniture and spending extra time in Jimmy's bedroom. She saw Louisa's picture sitting on the bedside table, the same photo she'd seen in Lynn's bedroom.

Was she insane to hope for a renewed romantic relationship between her and Jimmy? Until today she'd not considered she might be contending with a ghost for his affection. But there it was, as plain as day. Louisa still held his heart. Caroline had promised him they would take it slow, and keep their children uppermost in their minds as they tried to work things out.

Second marriages sometimes didn't work out when the new wife moved into the man's home. A home he'd shared with his first wife. Louisa had never lived with Jimmy in this house but Caroline felt her presence in a real way as she picked up Louisa's framed photo. She hadn't known Louisa but she'd been correct in her assumption that Louisa had been the girl she remembered from the mill.

~ ~ ~

"Lynn, I knew you'd be in here."

"Daddy!"

Lynn jumped into his arms and they shared a hug.

"The roast sure smells good." He lifted the lid from the large pot on the burner. "Good gracious, what a large beef roast. Think we can eat all that? You've never fixed one that big."

"We've got more mouths to feed now, Daddy."

"Where is everybody?"

"James is in the back. He's watching television if he hasn't fallen asleep again. Caroline is upstairs. I guess she's putting her things away in her bedroom. Daddy, we're staying a whole week. Off from school a whole week!"

"I'll just go up and see if Caroline needs any help."

Jim looked in all the upstairs rooms as he covered the upstairs hall, first to the left and then to the right. He found Caroline in his bedroom standing by his bed with her back toward him. He slipped into the room as quietly as he could. When he put his hands on her shoulders, she jumped in delighted surprise.

"You shouldn't slip up on a lady like that." She swatted him on the chest.

Then he saw what she held in her other hand. Louisa's photo. He'd never been able to put it away, out of sight. Would he ever be able to do that without thinking he'd been unfaithful to Louisa?

Jim took the photo from Caroline and placed it on the bedside table, making sure it sat just as he'd had it. He fought for the right words. Why had Caroline come into his bedroom? He'd been happy all day knowing Caroline would be here when he came home. Now, his excitement dampened, he hung his head.

He felt Caroline's hand beneath his chin. She raised his head and looked into his ebony eyes. "Jimmy, everything is fine. I was just walking through the house, remembering it from when I lived here."

He didn't return her smile. "You shouldn't have come into my bedroom."

"Perhaps. But I understand . . ."

"Understand what? You didn't even know Louisa."

"I know you and I understand your loyalty to Louisa. Y'all were married, she was the mother of your child. Of course, you would still have her photo beside your bed. I do understand. I shouldn't have come in here. You're correct. I apologize."

Jim hung his head again. "Caroline, I apologize. Even though Louisa has been gone over sixteen years, I'm doing the same thing I did as a young, arrogant seventeen-year-old—I'm seeing both of you. I'm spending happy times with you and sad times with Louisa. Callie and Shirley Ann have been after me for years to let her go. It's not easy. But since I found you last Christmas, I've wondered about my loyalty. Should it stay with Louisa, or should I give my loyalty to you? It's a hard thing to do—decide between the two of you, even if Louisa is not here."

"You leave Louisa's photo right where it is. You have all the time in the world to work this out to your satisfaction. And you will. We'll let everything work out, however long it takes."

Jim reached for Caroline and took her in his arms while at the same time looking over her shoulder at Louisa's picture. He felt like a heel. He closed his eyes, and welcomed Caroline's warmth. He tightened his hold of her.

From downstairs they heard people talking. Caroline leaned back and looked at Jim. "Who is that downstairs?"

"I think I hear my sister and maybe Bones. Let's go down and find out." Jim started for the bedroom door.

Caroline held Jim's arm, reluctant to follow him. "Why would they be here? Today?"

"I won't know till I go downstairs. You coming?"

"If it is your family, they will probably resent me being here. Do they usually just drop in like this? Maybe I should stay up here."

"No, really they don't usually just come by. I suspect Lynn may have invited them for supper. I came through the kitchen when I got home and the roast she's cooking is mighty big for the four of us."

"Jimmy, *I'm* cooking the roast. Lynn walked me through the steps, but I sure did not know I was cooking for your family."

"Let's go. It'll be okay. They all know I've been seeing you and James. They have no ill will toward you." He tugged her along toward the stairs.

~ ~ ~

Sure enough when they got to the living room it was full: Arthur and Callie, Shirley Ann and Henry Frank, and five teenagers.

"Hey, everybody! How'd y'all slip in on me like this?" He looked at Lynn who was smiling like a Cheshire cat. "Lynn, is this your doing?"

"Yes, it is." She clasped her hands beneath her chin as her mother had done when she was pleased and excited.

"Well, okay, then." He took Caroline's hand and pulled her forward. "Y'all, this is Caroline, James's mother. You met James last year at Thanksgiving."

The group crowded in toward Caroline. At first she wanted to flee, but then all their faces held a kindness unfamiliar to her. Jim's sister and Callie hugged her and the guys shook her hand. The teenagers just raised a hand and gave her big smiles.

"Caroline, welcome to this crazy bunch of family we have here." Shirley Ann hugged her again. "Lynn wanted us to be a surprise and come for supper. We get together like this often, so don't feel overwhelmed. We're all glad to see you."

Words of agreement flowed through the room. Caroline smiled and glanced at Jim. "Thank you for the gracious hospitality you have offered me." She looked at Callie and continued. "I appreciate your making me feel welcome among you. Please, let us all sit."

Everybody did so except the teenagers who went toward the television room. Caroline was tense to say the least. But conversation buzzed around her and every now and then they would draw her into it. She heard their talk about Emmajean and about Callie's boy, Art. As they talked, Caroline recognized the cohesiveness of Jim's family. She sensed the empathy among them. She perceived no animosity toward her, even from Louisa's sister, Callie. Caroline, like James, had not had family around her for twenty years. She looked at Jim and they exchanged a smile, much of her stressful expression leaving her face.

Caroline's apprehension faded away while everyone ate at the dining room table, talk coursed among them. Seeing the way his family had accepted her, Caroline knew a big hurdle now lay behind her and Jim. If the family had disapproved of her, Jim probably would have leaned toward their decision.

Lynn grinned at Caroline. "Caroline, this roast is delicious. You did a good job."

"Thank you, Lynn. But where did all this other lovely food come from? You and I didn't cook all this."

"Callie and I brought things along." Shirley Ann sent a smile Caroline's way across the table. "That's how our family does—everyone chips in when we get together, and we have plenty for everybody."

"It's all delicious. Thank you for including me."

"Caroline, you'll always be welcome with us." Caroline discerned the sincerity in Callie's words, even while she wondered how Louisa's sister could mean that. But Caroline sensed that she did mean it and Caroline felt grateful.

~ ~ ~

After all the family left, Caroline and Jim sat on the sofa. James and Lynn had gone with some of their cousins to get ice cream at a drive-in. Jim stretched his legs out in front of him and spread his arms across the back of the sofa, letting one arm rest on Caroline's shoulder.

She snuggled closer to him. "Jimmy, I just cannot put into words how I feel about your family."

"Why's that?"

"The way they welcomed me was unbelievable, especially even Callie."

"Callie's been telling me for a long time that her sister would want me to start a new life with someone. She feels that Louisa would want me to have someone and not be lonely in this big house."

"That's what I mean. I just can't comprehend people being so . . . nice to me. You know when James came down here last

Thanksgiving he tried to tell me when he returned that y'all made him feel like family. I know now what he meant."

"So you feel better? You tensed up when you heard them when we were upstairs."

"I did, didn't I? They all helped welcome me and my dread went away as soon as they greeted me. I must thank Lynn for asking them over."

"I already did thank her. She was all happy that things turned out so good. I think she's accepted you as being a part of my life. So she wanted everybody else to get in on it too."

"We have some wonderful children, don't we?"

"Yep."

"Since the family received me well, what about us? You and me? Are we getting any farther along with things between us?"

Jim grew silent and walked to the fireplace to stir up the logs. He replaced the poker in its stand. He sat on the sofa again and turned toward her, looking into her navy blue eyes. "I don't know. Sometimes I think so, and other times I think we're no farther along than last Christmas. I just don't know."

"Jimmy, what do you not know?"

Jim was slow to answer. "My brothers in the army would say it's the logistics of the matter. The details of the situation. Knoxville or Newton? Newton or Knoxville?"

"Jimmy, I am in love with you. I have been since that summer of 1929. There has been no one since then. I love you with all my heart."

He took her hand. "I love you Caroline, but I just can't work out the details in my mind of a relationship between us."

She kissed his cheek. Her warm breath was like a touch of the upcoming spring working its way into his life. He turned toward her, and his lips found hers for a brief kiss.

"Jimmy, I told you of my plan for us to be together. Have you thought about it at all?"

"Of course I have." He kissed her again, this time a little longer.

"Well?"

"Oh, Caroline." He pulled her against him, and held her there for a long time.

It seemed providential that their children should arrive at just that moment.

~ ~ ~

They put their coats in the closet and came into the living room. "Hey, y'all, did you eat the rest of that cake?" James came to the sofa and sat beside his mom.

"No, we left it for you. I thought maybe you might be hungry again."

"Mom, are you trying to say I eat a lot?"

"Of course you do, and I'm glad you do. Lynn, did you give him the grand tour of Newton?"

"Yes, he got dizzy I drove around the courthouse square so many times."

They all shared a laugh at James's expense.

"Daddy, we brought some textbooks home with us. Do you mind if we spread out in the television room and try to get some studying done?"

"Sure, go ahead. Let me know if it's not warm enough back there."

As they started out of the living room, the telephone rang. "Go on, I'll get it." Jim left the sofa and picked up the telephone. "Hello."

Caroline watched when Jim's jovial appearance faded as he listened to the caller. At his serious countenance, she moved to the edge of the sofa.

"Okay, Bones, I appreciate you letting us know. Call me again if there's anything I can do. . . Bye." He cradled the black telephone.

Jim turned toward Caroline, his hand still on the telephone. She stood and came to his side. "Why did Arthur call? You look so serious."

"When they got home they found a letter from Judge Franklin's office. They have to appear in his court next week. Bones sounded shook up. He said Callie's crying." One more domino had fallen in Art's problem but the boy's trouble may be about to get worse. Jim didn't know much about juvenile court but he'd asked around about the judge. Everyone he talked to said he was a tough man but mostly fair. The fair Callie would like, but the tough . . . well, maybe she could keep herself together whatever the judge did.

"Poor Callie. I can't imagine what I would be doing if James had gotten himself into something like Art has."

"Yeah, but James is a good kid."

"Didn't you think Art was a good kid until lately?"

"Sure did, but I knew he was having trouble staying in school. It's the drinking that's brought him to this. And you know how I feel about drinking."

She smiled. "Yes I do know. You learned your lesson back when you were working at the mill."

"Yeah, going with those guys from work that Saturday sure opened my eyes the next day. I promised myself that morning I'd never do that to myself again. My head felt like it weighed a ton, and would explode any minute." He stared at the floor. "I didn't want to turn out to be a drinker like Poppa."

"And you haven't."

"Poppa changed after that, stopped drinking, and started treating us all better." Jim remembered his Poppa and Momma. When they'd died from that wave of pneumonia that spread down from Knoxville, he had become the head of the family. All that and the Great Depression too. Jim had to grow up in a hurry. He and Louisa had taken over the care of Emmajean, just a kid then.

Emmajean. She had blossomed into a beautiful young woman. What in the world is going to happen down in Atlanta with her trial beginning in June? Another domino for him to try to prop up. He hoped the situation with Art would be settled before June.

"Jimmy, what are you thinking about?"

She probably knew like she did when they were younger but he answered her anyway. "Aw, just everything. I feel like I have too many plates in the air—you know, like the jugglers at the fair?"

"Art's problem is not yours to bear. I know he's your best friend's child and your nephew. But there's nothing at all you can do to alter the outcome."

"You're right." His facial expression didn't improve.

"Jimmy, what other *plates* are you concerned about?"

"Of course, Emmajean. I can't really change that situation either. I just have to wait and see. I think that's what's bothering me the most—having to stand by and watch things happen as they will. I don't have any control over anything."

She stepped closer to him but didn't touch him. She smiled knowingly. "What other plates are on your mind, Jimmy?"

He took a few moments to look at her, at her strawberry blond hair, her flashing blue eyes. "You. You and me." The solution to their problem seemed so simple, looking from the outside. But Jim stood smack in the middle and that's where it got difficult. It wasn't just a question of did he want to have a relationship with Caroline. The question was if he should. Not just for him but also for their children. What was best? How could he decide?

"You seem to think about that much of the time we're together."

"And when we're apart too."

"I can't understand why you can't get past the thinking stage on whether we should have a closer relationship. Jimmy, we've already lost twenty years we could have been together, and the more you think the more time we'll spend apart."

Jim felt like a two by four had hit him over the head. Why couldn't he get past the thinking stage about Caroline and him? Really, what was there to think about? As Caroline just said, the longer he thought, the more time they'd spend apart. Wasn't twenty years long enough to spend separated?

"Caroline, our twenty years apart gave us James and Lynn."

"Of course they did. And we have two children we can be proud of. But the twenty years are in the past. Can't we start anew? Can't we begin a new life beyond the past?"

Thinking they were getting into some serious talking here, he remembered the kids were in the television room. He also remembered where he and Caroline used to do most of their talking. "Caroline would you like to take a drive?"

"Sure." Jim surprised her with his abrupt change of subject. Would he refuse continually to talk about them?

"I'll tell the kids we're going out. You want to grab our coats out of the foyer closet?"

When he returned Caroline already had on her coat and offered his to Jim.

In the car, Caroline watched the landscape of Newton as they drove. When Jim turned south before reaching the courthouse square, Caroline asked, "Jimmy, where are we going?"

He glanced toward her. Because he knew where they were going and she didn't, he gave her a slight smile. "That's for me to know, and you to find out."

As the miles clicked past, Caroline began to put it together and thought she knew Jim's destination. She remained quiet, willing to let him think she would be surprised.

Nearer to Chattanooga than to Newton, Jim turned the car left onto a drive covered on each side by tall spiny pines and delicate mimosa trees. He drove to the end of the short drive and parked the car outside a small eating place.

He looked over at Caroline.

"The Evergreen Café. Jimmy, you're so thoughtful."

"This is where we did a lot of our talking. I remember on Sunday nights you would drive me down here in your little Buick, and sometimes we'd talk for hours after we'd eaten."

"Is that what we're going to do tonight—talk for hours?"

"You never know." He got out of the car, and ran around to open Caroline's door to help her out.

After they'd been seated, they ordered pie with milk to drink. Jim didn't know where to start. They looked at one another across the table, waiting for the other to start their conversation.

When they'd eaten their pie and sat back in their wooden booth, Jim reached across the table for Caroline's hand. He looked at her slender fingers and squeezed them. "Caroline, do you remember all the Sunday nights we spent here?"

"Of course, I do. And I've pulled them from my memory many times."

"Caroline." He held her hand in both of his. "You make it sound so simple for me to make a decision about us."

She nodded but didn't speak. She sure wasn't helping him out here. She waited for him to speak again.

"I've been waiting for time for us when the children weren't around. It's always the four of us. That's good." He was quick to assure her. "But I felt we needed some time for just us without interruptions."

"So, now we have some time for us."

"Caroline, you saw Louisa's picture sitting on the table beside my bed. If we get into a full blown relationship, her picture will have to go. I don't plan to try to be loyal to both of you at the same time—again. Louisa's been gone a little over sixteen years. You probably figure that's long enough to hold on to a memory."

"Actually, I don't. Jimmy, I've held onto the memory of you for longer than that. I thought of you every day. When I'd look at James as a baby and as he grew, I'd think of you, he resembled you so much. So, no, I don't question your loyalty to Louisa, however brief your marriage was."

"You're agreeing with me. That's not making this any easier." He flavored his words with a fleeting smile. "It's only been three months since I found you last Christmas. If there were just you and me, this decision would be easy. I would have already asked you to marry me."

He noticed Caroline's quick intake of breath.

"You look startled. Why does that surprise you?"

Caroline only shook her head and smiled, love radiating from her eyes.

"We love each other. We've said so. Marriage has to have love to build on, but we do have a couple of complications. Our child and my child."

She put her other hand over their clasped hands. "We all four love one another. That's obvious."

"Okay, plan for the kids to live in your home and remain in school is good. But at the same time you wanted to move here to Newton."

Her smiled broadened.

"Caroline . . ."

"What, Jimmy?"

The waitress came to their table asking if they needed anything, and left when they said no.

"Doggone it. I've just got a lot going on in my life right now. I can't think straight."

"Jimmy, of all the things you have on your mind, which is the most important. When you make a mental list of them, which one is most important?"

Jimmy looked at her in silence. Why couldn't he get the words out? And would they be words that would make them both happy?"

"Caroline, at the mill I've arranged for Bob Allbright to run the place while I'm in Atlanta for Emmajean's trial that starts on June 11. I have no idea how long that will last and neither does the lawyer. Will you wait till that trial is over before we make any big decisions about us?"

"Do you mean a decision of whether we will get married?"

She had hit it square on. "Yes."

"I don't want to wait, but I will."

That sounded like the Caroline he remembered from his youth—stubborn and getting what she wanted, when she wanted it. Jim smiled at the remembrance.

"It's fine with me if you still want Lynn to move out of the dormitory and into your home. I'd better call the school and arrange for that change in her living quarters. Have you mentioned this to Lynn?"

"No, I thought if you told her she might more readily agree."

"You've thought of everything. Again."

He moved his hands away from hers and stretched his arms across the back of the booth. He looked at her a long time. He would never tire of seeing her every day. Wake up with her every morning. Had he made a mistake asking her to wait till after Emmajean's trial?

"Jimmy, you've made the right decision." She could always know his thoughts.

~ ~ ~

Monday evening as they ate, Jim waited to get into the conversation circling the table. These two kids made them seem like a family of four with two adorable children. That's how it'd be if he could let go of the things that stomped around in his mind. But there was no way he would turn his back even for a weekend on his baby sister. Emmajean, frail and vulnerable, in Atlanta alone—her only bright spots when Jim and Terry visited her. If he and Caroline married that would weaken his loyalty to both of them, it would be like a competition for his time. Maybe his loyalty to all three of them. Jim still held strongly to his loyalty to Louisa.

He grabbed the lull in conversation and looked up the table at Lynn. "Hey, Lynn. I've got a question for you."

Lynn held her fork half way to her mouth. "Okay."

"How would you like to move out of your dorm, and live with Caroline and James in their beautiful home?"

Lynn looked from her daddy to James and then to Caroline. Jim saw surprise, yet hesitation in her eyes when she looked back at him. "Are you serious, Daddy?"

"Yes, I am. Caroline and I have discussed this. In fact, it was her idea. You'd probably be safer living with Caroline and James, and it certainly would make James's job of watching over you an easier one. What do think?"

"When, Daddy? Next fall?"

"No, next quarter."

"You mean when we go back to Knoxville for next quarter?"

"I do."

Lynn could suppress her smile no longer. She folded her hands beneath her chin in her excitement. James's grin was even wider as they looked at one another. Caroline gave Jim another *I told you so* nod.

"I called the university people today to see about how to get this done. They've approved of your moving out of the dormitory."

"You already set this up? You knew I'd be happy with this before you called, didn't you?"

"Caroline and I agreed that you probably would be." Seeing the happiness of his daughter caused his smile to broaden as much as James's.

Caroline smiled her acceptance toward Lynn. "I'm glad you're excited about moving in with us, Lynn. Our home is large enough for a family. You'll have plenty of room and a huge welcome."

And Jim's home also would hold a family. A family of four—the idea grew in his mind.

"James, looks like I'll follow you back to Knoxville. We'll have some moving to do."

"Daddy, we'll have to go back before the week is over so I can get everything packed."

"Yes, I thought so. We'll go up the middle of the week. I'll spend the rest of your quarter break with y'all and get back here by next Monday."

"Daddy, this makes quarter break more exciting than I had expected."

"Good. That's settled then."

"Oh, Dad, it won't be settled till we get Lynn moved in."

"And that won't be easy. I helped her move in up there. She had a bunch of stuff and it's probably multiplied by now."

Smiles all around. Just like a family.

~ ~ ~

James and Jim had accompanied Lynn to the dorm to begin her move. They took two cars, and made several trips loaded with her things. Caroline stayed at her house to supervise the unloading and moving in part. But Lynn, always resourceful and determined, knew just where everything went, and didn't call on Caroline to help much at all.

Mildred had prepared a light dinner before she left for the day. "I thought about us going out to eat dinner but thought y'all might not want to get dressed for that after all your work today."

"This dinner is great, Mom. With the snack you had for us this afternoon this dinner is fine."

"You think of everything, Caroline." Jim winked at her.

Well, maybe she thought of everything but she didn't always get everything to go her way. Looking around the table, she imagined them as a permanent fixture of a family of four. Specifically, she reflected on Jim and her as a married couple, and warmth flooded her body. She remembered the few times they had touched and the even fewer kisses they'd shared. She squirmed in her chair. The only intimacy they'd ever enjoyed happened that summer beside Caney Creek. Thinking on that, her heart quickened. If the love she had for Jim was based on only that one day its flame would have gone out long ago. Yes, she looked forward to sharing her body with Jim again, but her love for him was more than physical. She loved all of him, his mind, his heart, his laughter, his attentions to their children—Caroline loved Jim completely and totally. And she loved him with her entire being.

"Mom. Hey . . . Mom."

James brought her back to reality. "What?"

"You drifted away there. You okay?"

She felt the heat creep up her neck. "Yes, of course." She took a few sips of iced tea to compress her feelings.

When she looked toward Jim, he already looked at her like he knew where her mind had just wandered. He couldn't know. His smile told her otherwise and she reached again for her iced tea.

"Mom, Lynn and I are going to the Tennessee Theater. *Show Boat* started today. The movie's got Howard Keel and Kathryn Grayson in it and some of the stars are supposed to be there tonight. I hope Lynn can see Kathryn Grayson, she likes her singing."

"That sounds exciting. I wouldn't mind seeing that movie myself." Caroline looked at Jim.

"Let's go along with them, Caroline."

Again, their minds moved along the same path.

"Thank you, Jimmy, but let's stay here. We can see the movie over the weekend." She saw relief slip over their children's faces. Of course, they wanted to go without their parents. "Is that okay with y'all?"

"Sure," they both said.

"Lynn, we might need a light jacket inside the theater. Did you bring one with you?" She nodded. "Grab it, and we'll get going. Mom, Dad, we'll be back a little late. The movie stars that attend will probably make an appearance before the movie begins."

~ ~ ~

Jim and Caroline stood in the open doorway, waving bye to their children going off to the movie.

Jim closed the door and they returned to the living room. They sat in comfortable silence for a little while. Then Jim stood and paced around the room.

"Jimmy, is something wrong? Come sit with me."

"Well, I told you I do my best thinking when I'm on my feet. I'm just trying to think some things out." He returned to the sofa. "Emmajean called me today."

His words fell heavily in the room. "How is she?"

"She sounded down when she called. I tried to cheer her up but I don't think I did too good a job of that. It's been a few weeks since I've visited her. She didn't come right out and ask me to come down there, but I could hear it is her voice. The loneliness."

Jim looked at his watch. It was still early evening. Not too late to call Terry and see if he could go with him to Atlanta tomorrow. He dreaded to mention his idea to Caroline. He wanted to get to his feet again but knew she would call him back.

"Jimmy, I can almost hear the wheels turning in your head. What are you working out?"

"I think I might go down to Atlanta to visit Emmajean tomorrow."

"I thought the four of us were planning to spend the weekend here before you had to return to Newton on Sunday. You can't wait till next week?"

Now he'd done it. Caroline's impatience had slipped into their conversation.

"Caroline, I could wait, but I need to make sure Emmajean doesn't get too down on herself. I need to help keep her spirits up as much as I can."

"Jimmy, I don't really know Emmajean. You're her big brother and you must feel an obligation to watch after her. With her in Atlanta that makes it inconvenient for you."

"Doing for my sister will never be inconvenient for me. And she's not an obligation to me. I love my little sister."

"Of course you do. I wouldn't want you to feel any other way. I'm just concerned that you would decide so quickly to go, and leave the three of us here."

"Do you think Emmajean is more important to me than the three of you?"

"Is she?"

There is was. The elephant in the room. His concern for Emmajean bothered Caroline. "I didn't say Emmajean was more important to me than you and the kids."

"I almost think you feel that way."

Jim stood then and walked the length of the room and back. What could he say that wouldn't upset Caroline further? He sat on the sofa and took her hands in his. "Caroline, I love you deeply. And you know I love our children. You grew up as an only child so you probably can't understand where I'm coming from here."

"Jimmy, I think I understand you quite well."

"I took care of Emmajean since she was an adolescent. When our parents died, I was the only one she wanted to hold her. However, we haven't been close for the last ten to twelve years since she went to Atlanta. She let us believe she was working in the fashion business down there and was too busy to come home, and discouraged us to come there to visit her because of her work. But she was really living a hardscrabble life, working in a diner. Then she got in with this guy who got her into trouble with the police."

Jim pulled Caroline to him and relished the closeness. Did she think he was choosing his sister over her? That would be a tough choice to make. His family ties were strong and loving.

"Jimmy, I hoped we'd have this evening to talk without the children interrupting us. You put a damper on our time by talking about going to Atlanta tomorrow. Would you possibly consider going there on Sunday? I'd love it if you would."

She'd given him an out. A way to see Emmajean, and spend more time with Caroline. Why hadn't he offered that compromise before she did? He reached down and tilted her chin up with his fingers. He dipped his head till he found her lips and stayed there longer than ever before.

"Wow. I believe that changes my mind. I guess I'll go to Atlanta Sunday."

Relief washed over her face. She smiled as she pulled him closer for another kiss, which lasted as long as the other one. Jim was the first one to break away. "Caroline, we're alone in the house. It would be easy to forget any restraints. I would love to carry you up those stairs right now. I wish it were easy to push all the hurdles out of our way, and I'd do it."

She looked into his eyes, black as night, and snuggled closer against him. "I wish that too. I look forward to the day when our path is clear for us to think of us, and do what I think we both want to do."

"Get married?"

She smiled and nodded.

"I want us to be married as much as you do. I love you, Caroline. Don't forget that. I'll see you as much as I can until June, but remember I'll be in Atlanta pretty much every week then until Emmajean's trial is over."

~ ~ ~

Driving toward Atlanta on Sunday, Jim yawned. Last week had been a busy one, first in Newton and then in Knoxville. He didn't have a restful weekend. He'd enjoyed it, for sure, but not much time for relaxation. He'd telephoned Terry Saturday evening and he jumped at the chance to accompany Jim to Atlanta on Sunday.

Terry was fast becoming a fixture where Emmajean was concerned. Sometimes Jim wondered if she was as glad to see Terry as she was to see her brother. He chuckled thinking of the parallels of their little group of three with his little family of four.

"What're you chuckling about?"

"Terry, just thinking and letting some of my stress ooze out."

"I don't know too much about your personal life besides Emmajean but you do have a lot on your mind, don't you?"

"Yeah, but this trip is for Emmajean. Let's forget about the rest today."

"Sure."

"Have you talked to Mr. Cox lately?"

"I have. He's approaching her defense about like I would. He's more familiar with the system down there but I'm confident he'll do a good job once the trial begins."

~ ~ ~

"Y'all sure did surprise me. Out of the blue there you two were—standin' in the door to the cafeteria. You sure drew a lot of attention from all the females livin' here. The two handsomest men they've probably ever seen."

"Don't be throwing out all those compliments, it might turn Terry's head."

"Oh, Jim, you hush up." She swatted the air toward him across the table.

The folks at the YWCA let her leave her job early at the cafeteria, and now they were finishing a bite of lunch.

"Did you come down just to take me shoppin' again?"

"Not really. We just came to see you. If you need to go shopping, we can do that. Just say the word."

"Jim, I was just kiddin' you. I don't need to go shoppin'. Spendin' time with you and Terry will make the day special." Emmajean and Terry shared a contented look.

"Emmajean, at least today I won't be a lawyer, just a good friend."

Jim watched the exchanged glances shared by his sister and Terry. With each trip, they had become more comfortable with one another. Jim sensed the closeness developing between them. Not only was Terry building her confidence about the trial, but her self esteem had improved since that first day they saw her in January.

Emmajean nudged his shoulder as they sat side by side across from Jim in the restaurant booth. "Did you say a *good* friend?"

Terry nodded and a broad smile nearly cracked his face open. "I know you enjoy seeing Jim better than me. He's your brother so I don't mind. But next to him do I come in second?"

Happy to watch them and listen to their bantering, Jim allowed himself to relax. He leaned back on his side of the booth and let his body soak in their cheeriness. He admitted to himself that he had needed this visit as much as he had thought Emmajean did. While at Caroline's, he'd felt compelled to make this trip. Now he recognized that he benefitted from being here as much as his sister apparently did.

"I'd like to stay here and talk all afternoon, but the waitress is glaring at us. She probably wants us to leave so she can have another customer's tips." Terry looked at Emmajean. "Where to now?"

"I'd love to go to Callaway Gardens. I understand they have beautiful flowers already blooming this year. But it's over near the Alabama state line and we don't have enough time to go and y'all get back home before dark."

Jim noted Emmajean's excitement. Not only was she always stubborn, but if she liked anything she always showed a lot of enthusiasm.

"I've heard a lot about this thing called Stone Mountain right here in Atlanta. It's just a big old rock where somebody started carvin' out pictures of some Confederate heroes. But he never finished. The place where he started the carvin' is bigger than two football fields. It's over five miles around the base of the big rock."

"Why didn't he finish?"

"I've heard he left to go start another rock carvin' project in South Dakota. They call that place Mount somethin' or another. I've never seen Stone Mountain. It never sounded too interestin' to me."

"Well, then, guess we'll have to settle for each other's company for a couple of hours before Terry and I head back home."

Chapter 7

Jim slipped into the courtroom and took a seat in the back. He told Arthur he would be there but Jim doubted he even noticed him. The spectator area of the room was vacant except for Jim. Judge Franklin sat at his podium which loomed higher than where Bones sat. The four of them sat behind a long table, looking up toward the judge.

Terry whispered something to Art. Callie sat on the other side of Art and Arthur rounded out the quartet.

"Mr. Fields, this is my courtroom and I intend to make this meeting low key, no arguing, no objections. Understand?"

Terry stood. "Yes, Your Honor."

The judge looked down and shuffled some papers. "Mr. Fields, are you representing Art Gray and is he in the courtroom?"

"Yes, Your Honor, I am. This is Art Gray." Terry motioned for Art to stand.

Art looked stiff as a board and scared to death. His arrogance seemed to have disappeared. Maybe Terry had convinced him of the seriousness of today.

"You may be seated. Now, in my papers here I have plenty of information about you, Art. You know what all it is as well as I do so let's talk about everything for a while. We'll just take it slow and easy. That alright with you?"

"Yeah." Terry nudged Art. "Uh, yes, Your Honor, it's okay with me."

"First, I don't like what I read about you and your school attendance record. It appears you're just one step ahead of the truant officer hauling you in. Why is it that you're absent or tardy so much?"

Art started to stand but the judge waved him back to his chair. "Well, I really don't like school."

"Why is that?"

"Well, uh, I just don't like to be told what I can and can't do all day."

"Art, what do you plan to do if you graduate from high school?"

"I haven't thought much about it, I guess. Probably get a job, maybe work for my dad."

"So if you get a job do you think you can go in to work whenever you want to and not go to work when you don't want to?"

"I guess not." Another nudge from Terry. "Uh, no, sir."

"You're absolutely correct. If you don't like your teachers telling you at school what you can and can't do, tell me how you think you'll like working for someone whose orders you'll have to follow."

Several beats of silence passed before Art answered. "I probably won't like it."

"How long do you think you'll keep your job if you treat it like you do school?"

"Probably not long?"

"You're correct again. I would suggest you begin preparing yourself for a job by attending school regularly. If you don't, the truant officer will be called in and you might not graduate this year. Do you understand me?"

"Yes, sir."

"Now, let's move on to this car accident you had recently. You got banged up a little but the biggest thing here is that you'd been drinking. The police officer covering your wreck used the Drunkometer on you and you registered above the legal level of alcohol you can drink and drive safely. You skipped school and you drank a lot of alcohol. Why, Art? We know you don't like school but why in the world were you drinking in the middle of the day?"

"I guess I just was."

"Art, do you drink during the day every week?"

"Yes."

"How many days a week do you drink?"

"It depends on how many days I skip school."

Silence galloped through the almost empty room. Jim kept his eye on Judge Franklin who had leaned back in his chair, apparently considering all that had been said so far. He leaned forward.

"Art, I've got here a list of the teachers you have class with each school day. Beginning tomorrow, you will have each teacher sign a piece of paper dated for that day. You will bring that piece of paper home and give it to your dad. Every day. Do you understand me?"

"Yea . . . Yes, sir."

"Now, as for your drinking, I'm suspending your driver's license for two months . . . . Mr. Fields, keep your client under control with his mouth shut. If you attend school regularly I'll return your license to you. Mr. Fields, please give me Art's driver's license."

The judge waited while Art fished his license from his billfold. Terry walked to the judge's podium and handed the piece of paper to him. Jim saw Arthur put his arm around Callie's shoulders. They both turned toward Art and looked downhearted and glum.

Judge Franklin gave a light tap of his gavel. "I also order you to attend an Alcoholics Anonymous meeting each week. Mr. Gray, will you be able to drive Art to these meetings?"

"Yes, Your Honor."

"They hold their meetings at the Episcopalian church, 7 p.m, Fridays."

"Yes, sir."

"Art, you are to be in church every Sunday morning unless you're truly sick. And you will do community service each weekend until school is over this year. The truant officer will get in touch with you and let you know what you have to do. Also it looks like you're working on saying yes, sir and no, sir. See that you continue to do that."

Jim felt like he was watching a bad movie that wouldn't have a happy ending. He saw Art lower his head.

"And finally, I fine you 200 dollars. You can take care of that at the clerk's office. Mr. Fields, do you or your client have any questions or anything to say?"

Terry looked at Art and his parents who all shook their heads. "No, Your Honor."

"Art, I'll see you back here in two months, and we'll talk about how you did with all this."

Another slight tap of his gavel and the judge left the room.

~ ~ ~

When they all stood at Art's table, Jim moved forward and shook hands with Terry and Arthur then offered his hand to Art. Surprisingly, Art shook his hand. Jim noticed the track of a tear across Art's cheek. This was one somber bunch of people, including Art.

Jim looked again at Callie. She looked up at him with red, puffy eyes. Her face held the expression of "Why me, God?" But Jim couldn't imagine her letting those words cross her lips. Callie and her sister, Louisa, both loved God. Callie would never question God's plan for her and her family's lives.

Jim gave her a shoulder hug and an extra squeeze. He didn't know if it would help her, but that's all he could do. Arthur talked with Terry, and Art stood still with his hands stuffed in his pants' pockets.

"Well, okay, what happens next?"

"Jim, Terry says I can go to the clerk's office down the hall and pay Art's fine, so I'm on my way to do that."

"Arthur, it won't take you long to finish up down there." Terry closed his briefcase then turned to Jim who still held Callie's shoulder.

"Terry, it's nearly lunchtime. What's your schedule?"

"I can get lunch now. Art, you hungry?"

Art looked at the floor, and spoke barley above a whisper. "Yes, sir."

"Callie? You up to going someplace for lunch?"

"Jim, I'm not hungry but I'll drink some iced tea with y'all if we go."

Terry stepped forward. "Let's go then. After we eat I'll take Art to school."

"School?" Art's head snapped up. "The day's half gone. Can't we forget school for the rest of today?"

"Art, I don't think Judge Franklin would be happy to hear that."

Callie's voice was weak when she hugged Art. "Son, you have to go to school. You heard the judge tell you what all you have to do."

They all turned when the courtroom door opened. "I got the fine all taken care of. How about getting lunch? My treat."

"I've already beat you to it. Let's go then. The Blanchard Hotel?"

Callie looked at Jim in surprise. "The Blanchard Hotel? We go there just for celebrations. I don't think we're in the mood to celebrate today."

"Callie, look at it this way. Art possibly couldn't be leaving here with us today. The judge could probably have put him in jail for a while. But we're all here together. There's always a bright side— let's go eat."

~ ~ ~

Back in his office after lunch, Jim stood at his window watching the traffic go by on four-eleven. He ran this morning with the judge through his mind. Judge Franklin lived up to his reputation as tough, but fair. Would Art go to those AA meetings? If not, he'll be in trouble with the judge.

Watching the cars on the highway, he wished he could see Caroline drive past on her way to his house. It wouldn't happen today, not in the middle of the week. He turned toward his desk and punched the intercom. "Peggy, please get Mrs. Hensen on the telephone."

He sat just as his intercom clicked on. "Mr. Callaway, I have Mrs. Hensen on the line. I'll transfer her now."

Jim didn't wait long enough for the first ring to finish before he picked up his telephone. "Caroline?"

"Jimmy, I'm so glad you called. How did it go with Art this morning?"

Jim explained the morning with as little detail as possible. He knew Caroline had wanted to know but he'd really called just to hear her voice. When he stopped talking, she questioned him. "Jimmy?"

"Yeah."

"Jimmy, you're so quiet. Is there something you're not telling me?"

"Not a thing."

"You're not talking to me. Are you sure?"

"Caroline, I just wanted to hear your voice. Thinking about you is great but hearing your voice is even better. How are you and the kids? Has Lynn got all her things where she wants them?"

"Jimmy, yes, Lynn seems so happy and relaxed here. She's accepted me and the situation better than I had hoped for. She and James left this morning for the campus."

"That's good news. So, y'all have everything going along okay then. The kids are doing great. How about you? Lynn won't be a burden on you?"

"Absolutely not! Jimmy, you should know better than to ask such a question. The only burden on me is you not being here."

"Now wouldn't that be something? I could just walk away from the mill and move in with you too." He leaned back in his chair and chuckled.

"Yes, it would be something. But the telephone is not where we should be talking about this. When are you up for some company?"

"How about a week from Friday? Could y'all come down for the weekend?

"Jimmy, why not this Friday?"

"I want to be here for Bones and Callie this coming weekend. Art starts his community service Saturday. And, besides, I just saw you last Sunday morning."

"There you go, trying to take care of everybody. I know you have some things on your mind. But, Jimmy, you can't let them consume your every day. The kids and I aren't in trouble with the law, but we do need to see you."

Jim remembered similar words coming from his momma when his new sister, little Ollie, had died: *"Jim, I wish you'd come home more. The children need to see you and I miss you."*

"Caroline, I love all of you—you and the kids, Bones's family, and Emmajean. I love *you*. Remember that. We're all in a tough spot right now. And until Art cleans up his life and Emmajean is free to come home to Newton, I guess you'll just have to put up with my ways."

"I realize that's a part of you I love—wanting what's best for everyone. So, a week from Friday it is then. You'd tell me if anything was bothering you, wouldn't you?"

"Of course. I'm sharing everything with you now. I've not shared much with anybody expect Arthur for over sixteen years."

"You can depend on me anytime you want to talk."

"Thanks. Well, I'd better stop doing personal stuff on my shift here at the mill. Some of the folks around here might get the idea they can do the same. I miss you. See you a week from Friday."

"We'll be talking before then. I'm glad you called. Bye, I love you."

"I love you. Bye."

God, thank you for your precious gift of love. You told us to love one another with a brotherly love. I love Caroline and it's fast becoming a love that I want to act on. I want to marry Caroline but I don't want to if it means bringing her into this heap of problems I'm swimming in. I know I've taken on others' troubles, and I'm trying to help. Emmajean, Art and his family, and Caroline and our family. At least we could have a family. Please give me Your strength and guide me in my decisions every day. Amen.

~ ~ ~

"Good morning, Arthur. Good to see your family in church today."

"Thank you, pastor, and good morning to you."

Arthur was really glad his family came to church, especially Art. Art could still adjust his attitude some but at least he came with them. He felt a hand press his shoulder, and he turned.

"Morning, Bones, how's the weekend going?"

"Jim, pretty good, I guess."

Arthur and Jim followed Arthur's family into a pew and took their seats.

Jim shot a glance at Art. "How did Art do on his community service yesterday?"

"Good, I reckon. They kept him busy pickin' up trash beside some roads and the grounds of his school. He's still broodin' but I guess he'll just have to get used to it. He really hated goin' to the AA meeting. Said it was just a bunch of drunks who'd lost their jobs and families and he didn't belong there."

"Bones, he hadn't caught on yet that the reason those men have lost their jobs and families is because of drinking. He may not admit catching on but it won't take him long."

The choir and pastor entered the sanctuary and a hush fell over the crowd.

Chapter 8

A couple of months later, on June 11, Jim and Terry rode toward Atlanta. Not much traffic on the road in the wee hours of the morning. Jim wanted to start early so they could get there when the jury selection began at nine o'clock. Emmajean couldn't be present but he and Terry could.

Neither of them talked much at this time of day. Jim glanced over to see if Terry had gone to sleep but he hadn't. "I guess I'll be learning a lot today."

"You've never received a summons to appear for jury selection, Jim?"

"No and I'm relieved I haven't."

"Jurors are picked from a jury pool from lists of citizens living in the jurisdiction of the court. Sometime they pull names from registered voters or from those who have driver's licenses. I don't see how you've never been picked."

"Just lucky, I guess. From what I hear, it's no picnic being on a jury."

"No, it's not. It's a serious undertaking, making decisions that impact others' lives."

"What will they be doing down there today?"

"Picking the twelve jurors, which usually takes a lot of time, sometimes even longer than one day."

"Really?"

Jim continued to drive toward Atlanta. He wanted to get all this over with but dreaded it all for Emmajean's sake.

When Jim and Terry entered the courtroom assigned for Emmajean's case, nothing had started. Jim saw some twenty-five to thirty people who looked as confused as he was. "Terry, why are so many people standing around here?"

"They are the jury pool that's been collected for this trial."

The bailiff commanded, "All rise."

Judge Orr appeared, coming through a door at the front left and into the courtroom.

"Be seated," the bailiff instructed.

A professionally dressed woman walked over to the group of potential jurors. "Let me have your attention, please. I'm the county court clerk. I'm going to get you seated in the order your names were originally drawn for this jury pool."

She began going down her list of names and when she called a name that person went to the seat she assigned. Once everyone had correctly taken a seat, the clerk moved to stand before the group. "You have been sent to this courtroom to take part in *voir dire*, the oath to speak the truth in the examination of testing competence of a juror." She turned and nodded to the judge who stood at his place on a podium.

The judge took his seat and tapped his gavel on the wooden block. An immediate quiet draped the room. The judge looked toward the jury pool and spoke to them.

"In order to have a fair and lawful trial, there are rules that all jurors must follow. A basic rule is you must decide the case only on the evidence presented in the courtroom. You must not communicate with anyone, including friends and family members, about this case, the people and places involved, or your jury service. You must not disclose your thoughts about this case or ask for advice on how to decide this case.

"You must not do any research, or look up words, names, maps, or anything else that may have anything to do with this case. This includes reading newspapers and watching television, or any other means at all, to get information related to this case or the people and places involved in this case. This applies whether you are in the courthouse, at home, or anywhere else."

The judge continued to speak to the jury. "Unlike questions you may be allowed to ask in court, which will be answered in court in the presence of the judge and the parties involved, if you investigate, research or make inquiries on your own outside of the courtroom, the trial judge has no way to assure they are proper and relevant to the case. The parties likewise have no opportunity to dispute the accuracy of what you find or to provide rebuttal evidence to it. That is not the way our judicial system works, which assures every party the right to ask questions about and rebut the evidence being considered against it, and to present argument with respect to that evidence. Non-court inquiries and investigations unfairly and improperly prevent the parties from having that opportunity our judicial system promises. If you become aware of any violation of these instructions or any other instruction I give in this case, you must tell me by giving a note to the bailiff.

"All of us are depending on you to follow these rules, so that there will be a fair and lawful resolution to this case."

He rapped his gavel again.

"Gentlemen, you found on your seat a list of questions pertaining to your name, occupation, education, family relationships, and time conflicts you may have for the anticipated length of this trial. Several other questions you see there are uniquely pertinent to this particular trial."

The judge began with the man seated in the first chair and proceeded to ask all those in the pool the same questions. After each person was questioned by the judge, he deferred to Emmajean's attorney, Mr. Cox, to Barry Wagner's attorney, and the prosecutor.

Looking toward the two attorneys and the prosecutor, the judge directed them. "You each are allotted five challenges to remove prospective jurors from consideration. You may state your challenges during *voir dire* or to me at the end of *voir dire*." He waved a hand to indicate they could each ask follow up questions of the prospective juror.

Terry leaned close and whispered to Jim. "The judge's questions are to familiarize the attorneys with the jurors so they can pick up on any biases, experiences, or relationships that could possibly jeopardize the proper course of the trial."

Mr. Cox cleared his throat and stood. "Sir, have you ever used illegal drugs?"

The first prospective juror answered, "No, sir."

"Do you have any relatives who have used illegal drugs?"

"No, sir."

"Do you have any children or grandchildren who are teenagers?"

"Yes, sir."

"Which ones, children or grandchildren?"

"Grandchildren."

Mr. Cox looked at his notes. "Have you ever served on a jury?"

"No, sir."

Mr. Cox nodded to the judge indicating that he approved of potential juror number one. He sat and shuffled through his papers on the table while the other attorney and the prosecutor went through their list of questions directed toward likely juror number one. When finished, they, too, indicated to the judge that they approved.

One by one, each person in the jury pool was questioned by the judge and then by the two attorneys and prosecutor. Jim recognized that Terry had been correct when he talked about how long picking the jury would take.

The prosecutor finished his questioning of likely juror number twenty and sat. As Mr. Cox prepared his notes to stand, the judge rapped his gavel.

"We'll take a recess for lunch and reconvene at two o'clock." He tapped his gavel again, stood and walked out of the courtroom.

The court clerk stood in front of the jury pool. "We will all go by bus to lunch together. Follow me."

"They have to stay together till this thing is over?'

Terry stood. "Yeah, this group now and then the twelve that get picked will be together for a while."

Jim stood and stretched. "We've got a couple of hours. Want to go by and see Emmajean and then grab a hamburger?"

"Sounds good." Terry couldn't conceal his smile.

~ ~ ~

When Jim and Terry arrived at the YWCA it was lunch time. They looked into the cafeteria and spotted Emmajean. After a few minutes she looked up and saw them. A wide smile filled her face, replacing her working face. She rushed to them and hugged them both. "I've got to finish servin' lunch but it won't be much longer."

"Okay, little sister, we'll go grab a bite to eat and come back in a while."

After hurrying through their lunch, Jim and Terry had only thirty minutes before court resumed. They found Emmajean waiting in the common room. "Tell me about the trial. I want to know everythin'.

Jim looked at Terry, indicating that he should do the telling.

"Not much to report, Emmajean. They spent all morning on picking people to serve on the jury and they haven't finished doing that. The judge recessed until two o'clock."

"You don't have long to stay here. When do you think they will finish gettin' the jury? When will my trial start?"

"Whoa! Not so fast. Picking the jury is a slow process. They will probably finish that tomorrow or Wednesday at the latest. Then after that the judge and lawyers will probably do some talking in the judge's chambers. The trial may start sometime the end of this week. Or, possibly, the judge may start the trial next Monday."

"Well, they can take all the time they want to pickin' that jury. I'm not lookin' forward to the trial. Jim, are y'all goin' to stay down here through all this?"

"Yes, I've got my chief financial officer looking after the mill, and Terry's law firm will allow him to stay. We may go home on the weekends just to catch up on things."

"I'm sure glad of that. I couldn't get through any of this if both of you weren't here." She shot a sweet glance toward Terry. They both blushed.

"Okay, we'd better get back to the courthouse. We'll come by when the judge calls it a day. If you don't have to work supper, we'll all go eat together."

"I'll see if I can get off supper duty."

~ ~ ~

When the judge reconvened court, things progressed in slow motion just as they had that morning. By four o'clock they still hadn't finished questioning all the jury pool. They had a half dozen people remaining to question.

The judge hit his gavel hard against the block of wood. Everything screeched to a standstill. "Court will recess and resume tomorrow morning at eight o'clock." Again, he banged his gavel, rose, and left the courtroom.

The court clerk took her place in front of the jury pool. "I urge you not to discuss any of the proceedings of today. We've not started the trial yet and you've not heard any evidence, but it would be best if you didn't talk with one another about any of today's happenings."

~ ~ ~

The next day Jim and Terry observed the same scenario as the day before. Late in the afternoon all potential jurors had been questioned. The two lawyers and the prosecutor followed the judge to his chambers. The clerk told the jury pool to remain in their seats.

"What's going on now, Terry?

"This is a time for both lawyers and the prosecutor to voice an opinion to Judge Orr if they want to eliminate a person from the jury pool. When they come back into the courtroom the judge will call out the names of the anonymously challenged prospective jurors as well as those who had been challenged openly during the questioning. Those people return to the pool and will be considered for other trials. A jury is then formed of the potential jurors in the order that their names were originally chosen."

When the judge and three lawyers, along with their assistants returned, the procedure Terry had explained took place. The jury of twelve had been selected.

Mr. Cox motioned for Jim to move toward him. Jim and Terry went to where Mr. Cox stood beside the defendant's table.

"Jim, while we were in the judge's chambers I asked the judge to order the prosecutor to supply a bill of particulars—a brief statement of the core facts of the case. The prosecutor did and we had a detailed discussion while looking at the facts the prosecutor will be using against Emmajean and Barry in the trial."

"Did he have much against Emmajean?"

"No, Terry, he did not. Not nearly enough. He had substantially more evidence against Barry. Since the jury may be swayed by the evidence against Barry to improperly convict Emmajean, I made a motion to sever." He looked at Jim. "That's a request for Emmajean and Barry to have two separate trials."

"What did the judge say then?"

"Well, Jim, he granted my motion. That's good news. Now Emmajean will be tried separately. The jury we just selected will be the jury at Emmajean's trial and her trial will be first."

"That will certainly be good news for my sister. She's anxious to get the trial over with but also dreading it."

"How is Emmajean doing overall?"

"Considering what's hanging over her head, she's holding up fairly well. Would you agree, Terry?"

"I would. A weaker person wouldn't be doing as well."

"Mr. Cox, would you like to go to supper with us? We're going to pick up Emmajean, and we'd be pleased if you'd join us."

"Please call me Bert—short for Bertrand. I think we're spending enough time together to get on a first name basis." He chuckled, the first Jim had heard from him.

"Okay, Bert it is. How about supper?"

"My wife is expecting me home. Some days it's impossible for me to get home for a regular family supper and when I can, I try to make it. Thanks for the invitation to join y'all and tell Emmajean about her trial being first. It starts Monday."

~ ~ ~

Emmajean was giddy about not having to be in court with Barry. Yet apprehension showed on her face. "Terry, how do you really think it's all goin'?"

"Good. I think it's going good. When the judge granted Mr. Cox a separate trial for you, he agreed that the evidence against Barry weighed heavier than any evidence against you. That's a good sign."

"Emmajean, I guess Terry and I will go back to Newton tomorrow. We'll probably come back down Sunday afternoon." He looked at Terry. "That okay with you?"

"Sure. Emmajean, you'll be busy with your work so don't let your mind dwell on this upcoming trial. You can't change anything that's already done. We'll all just hope for a short trial and a sensible jury that will see that you're not guilty."

Terry reached for her hand and squeezed it. To Jim it looked like the two of them were paying a lot of attention to each other. When this trial is over would they start dating? Or would Terry think that Emmajean didn't measure up to his station in life?

Chapter 9

Jim wanted to telephone Caroline with an update from his time in Atlanta. He couldn't do that because he had to check in at the mill. He found his office empty.

"Peggy, how's everything going?"

"Fine, Mr. Callaway."

"Bob and you getting along okay? Is the mill as normal as if I was here?"

"Just about. I've nudged Mr. Allbright a few times so he would do things like you would do them. Other than that he's doing a good job."

"Good. Glad to hear that. Peggy, I'll be here the rest of the week and be going back to Atlanta on Sunday. Emmajean's trial starts Monday. I'll be away again but I don't know for how long. You think y'all can keep things running around here?"

"Sure, Mr. Callaway. Anything I can get you?"

"Thank you, no. I'm going to start going through all the papers I see on my desk."

"I think Mr. Allbright has them in different piles so you should be able to look at them without any trouble and still know what went on here while you were away."

"No time like the present, so I'll get started. Thanks, Peggy."

As Jim retreated into his office it all seemed quite tame compared with the activities of court procedures he'd sat through in Atlanta. He wanted to talk to Caroline but didn't want Peggy to know that was the first thing he did upon returning to the mill. He could use the telephone and he knew Caroline's number. He'd put in the call himself.

After pushing button after button, Jim finally heard Caroline's voice.

"Jimmy!"

Her calling him Jimmy was music to his ears. Nobody called him Jimmy except Caroline. Twenty years ago when they were together she'd not wanted to call him Jim—everybody did that she'd said. So she chose his name to be Jimmy.

"Caroline, I've missed talking to you. Tell me how you and James and Lynn are. What's going on with y'all?"

Jim could hear some of the excitement fade from her voice. Maybe he shouldn't have mentioned the children so early in their conversation. "Oh, we're all doing fine."

~ ~ ~

When Jim and Terry returned to Atlanta Sunday afternoon, they went directly to the YWCA. Emmajean watched out the window of the common room and saw them approach. Two of the most handsome men in Atlanta. She was at the front door by the time they opened it.

"Jim!" She gave him a big hug, which he returned. She looked toward Terry. Turning away from Jim she gave Terry a hug, although more restrained. "Am I glad to see y'all. These several days waitin' for Sunday to get here wasn't easy. Come on in."

They sat in the common room. Their conversation danced around all the mundane things except the trial. "Okay, let's not put it off any longer. Let's talk about my trial."

"You got any questions?"

"Terry, I'm full of questions. You spend a lot of your time in a courtroom so you're probably comfortable there. The only time I've been in a courtroom was that one time for the . . ."

"Arraignment," Terry gave her the word she was searching for.

"Yeah, the whatever you said. But come tomorrow I'll be there all day."

"Speaking of tomorrow, Emmajean, remember those two suits we bought at Rich's on one of your shopping trips?"

"Yeah, Terry, what about them?"

"You need to look as innocent as you really are. You need to appear calm, not a show-off. So wear one of those suits tomorrow with a nice blouse that matches. You can wear high heels or flats, whichever you'd be more comfortable with."

"Flats. No decidin' needed."

"Those two suits will do you for however long the trial is. Just change the blouses and you'll be fine."

She looked at Terry as he talked to her, then glanced at Jim. Does Jim have any idea how attracted she was to Terry? Terry appeared interested in her, but they had no time to be alone. Could he really want to spend time with Emmajean whenever they got through with this trial? When she looked at Terry she saw concern for her in his eyes. Was this the way a lawyer acted with a client?

"Emmajean . . . Emmajean, where did you go there for a minute? Did you hear what I said?"

"What, Jim? What did you say?"

"I told you we'd be right behind the table you'll be sitting at tomorrow and all through the trial, for however long it takes."

She turned her attention toward Terry. "How long will this trial take?"

"We can't ever tell for sure. But Mr. Cox told us that the prosecutor has more factual evidence on Barry than on you. That could mean a short trial but really there's no telling."

"I'm sure glad I won't have to see him durin' my trial."

"I am too, little sister. He's done enough damage to you by bringing you into his drug dealing."

"What time does the trial start tomorrow?" She looked at Terry for her answer.

"Eight o'clock. And we can't be late and get on the judge's wrong side right out of the box. I want you in the courtroom even before eight. We'll come by to get you at seven-thirty. Be ready please, we won't have any time to waste."

Chapter 10

Not many spectators sat in the courtroom. A few photographers and one who sketched away on his large tablet. Bert Cox talked to Emmajean, never letting his attention stray from her. He kept her engaged until the judge appeared. "All rise" came from the bailiff.

When Judge Orr sat behind his desk, the bailiff spoke to the courtroom. "Be seated."

"Bailiff, please escort the jury into the room." The bailiff walked out of the courtroom and shortly returned, the jurors following him in single file. He motioned for the jurors to be seated in the front row of seats and when those were filled he motioned for the others to sit in the second row.

When all were seated the bailiff stood below the judge's platform. He held a few legal size pages in front of him and read: "We're about to hear the criminal case of the state of Georgia versus Emmajean Callaway. The charges on the defendant are aiding the possession of an illegal substance with intent to distribute and sell, a misdemeanor."

The judge spoke to the jury. "Members of the jury, the attorneys must prove with their words. I mean that the attorneys must persuade you, by what's presented in court, that what they are trying to prove is more likely to be true than not true. This is sometimes called 'the burden of proof.' Let me put it another way. If you believe a set of facts, you must find the verdict *that* lawyer asks for."

The judge looked around his courtroom. "Mr. Prosecutor, are you ready for your opening statement?"

"Yes, Your Honor."

The prosecutor tilted his chin upward and walked toward the jury. His opening statements held little substance to prove that Emmajean sold illegal drugs. He had no solid grounds for what he said to the jury.

When he had finished, Mr. Cox patted Emmajean's hand and rose. He deliberately slowed his steps to the jury box. He made eye contact with each juror before he spoke

"Gentlemen, thank you for giving this court your service as a juror." He pointed slowly to Emmajean. "Emmajean Callaway's involvement in the case we're trying today is minute and innocent. Barry Wagner befriended her when she worked at Baker's Diner where Barry frequently ate. He paid attention to her when she was way down in spirits in her life. Barry's attentions perked her up, and she conversed with him a lot at the diner. When Barry first asked her to go out with him one evening, she accepted his invitation. He took her to a food drive-in north of Atlanta. While there, Barry trolled for potential customers for his sales."

"Objection!"

Mr. Cox turned toward the bench and spoke to the judge. "I have witnesses to prove this point."

"Objection overruled."

Mr. Cox continued with his message to the jurors. "Soon, after several dates going to the same food drive-in, Barry asked Emmajean for a favor. He asked her to carry a small brown sack to a specific car, not to look in the sack or she might be embarrassed, and bring cash from those in the car back to Barry."

Mr. Cox looked at some papers he held, letting the jurors have some time to absorb what he'd said. "When Emmajean Callaway finished high school in Newton, Tennessee, she took what savings she had and came to Atlanta. Newton, Tennessee. Atlanta. Quite a jump for a somewhat sheltered young lady. She wanted to get involved in the fashion industry Atlanta offered. Instead, she became involved with Barry Wagner, resulting in why we are here today."

Mr. Cox took a minute to turn away from the jurors and coughed. Another gesture to allow the jurors to let what he'd said to them sink in.

"In this courtroom I intend to prove to you that Emmajean Callaway is innocent of the charges leveled against her. With facts, I will prove that this young lady had no knowledge of what Barry Wagner did or why he asked her to help him." He turned and walked unhurriedly back to the table where Emmajean sat.

"Is the prosecution ready to proceed?"

"Yes, Your Honor, we are."

"Then let's get started. Call you first witness."

"I call Jerry Whitnow to the stand."

All heads turned toward the back to see the witness enter.

Mr. Cox leaned toward Emmajean and whispered, "Do you know this guy?"

"No, sir, I don't."

The bailiff stepped up to the witness chair and before Jerry Whitnow sat, the bailiff instructed him to place his hand on the Bible. "Do you swear to tell the truth, the whole truth, and nothing but the truth, so help you God?"

The young man stammered and finally croaked, "Yes." Then he took his seat to the left of the judge.

"Mr. Whitnow, have you ever been a witness in a court trial?"

"No."

"You seem a little nervous. We want you to be comfortable while we talk. Can you calm yourself a little?"

"Objection. Completely irrelevant to this case."

"Sustained." The judge gave a warning look at the prosecutor.

"Very well. Please state your name and occupation."

"My name is . . ."

The judge interrupted. "Young man, you need you to speak up. We all want to be able to hear you."

Whitnow swallowed and Jim saw his Adam's apple move up and then go down and he raised the volume of his voice. "My name is Jerry Whitnow and I work at the Dixie drive-in."

"Is this Dixie drive-in a place where the customer stays in his car and you and others bring their orders to their car?"

"Yes." The young man could not sit still nor keep his eyes focused long on anything.

"Mr. Whitnow, have you ever seen the defendant at Dixie drive-in?"

A wide grin spread across the boy's face as he looked toward Emmajean. "Yes, I have. She's the prettiest red headed girl I've ever seen."

"Objection. Irrelevant."

"Sustained. Mr. Prosecutor, let's stick to the charges against the defendant and don't go off on any rabbit trails."

"Yes, Your Honor. So, Mr. Whitnow, you have seen the defendant at the Dixie drive-in where you are employed. Is that correct?"

"Yes."

"How often did you see her at the Dixie drive-in?"

"Well, I didn't count how many times she came there."

Snickers flowed through the spattering of spectators in the courtroom.

"When you saw her was it usually in the afternoon or at night?"

"At night. I work another job in the day."

"Did you usually see this red headed girl on week nights or weekends?"

"Mostly on weekends but some times during the week."

"So, Mr. Whitnow, when you saw her at night while you worked, was she alone?"

"No. Never. She was always in a car with a guy."

"Was she with the same guy every time you saw her?"

"Yes."

The prosecutor walked over to his table, shuffled through some papers, and picked up one.

"Would you be able to describe the guy the defendant was with in the car?"

"I don't know. It was always night. Unless I had to deliver an order to a car close to hers I couldn't see the guy."

The prosecutor held up a glossy black and white photo of a male. "Did the guy look like this?"

"Objection. Irrelevant. Your Honor, this case concerns one person, Emmajean Callaway."

"Sustained."

Before the judge turned his head toward the prosecutor, the prosecutor was already asking his next question. "Mr. Whitnow, you said you couldn't see the guy in the car with the defendant, but did you ever get a good look at her?"

"Yes."

"Could you describe her please?"

"Well, she was pretty tall and had beautiful red hair, I guess you could call it auburn hair. She always seemed to walk fast."

"Where was she walking fast to?"

"She would hurry to one car and then hurry back to her own car."

"Did you ever see her carrying anything?"

"Yeah, she did, come to think of it."

"What was she carrying?"

"The best I recollect, she carried a small brown sack. Like the ones you might carry your lunch in."

"Now, Mr. Whitnow, can you point out anyone in this courtroom who looks like the same girl you saw at the Dixie drive-in mostly on weekends at night?"

"Yes. That girl." He pointed directly at Emmajean.

"For the record, Your Honor, the witness has identified Emmajean Callaway as the girl who came with Barry Wagner to the Dixie drive-in.

"Objection."

"Sustained. Both counsel approach the bench."

Mr. Cox and the prosecutor walked up to the judge's platform. He looked down at them and shook his head. "We are here to find Emmajean Callaway guilty or not guilty. Only the young lady. Mr. Prosecutor, you will not mention the name of Barry Wagner in this courtroom during this trial. Is that understood?"

"Yes, Your Honor."

"Are you finished with this witness?"

"Yes, Your Honor."

"Mr. Cox, do you wish to question this witness?"

"Yes, Your Honor."

"Proceed."

Emmajean's lawyer walked to stand in front of the witness but faced the back of the courtroom. "Mr. Whitnow, you're employed at the Dixie drive-in?"

"Yes."

"Is it your habit Mr. Whitnow while working your shift to watch girls or deliver food to the car customers?" Mr.Cox spun toward the witness, startling him.

"Mr. Whitnow, please answer counsel's question."

"Uh, I deliver food."

"And watch girls?"

"Yeah, I guess I do."

"So while you do both, do you do either one of them very well?"

"What?"

Mr. Cox looked at the witness and then at Emmajean. "If you're delivering food to the cars *and* watching girls, are you doing a good job at either one of them?"

"I don't know. I've never thought of it like that."

"Thank you. Now, you described that the defendant carried a small sack when she went up to a car. Did you see what was in the sack?"

"No."

"Could it have been food, or candy, or bubble gum?"

A blank expression fell across the witness's face. "I guess it could have."

"So you watched a tall girl with auburn hair go to a car carrying a small sack, but you didn't see what it contained. Did you see any money exchange hands before she returned to her car?"

"No. The lights are not too bright at the drive-in."

"So, you saw her auburn hair even in the dim light but you didn't see what was in the sack or if any money was exchanged?"

"Yes. That's right."

"No further questions, Your Honor."

"Mr. Prosecutor, do you have redirect?"

"No, Your Honor."

The judge looked toward the witness. "You may step down." The boy crisscrossed the path of Mr. Cox as they returned to their places.

Looking up at the big clock on the wall, the judge rapped his gavel. "Court is adjourned and will reconvene at two o'clock."

Jim's heart ached as he watched the matron jailer lead Emmajean through a door on the left near the front of the courtroom. Terry had told him she would be confined until the trial ended.

~ ~ ~

After a quick lunch Jim and Terry returned to the courthouse and found the courtroom almost empty. As they stood before their seats on the front row, the spectator spaces began to fill. Shortly, the bailiff appeared.

"All rise."

The judge took his place on the podium and rapped the gavel once. Every one sat. "Mr. Prosecutor, do you have another witness?"

"Yes, Your Honor."

"Then call it."

"I call Angela Harvey to the witness stand."

Jim exchanged a questioning look with Terry as they looked toward the back door. A young lady appearing to be near the age of Emmajean walked the aisle toward the judge.

"Do you know her, Emmajean?"

"Yes, Mr. Cox, she used to be my roommate."

After the bailiff swore her in she sat in the witness chair.

The prosecutor stood before her. "Please tell the court your name and where you live."

"My name is Angela Harvey and I live in College Park, Georgia."

"Thank you, Miss Harvey. Where do you work?"

"Presently I'm working as a sales clerk at Hammer's department store."

"Thank you. Do you know the defendant, Emmajean Callaway?" He pointed at Emmajean and Miss Harvey followed the direction of his hand.

"Yes."

"How do you know the defendant?"

"We were roommates for a year. We rented a place together."

"The time you lived with Miss Callaway, did you work at Hammer's?"

"Yes."

"At that time where did the defendant work?"

"Objection! Irrelevant."

The prosecutor turned toward the judge. "Your Honor I intend to establish the working schedules of both women and show the relevance to the case."

"Objection overruled."

"Now please tell me where Miss Callaway worked when you were roommates."

"She worked at Baker's Diner."

"And what was her job at Baker's Diner?

"She was a waitress."

When the prosecutor asked her questions Miss Harvey's eyes darted from him to Emmajean and back.

"Now, Miss Harvey, what hours did the defendant work at the diner?"

"She worked from breakfast till the middle of the afternoon."

"And when you say she worked from breakfast, what time would that be?"

"She had to be at the diner at six thirty in the morning."

"You said she worked until the middle of the afternoon, correct?"

Miss Harvey squirmed in her chair like she knew where his questions were going and she didn't want to answer him. She darted a glance toward Emmajean with apology in her eyes. "Yes, that's correct."

"So if she left work at the diner did she arrive home shortly thereafter?"

"I don't know. My work at Hammer's was noon to nine o'clock."

"So, if you went straight home after your shift at Hammer's, Emmajean was already at your house. Is that correct?"

Miss Harvey readjusted her position in the chair and again appeared to apologize to Emmajean even before she answered the prosecutor's question.

"Sometimes she was."

"Sometimes." When the witness said nothing, the prosecutor continued. "And sometimes when you got home after work, she was not at the house?"

"Yes."

"Yes she was at the house or yes she was not at the house?"

"Yes she was sometimes at the house when I got home and yes sometimes she was not at the house."

The prosecutor walked toward his table only to turn around and face the witness again. "Did the two of you go out at night together, socially?"

"No."

"No. You and the defendant didn't socialize together after work?"

"That's right. We just lived at the same place. We didn't go out together."

The prosecutor deliberately walked to his table again, pushed some papers around, stacked them neatly and moved again toward the witness.

"Now, Miss Harvey, when you returned home from work and your roommate was not there what time did she come home?"

"I don't know."

"You mean you lived with the defendant and you don't know when she came home at night?"

"Yes. I usually was asleep when she came home."

"You were usually asleep. What is your usual bedtime?"

"I'm usually in bed after the eleven o'clock news goes off."

"So, some nights your roommate was not at home at eleven thirty?"

"Yes."

"Did this occur during the week or mostly on weekends."

"Mostly on weekends."

"Did you ever question her about how late she came home?"

"Objection. Irrelevant."

"Your Honor, I intend to relate this information precisely to this case."

"Mr. Prosecutor, proceed cautiously."

"Yes, Your Honor."

"Miss Harvey, did you ever question your roommate about how late she came home?"

"Yes."

"What did she answer?"

"She kinda brushed me off."

"What do you mean when you say she brushed you off?"

"Uh . . ."

"Uh, what?"

"Well sometimes she ignored me when I asked."

"She ignored you. She wouldn't tell you when she got home because she wanted to keep it a secret from you?"

"Objection! Badgering the witness."

"Sustained. Mr. Prosecutor, don't be leading the witness in her answers."

"Yes, Your Honor."

Before the prosecutor could rephrase his question, the judge's gavel fell onto the block of wood. "We'll take a recess here and reconvene tomorrow morning at eight o'clock.

~ ~ ~

When Jim and Terry left the courthouse, they stopped off for an early supper.

"It just breaks by heart watching this trial. Especially when the matron leads Emmajean off through that door."

"Jim, where they take her during the trial is a much better place than where you saw her in the precinct jail. She's staying in a women's detention center close to downtown Atlanta."

Jim didn't seem buoyed by Terry's information. "Still she is alone, without family. Can we visit her there?

"No." Terry's blunt answer made Jim wince.

They ate their meal in silence before going to their hotel for the night.

Chapter 11

Emmajean lay on her cot in her private cell when she heard the whistle and all the barred doors unlocked and slid open, metal scraping on metal. It was supper time but Emmajean had decided she wouldn't go. She was tired and lonely and would just stay where she was.

Out of nowhere a strong arm jerked her off her cot and dragged her into the line of women going to the dining hall.

"What are you doin' . . ."

"Shut up, and stand straight. If you stay in your cell the guards and other inmates will take notice of you. From then it will get tough on you. You'd better straighten up, and don't bring any attention to yourself."

"Who are you?"

"Just a friend who's trying to keep you out of trouble."

"Why would you want to help me?"

"Girl, you ever been locked up?"

"Yeah, the night they arrested me but it wasn't as nice as this place."

"If you don't follow orders here you won't think this place is nice."

"You got a name?"

"Yeah, it's Pauline."

"Pauline. What's your last name"

"Emmajean, last names in here don't matter."

"How'd you know my name?"

The line of women began to move, single file, toward the dining area.

"I've been here a while and I listen real good. I heard one of the guards mention your name when they brought you to your cell. What're you in for?"

Emmajean had learned a few things herself in the last few weeks. She shouldn't talk to anyone, like Jim had told her at the beginning, without her lawyer. She just shrugged her shoulders at Pauline.

"That's okay. Your lawyer probably told you not to talk to anybody. But I'll eventually find out. I'm in here for manslaughter— they say I killed my boyfriend. My lawyer who's pleading my case is saying I did it in self defense."

Emmajean's eyes widened as she looked at Pauline. She couldn't imagine Pauline killing someone, even in self defense. Looking at her she would have had no idea. Emmajean looked around at the other women, wondering what they had done. She shivered just thinking about it.

When they got to the dining area, Emmajean allowed Pauline to tell her where to go and when, and where to sit. They sat at long metal tables with metal benches attached. Emmajean looked at her metal plate. Its contents didn't appear much better than the slop they fed their hogs at the farm.

Pauline gave Emmajean a stern look. "Eat it no matter what you think it looks like. You'd better clean your plate or you'll get in trouble for that too."

Emmajean choked down the food. At least it would provide her strength to stand upright, get back to breakfast in the morning, and return to the courthouse.

After they ate and disposed of their plates and utensils in their proper places, the guard guided them to the outside door. They received an hour out on the dusty grounds. Emmajean and Pauline walked about together. Pauline offered Emmajean a cigarette, which Emmajean declined. As Pauline smoked her cigarette, they walked and Pauline told Emmajean all the ins and outs of being at this detention center.

All too soon, the guards herded them back into the building, and in single file they returned to their cells as they had walked out of them earlier. Emmajean went into her cell and noticed that Pauline went into the next one. Emmajean wondered if they could talk to one another. Probably not. Emmajean heard very little chatter in the building.

In each cell Emmajean had noticed a Gideon Bible. She reached for it and sat on her cot, leaning her back against the cool concrete block wall. It wasn't like reading the Bible Terry had given her. His grandmother's Bible was well-read and felt good as she held it. The pages of this Bible were not as soft as Terry's grandmother's Bible.

Emmajean had found some favorite verses while reading her Bible at the YWCA. She leafed through the pages to find one verse that had particularly strengthened her—Philippians 4:8. If she could think on the things the verse mentioned it would keep her mind off her trial and the position she was in.

When Emmajean had finished reading she dressed in her pajamas—fashionable detention center issue. Soon the first call for lights out blared from the public address system. She replaced the Bible on its small table and crawled under the covers on her cot. When the lights were turned off, she could not see a slither of light. But she was used to the total darkness on their farm in the country and had no apprehension or fear. She was locked in and, thank goodness, the other inmates were locked out.

Chapter 12

"All rise."

At the bailiff's call for everyone to stand, Judge Orr entered the courtroom from the front left. He took his seat and pounded the gavel one time. Everyone in the courtroom resumed sitting.

The judge looked over his courtroom without a word. Everyone was where they should be—the prosecution seated on his left and the defendant on his right. "Angela Harvey, please take the witness chair." Angela did as he had said. "Miss Harvey, remember you are still under oath to tell the truth, the whole truth, and nothing but the truth."

The prosecutor approached the witness. "When this trial recessed yesterday you and I were talking about your roommate—Emmajean Callaway—coming home quite late. Now when you asked her why she came home so late, what exactly did she say?"

"Well, I said to her that she surely didn't stay out so late in College Park because they practically rolled up the sidewalks when dark fell." Low laughter rumbled through the room.

"Miss Harvey, we are not here to determine when activity in College Park ceases. Mr. Prosecutor, let's don't get started off on the wrong foot like we ended yesterday. Keep your witness answering questions pertaining to this case."

"Yes, Your Honor." He stepped close to the bar separating him and Miss Harvey and looked her in the eye. "Did the defendant ever explain her returning home past normal bedtimes?"

"Well, yes, one day as she left for work at the diner I was questioning her. She was running late, as usual, and told me that when she got home from the diner we would sit down and talk about it."

"And did that happen?"

"Yes, we sat at the kitchen and drank iced tea and she explained things."

"What did she say?"

"Objection. Hearsay."

"Objection sustained. Mr. Prosecutor, be careful."

"Your Honor, I'm trying to get this witness to corroborate the earlier witness, Mr. Whitnow."

"Proceed but do it quickly."

"Yes, Your Honor." He stepped over in front of the witness. "Now Miss Harvey, what did your roommate, the defendant in this trial, tell you."

"She said a friend of hers would drive them to a North Atlanta drive-in food place. He told her to take a small sack to a specific car and not look in the sack or she might be embarrassed. Just hand over the sack and bring back the money to him."

"How did you reply to that? Did that satisfy your curiosity as to your roommate's late night activities?"

"Yes. And I told her I thought her friend was having her do something he didn't want to be seen doing himself. I told her I thought something illegal might be going on. That surprised her but she said her friend wouldn't do that to her."

"Did she defend her friend anymore?"

"No."

"Was that the end of your conversation with Miss Callaway?"

"Almost. I told her I didn't want to be around if something illegal was going on and that I'd be moved out by the weekend. She said she couldn't pay the entire rent and what would she do if I moved."

"And did you move out by the weekend?"

"Yes."

"What did the defendant do about paying all the rent? Did she pay her rent with money she made selling drugs?"

"Objection!"

"Sustained."

The witness answered the prosecutor's last question. "I don't know. I moved out and didn't see her again until yesterday when I walked into the courtroom."

The prosecutor walked toward his table. "Your witness, counselor."

Mr. Cox resumed his stance before this witness. "Miss Harvey, how long did you and the defendant live in the same apartment?"

"Almost a year."

"Almost a year and you didn't have a conversation with her about her late night activities until recently?"

"That's right."

"Why not?"

"I'd never been suspicious until a few months ago."

"Why did you become suspicious of the defendant when you did?"

"Well, this guy would come by to pick up Emmajean but he never came to the door. He just sat in his car and honked the horn."

"Did the defendant give you a reason why she went to his car instead of him coming into the house to pick her up?"

"She wouldn't talk about it."

"Why do think this was?"

"Objection. Leading the witness."

The judge looked toward Mr. Cox. "Sustained."

"Miss Harvey, did you ever meet the guy Emmajean would go out with?"

"No."

"Did you ever see the defendant with one or several small paper sacks?"

"No."

"Did you ever see her with anything that caused you to suspect her of doing anything illegal?"

"No."

"Did your roommate ever lock her bedroom door?"

"No."

"Did you ever get the feeling she was trying to hide something?"

"No"

Mr. Cox started toward his table. "That will be all, Your Honor."

"Any redirect, Mr. Prosecutor?"

"No, Your Honor."

The judge hit the block with his gavel. "Court recessed and will reconvene at two o'clock."

~ ~ ~

After the recess Jim and Terry returned to their seats and sat in the first row, directly behind Emmajean.

"Mr. Prosecutor, do you have any more witnesses."

"Yes, Your Honor. I call Atlanta Police Department detective Mr. Larry Hamilton to the stand."

After he was sworn in and sat, the prosecutor approached the detective. "Please state your name and where you work."

"My name is Larry Hamilton. I work for the Atlanta Police Department, Precinct #312."

"Mr. Hamilton, were you working on New Year's Eve, 1950?

"Yes."

"Who were you watching?"

"We'd had some reports of illegal drugs north of Atlanta. We were zeroed in on a drive-in up there. My partner and I were in an unmarked car watching the people going in and coming out of the drive-in."

"What did you see that night that was important to you?"

"We'd been watching the drive-in for a while, and we regularly saw this green older model Plymouth."

"What did you observe the car and its passengers doing?"

"Mostly on weekends we saw the same car come in and park near the last parking place. We'd see a redheaded girl leave the car, carry a small sack to another car. She passed the sack to someone inside, they passed some money to her, and she'd return to the Plymouth."

"That New Year's Eve night did you do anything differently?"

"Yeah. We tailed him when he left. We already had a search warrant on our suspicion. After quite a while when we knew they'd turned out the lights and gone to bed, we entered the house, served our search warrant, and found the marijuana."

"And what happened then?"

"We arrested them both and took them to the station."

"That's all, Your Honor."

"Mr. Cox do you want a cross examination?"

"Yes, Your Honor."

The judge waved Mr. Cox toward the witness stand.

"Detective Hamilton, where did you find the marijuana?"

"In Mr. Wagner's bedroom."

"You had a search warrant. Did you search every part of the house?"

"Yes, we did."

"Did you search Miss Callaway's bedroom?"

"Yes, we did."

"Did you find any marijuana or other illegal drugs in Miss Callaway's bedroom?"

"No, we did not."

"That's all, Your Honor."

"Mr. Prosecutor, any redirect?"

"No, Your Honor. The prosecution rests its case."

The judge hit his gavel on the block of wood. "Court is recessed and will reconvene tomorrow morning at eight o'clock."

~ ~ ~

Over supper Terry could tell Jim was full of questions. He waited until his friend opened up.

"Terry, what did the prosecutor mean when he said the defense rests its case?"

"That means he has no more witnesses to call. I told you he didn't have much of a case against Emmajean. That's how Mr. Cox was able to get the judge to grant his motion to sever and he got Emmajean a separate trial."

"Do you know much about Bert's defense plans and his witnesses?"

"No, I don't. Let's get to the courthouse a little earlier and ask him to share his plans."

~ ~ ~

"You're what?"

"Now, Jim, wait a minute and let me explain."

"It'd better be a good explanation why you're going to put Emmajean on the witness stand."

"You heard how weak the prosecutor's witnesses turned out to be. I got them to say more in favor of Emmajean than he got them to say anything against her. Have you been watching the jury members, Jim?"

"No."

"I have, sir. I see where you're going."

Jim looked at Terry. "If you understand what Bert's doing why didn't you tell me?"

"Well, I know that's the way I'd be handling her defense and as it turns out Bert thought so also."

"Jim, I've been watching the jury." Bert sat on the edge of his table. "They're showing sympathy for Emmajean like they think she is completely innocent. When they look at the prosecutor their faces appear as though they had just swallowed a big spoonful of kraut. They don't like him. They like your sister."

Jim shook his head to clear his thinking. He trusted Bert and Terry. They knew the law better than he did. If that's the best way to go, then he'd not make a big fuss. "Does Emmajean know you're calling her as a witness?"

"Yes, I told her what I've just told you, that she's the best person that could help her on the witness stand. I told her to stay calm, be herself, and answer the questions simply and truthfully. She said she could do that."

"But the prosecutor will try to trip her up with his questions. You know that."

"I explained to Emmajean what the prosecutor would try to do. She's brave. When she understood that she could help herself, she agreed to be a witness."

~ ~ ~

After the bailiff told everyone to stand and the judge sat at his podium, everyone took their seat when he pounded his gavel. Again he looked out over the courtroom as if he were counting the people or even reading their minds.

Finally he spoke. "Before the recess the Prosecution rested their case. Mr. Cox are you prepared to present the defendant's case at this time?"

"Yes, Your Honor."

"Call your first witness."

"I call Emmajean Callaway to the witness stand." Jim heard several gasps among the spectators, and noticed that the reporters scribbled faster on their notebooks.

Beyond the Past

Chapter 13

Dressed in one of her new suits and wearing a blouse of a pretty shade of light pink, which highlighted her auburn hair, Emmajean rose and walked alongside Mr. Cox. He held her hand when she stepped up to the witness chair.

The bailiff approached. "Place your hand on the Bible. Do you swear to tell the truth, the whole truth, and nothing but the truth, so help you God?"

"Yes."

Jim could hear the slightest tremble in her voice. She darted her eyes toward where Jim and Terry sat. They both gave an encouraging smile.

Mr. Cox stood in front of his table and started his questioning. "Now, please tell us your name and where you work."

"I'm Emmajean Callaway and I work at the YWCA here in Atlanta."

Mr. Cox went to stand before the jury before he asked his next question. "Please tell me, Miss Callaway what do the letters stand for."

"Young Women's Christian Association."

Still facing the jury, Mr. Cox repeated the words. "Young Women's Christian Association."

Jim watched as Mr. Cox turned toward Emmajean deliberately and unhurriedly, giving her time to work out her response without haste.

"What does your work there entail?"

After a pause she answered. "I serve food in the cafeteria three times a day."

"I see." He started toward his table, then stopped and turned toward Emmajean as if to gauge her state of mind. "How long have you worked there?"

"Let's see." Emmajean looked in deep thought before answering. "My arra, uh, arraignment was January 4 and on that day I moved into the YWCA to live. So I think I was working there by the end of January."

112

"How did you get your job in the cafeteria at the YWCA?"

"I had to fill out an application to live there. So they probably saw on the application that I had worked in a diner back home. Anyway, they offered me the job and I took it."

"Before you lived at the YWCA where did you live?"

"In College Park and then in Cabbagetown."

"That would be College Park south of Atlanta?"

"Yes."

"Did you have lots of friends in College Park?"

"Not many."

"How about at the diner? Did you make friends there?"

"Yes. All those I worked shifts with were friends."

"What about the customers? Did you make friends with any of them?"

"Well, yes. A few of the regular customers."

"You're a good looking young lady. Did any of the regular customers ever try to flirt with you?"

"Yes."

"How did you react to their flirting?"

"I just treated all my customers the same way. I just was nice to them all."

"Did any one of those who flirted with you ever ask you to go out with them?"

"Uh, well, yes one did."

"And did you go out with him?'

"Yes."

"Would you call it a date when you went out with him?"

"I guess. Maybe."

"What did you do on this date with your customer?"

"Objection. Irrelevant."

"Sustained. Hurry it along, Mr. Cox."

Mr. Cox rephrased the question. "When you had a date with this customer did the two of you go out in public, say, to the movies or a restaurant for a nice dinner?"

"No."

"Then where did you go on your dates?"

"We went for hamburgers or milkshakes at a drive-in food place."

"Did you go to the same drive-in every time you went out?"

"Yes."

"Which drive-in did you go to?"

"The Dixie drive-in north of Atlanta."

"Every time you went out with this customer you went to the Dixie drive-in?"

"Yes."

"Did your customer-friend know the people who were also there?"

"Yes. Some of them."

"Did he ever say how he knew them?"

"Objection. Hearsay."

"Sustained."

"Okay, you and your friend always went to the Dixie drive-in and he saw people that he spoke to or nodded toward?"

"Yes."

"Did you ever do any favors for your friend?"

"Not at first, but after I'd known him for a while I did."

"What did you do for your friend?"

Jim saw Emmajean readjust the hem of her skirt and uncross and then recross her legs. Jim leaned toward Terry. "I can tell she's nervous."

Terry's face looked solemn.

The judge spoke. "Answer the question Miss Callaway."

"He asked me to carry small lunch sacks to certain cars but I shouldn't look inside the sack or I might be embarrassed."

"Did you ever look into any of the sacks?"

"No. I thought there might be man-stuff in them."

"You never looked inside the sacks?"

"That's right."

"Were the sacks heavy?"

"No."

"So you took sacks to cars. What else did you do?

"I took the money from someone in the cars, walked back to his car, and gave him the money."

"How many times did you do this for your friend?"

"Lots of times. I didn't count them."

"Miss Callaway, would you say you carried the sacks for your friend more than ten times?"

"Yes."

"Did you carry the sacks for him more than twenty times?"

"Yes."

"Did your friend pay you for doing these favors for him?"

"Yes."

"Were you still living in College Park by then?"

"No. When Angela moved out I couldn't pay the rent all by myself. My friend lived in Cabbagetown and he offered me his extra bedroom. Just to live there. Nothin' romantic at all."

"I see. So then you're living in his house, and you continued to do these favors for him?"

"Yes."

"How many bedrooms did his house have?"

"Two."

"Were you ever in your friend's bedroom?"

"No."

"In the evenings did he stay in the living room and watch television or read? Did he stay in the living room for anything?"

"No, he always went in his bedroom every evening and shut the door."

"So you did not ever have the opportunity to be in his bedroom?"

"That's right."

"You never saw what was in the sacks you delivered to cars and you never were in your friend's bedroom. Is that correct?"

"Yes, that's correct."

"No more questions, Your Honor."

The judge's gavel fell on the wooden block. "Court is recessed and will reconvene tomorrow morning at eight o'clock."

~ ~ ~

The next morning after the judge entered the courtroom, sat, and rapped his gavel, everyone took a seat.

"Mr. Prosecutor, do you wish to question the previous witness?"

"I do, Your Honor."

"I call Miss Emmajean Callaway to the stand."

Emmajean looked fresher than she did yesterday and she briskly walked to the witness chair, chin up and neither looking to the right nor the left.

"Miss Callaway, remember you are still under oath to tell the truth, the whole truth, and nothing but the truth, so help you God."

Emmajean nodded her head toward the judge.

The prosecutor rose and spoke from behind his table. "Please state your name and residence."

"Emmajean Callaway. I live at the YWCA."

The prosecutor looked down at his papers on the table, and rubbed his chin. He stepped out from behind his table and wandered across the floor toward the witness chair.

"We heard you speak earlier about your "customer-friend." Does this friend have a name?"

"Yes?"

"Please tell us his name."

Emmajean darted a look toward her lawyer, who gave a soft nod to her.

"His name is Barry Wagner."

"Fine. Now we also heard you tell the court that you lived with him. Is that correct?"

Another look toward Mr. Cox, who again slightly nodded.

"I lived in his house."

"Now, Miss Callaway, we're all adults here so please admit that you and Mr. Wagner lived in his house and had a romantic relationship."

"No. I will not tell you that. We did not have a romantic relationship."

Emmajean's words were spoken evenly with no increase in volume. But Jim recognized the fire in her blue eyes that was always present when her temper tried to burst forth. She had to stay calm. She couldn't let the jury see her lose control.

"Remember, Miss Callaway, you're still under oath to tell the truth. Now, did you and Mr. Wagner have a romantic relationship?"

"Objection! Question already answered."

"Sustained."

"Very well." The prosecutor walked around the floor in front of Emmajean, his head down, rubbing his chin, looking as if he didn't know where to go next.

"Now, you said you didn't ever go into Mr. Wagner's bedroom."

"That's right."

"Did you ever see about ninety pounds of marijuana—an illegal drug—in his bedroom?"

"Objection. She said she's never been in his bedroom."

"Sustained." The prosecutor sent a sly smile toward Mr. Cox.

"Miss Callaway, again, did you ever see about forty kilograms of marijuana in his bedroom?"

Emmajean steadied her eyes to the prosecutor's face. "I don't even know what a kilogram is."

"What did you see in his bedroom?

Jim watched while Emmajean waited a few moments, calming herself, before she answered. "I never went into his bedroom so I never saw anything in his bedroom."

Jim and Terry exchanged a glance and both smiled. She was holding her own toe-to-toe with the Atlanta prosecutor.

"How long did you do these favors for your friend?"

"Objection. Irrelevant."

"Sustained."

The prosecutor walked over to his table, looked at his assistant, and moved some papers around. He picked up one sheet of paper and approached the witness. Jim wondered what was on the paper and if it would trip Emmajean up. She was doing so well.

The prosecutor held up the sheet of paper before Emmajean. Her facial features never changed. "Do you recognize the building in this photo?"

"Yes."

"Please tell me what the photo shows."

"It's a photo of Baker's Diner."

Jim cast a look at Terry who returned lifted shoulders.

"Did you used to work at Baker's Diner?"

"Yes."

"What was your job there?"

"A waitress."

"How long did you work at Baker's Diner?"

"Objection. Irrelevant."

"Sustained."

"While you worked at Baker's Diner, were you friendly with the customers?"

"Yes. The customer is always right."

"Of course. And did you receive tips in money for your waitressing work?"

"Yes." Emmajean and the prosecutor locked eyes with each other. Who would look away first? Still holding her gaze at him, Emmajean broke the silence. "If they do their job good, all waitresses receive tips for the waitressin' work."

"Did you regard some customers more special than others and gave them extra attention for greater tips?"

"Objection."

"Sustained. Mr. Prosecutor it appears you've turned onto another rabbit trail. Please bring your questioning back to the charges at hand."

Jim noticed Terry trying to hide his grin. Jim figured Terry thought the prosecutor's questioning wasn't going well.

Finally the prosecutor spoke. "No more questions, Your Honor."

"Mr. Cox, any redirect?'

Mr. Cox rose. "Yes, Your Honor."

The judge's gavel hit the block of wood. "Court is recessed and will reconvene at two o'clock."

~ ~ ~

That afternoon Mr. Cox strode to where Emmajean sat in the witness chair. Jim could see her shoulders drop to a more relaxed position when he approached.

"Miss Callaway, your customer-friend befriended you by flirting with you while you worked at Baker's Diner, is that correct? He initiated the talk between the two of you?"

"Yes."

"He offered a bedroom in his house for you to live in after your couldn't pay your rent. Is that correct?"

"Yes."

"Where are you originally from, Miss Callaway?"

"Newton, Tennessee."

"Is it a very small town?"

"Yes."

"Coming from Newton to Atlanta was a big, big step for you, wasn't it?

"Yes. Atlanta is a lot bigger than Newton."

"Objection."

"Sustained."

"Atlanta and certain people who live in Atlanta have not treated you well, have they?"

"No."

Jim noticed the bravado in her voice weakened a little.

"But before your friend from Baker's diner came into the picture you were doing fine, you were working, earning a check, had a roommate, paying your rent, buying your groceries, and were never in trouble with the law. Is that correct?"

"Yes." Even though her voice was weaker she held her chin level.

"Thank you, Miss Callaway. No more questions, Your Honor."

Mr. Cox sauntered to his table, stopped, then turned toward the judge. "The defense rests its case."

The judge smacked his gavel on the block once. "Court is dismissed and will reconvene tomorrow morning at eight o'clock."

Chapter 14

Leaving the courthouse, Jim had to make his feet move one in front of the other. "Terry, I'm just plain worn out. I guess having to watch Emmajean up on the witness stand all by herself, and I couldn't help her. I'm here in Atlanta every day of the trial, but I can't do a thing for her."

"Jim you're here for support. Emmajean knows that and she really appreciates you being here."

"Terry, I'm really tired. How about we get back to the hotel and rest a while then order room service for supper? My treat."

"Sounds good. Let's head for the hotel."

Once at their hotel they headed for their separate rooms for a while before ordering their supper. Jim lay on his bed, stretched out, and tried to clear his mind. He was asleep in moments.

Caroline walked toward him, coming down the hall. Her loveliness spread a glow around her in her white nightgown. They met and embraced as they had twenty years ago. He led her into his room where they snuggled on the sofa. No talk of the children, no talk of Emmajean's trial or Bones's boy's troubles. Jim felt release, freeing. He found her lips and she kissed him back. They smiled and kissed again. They talked about getting married. It was easy, there were no obstacles, no hindrances. Just smiles and kisses. No blaming, no guilt. They were liberated from everything but themselves.

The shrill ring of the telephone brought him back to reality. "Uh . . . hello?"

"Jim?"

He scooted to sit on the side of the bed. "Yeah."

"Jim, it's Terry. You about ready to order room service?"

"Sure. Do that. I want a steak, well done, and whatever comes with it. Iced tea to drink. You order it and we'll eat in here. Come on over when you want to."

"Will do. Hey, if I woke you, I'm sorry."

"That's okay. I needed to get up and eat. See you in a while."

Jim couldn't shake that sweet, impossible dream. He walked over to the window and looked north toward Knoxville and Caroline. Then he looked to his right spotting the courthouse. He remembered the YWCA was just a few blocks beyond there. Emmajean was at the women's detention place, but where was that?

He looked again to the north. Jim had put on the brakes of Caroline and him working out a relationship together. He knew her well enough to know her patience was wearing thin. She just couldn't see the problems blocking them and any potential detours in their future together. He would have to do all the serious thinking on their outcome while she did the romanticizing of it. Everything had always worked out the way she wanted, except getting disowned by her parents. He could see how easily she faced things that seemingly dissolved before becoming a full-blown problem.

But the problems surrounding their getting married . . . a knock sounded. Jim stepped to the door, moved aside so Terry could enter the room. As he started to close the door, the room service cart neared. It stopped at Jim's door and Jim stepped all the way to the side of the doorway. The young man moved his cart toward the table to transfer the food. Jim signed the bill, adding a nice tip to the total.

Jim and Terry lifted the domes over the food and placed the food where it belonged. They sat and began to eat. Jim bowed his head for a brief moment and Terry stayed silent until he finished praying. "Jim how do you eat like you do and stay so trim?"

"I just quit when I'm full."

Terry laughed. "I guess I need a little more self-discipline."

"That might help. But as you grow older you'll need the self-discipline even more."

They chatted through the meal about everyday things. When they started their desert, their talk turned serious—Emmajean.

"Terry, what will we see in the morning?"

"Remember when the trial started—the prosecutor and Mr. Cox each had time to talk to the jury, introducing to them their side of the case?" Jim nodded. "Tomorrow they'll each have another chance to talk to the jury. This time both men will summarize what has been said about the case throughout the week. They can add other thoughts they may have. They'll do all they can to convince the jury to believe them."

"The prosecutor didn't really have much of a case against Emmajean, did he? He asked some good questions I guess, but

Bert came up and more or less turned around every one of his questions to make it work in Emmajean's favor."

"I see it the same way, Jim. I'm so glad the judge granted Mr. Cox's motion to sever or Emmajean's trial would have been presented with Barry's. That would have been a disaster because they have much more to convince a jury that he is guilty. Mr. Cox let me look at his copy of the prosecutor's bill of particulars, which was a brief statement of the core facts of the case. When we looked over the facts, it was obvious the prosecutor didn't have much at all that he could use against Emmajean."

"Do you agree with Bert when he says the jury likes Emmajean and doesn't like the prosecutor?"

"I've been watching the jury members since Mr. Cox said that, and I get the same feeling. Especially when the prosecutor questioned Emmajean, trying to get her confused. It just looked like the jury members were pulling for Emmajean."

"Boy, I sure hope you're both right on that."

Terry pushed away from the table. "Yeah, I hope we are too."

Shortly, they moved their room service cart out into the hall against the wall. Terry went on to his room. "Good night."

"Good night, Terry."

Jim watched a little television. Bored, he prepared to go to bed. Early, but his body could use the rest. After he was under the covers, his dream played on in his mind although this time he wasn't sleeping, but wide awake. He wanted Caroline close to him right then. He wanted to hold her. Of course, she wanted that too. But she wasn't looking any further.

She wanted them together, but wasn't considering how they would manage their living arrangements unless they married. Jim wasn't sure it was the right time to think about marriage. Once this tumultuous summer ended maybe things would be calm enough for bringing up marriage. Even if the jury said Emmajean was not guilty, where would she go? Would she go home and live in his house in Newton? That might not set well with Caroline. He'd always heard two grown women couldn't live under the same roof and keep peace in the house.

And there was Lynn. Bless her heart. He hadn't spent nearly enough time with her lately. Now that UT was out for summer quarter, Caroline had both their children in her home all to herself. Should he be there too? Make it a family of four?

And then Bones. He and Callie had troubles with Art. Would he be able to help them whenever he got home? Of course he would, for moral support if nothing else.

And, of course, the mill. Bob had done a good job keeping things running smoothly while he was away. But he needed to be a presence in his own mill. He got along well with all his employees, and he didn't want to jeopardize that.

Jim realized he was making observations and only asking questions. He couldn't answer even one of them without it being entangled with another.

God, please help me. I'm carrying a buddle of cares and can't fix any of them. Help me to let you stand alongside and share these cares. Without You I can do nothing. Amen.

These things ran through his head for a couple of hours before he finally drifted into restless sleep. The next morning he felt almost like he'd had no sleep at all. He and Terry ate breakfast and got to the courthouse before eight o'clock. They wanted to speak to Mr. Cox but he appeared to be deep in thought, hunkered down at his table with some books lying open. He occasionally made notes on a tablet in front of him.

"He's getting things ready for his closing statement," Terry said.

"We'd better not disturb him." They took their seats.

When the judge sat at the podium, he looked over the courtroom, and rapped his gavel. He turned toward the jurors.

"Terry, what's he doing?"

"He's giving the jury instructions and guidelines they must follow in coming to a verdict. This is commonly referred to as the judge's charge to the jury."

The judge proceeded to instruct the jurors about the relevant laws that should guide their deliberations. He read from papers he held, giving the jury instructions. In doing so the judge stated the issues in the case and defined any words that might not be familiar to the jurors. He read the standard of proof that jurors should apply to the case—beyond a reasonable doubt.

Then he looked up from his papers and spoke to the jurors: "You are the sole judge of the facts and of the believability of witnesses. You are to base your conclusions on the evidence as presented in the trial. The opening and closing arguments of the lawyers are not evidence. When I tell you that a party must prove something, I mean that the party must persuade you, by evidence presented in court, that what he is trying to prove is more likely to be true than not true.

"Finally, my instructions contain the interpretation of the relevant laws that govern this case. You jurors are required to stick to these laws in making your decision, regardless of what you believe the law is or ought to be. In other words, you will determine the facts and reach a verdict, within the guidelines of the law as determined by this court."

The judge swiveled his chair toward the courtroom.

"Mr. Prosecutor, are you ready to give your closing arguments?"

"Yes, Your Honor."

The prosecutor stood at his table then walked to the jury box. He glanced across their faces then spoke. "We're here to prove that Emmajean Callaway did indeed possess an illegal drug with intent to sell and distribute. You've heard the witnesses answer our questions. You must weigh carefully what you've heard and arrive at your verdict—guilty or not guilty.

"I submit to you that Emmajean Callaway was in a relationship with Barry Wagner, they possessed marijuana, and according to a witness went to the Dixie drive-in and distributed. Miss Callaway delivered the marijuana, received money for it, and brought the money back to her friend. How simple is that? She had marijuana, she delivered, and she received pay for it.

"Marijuana is illegal to possess and thus illegal to sell. Emmajean Callaway did both—possessed and sold marijuana. She and her friend had a good little scheme for their business with marijuana."

Jim saw Mr. Cox lay a hand over Emmajean's to keep her from standing and speaking. She did neither.

"But they got caught." The prosecutor smirked toward Emmajean. "In their house they had marijuana, at the Dixie drive-in they sold marijuana, and at the Dixie drive-in they accepted money for their marijuana. These are facts. You heard the employee of the Dixie drive-in testify to the presence of Miss Callaway at the drive-in and to the trips she took to different cars, always returning to her car without the sack she carried when she initially left her car.

"You heard Miss Callaway's former roommate tell how she reacted to the activities of Miss Callaway and her friend. Her roommate suspected that Miss Callaway was mixed up in something illegal and her roommate immediately moved out of their apartment rather than possibly being found guilty by association with Miss Callaway.

"You also heard the Atlanta Police Department detective say his people had been watching Miss Callaway's friend's car.

Watching the places they went and what they did. They had a search warrant. May I remind you that suspicion must run high for a judge to sign a search warrant. Every move Miss Callaway made was followed and documented.

"You cannot dismiss the facts you've heard here in this trial. Put all the facts together you've heard from witnesses and the only verdict you can come up with is guilty. Guilty! Guilty of possession of an illegal substance with intent to distribute."

The prosecutor walked back to his chair. He smiled at Mr. Cox and looked out over the spectators and cast a smile toward them. When he sat, he and his assistant put their heads together. Jim wondered if they talked about what Mr. Cox would say.

The judge's gavel rapped on the block, causing some in the room to jump, startled, including Jim. Why was the judge getting their attention at this point?

"Court will adjourn and reconvene Friday morning at eight o'clock."

Jim looked at Terry. "Why can't he reconvene this afternoon? He's been doing it that way all week."

"He probably has something important scheduled for this afternoon. He has adjourned court till tomorrow morning. Nothing we can do to change that."

"I hate that Emmajean will have to stay longer at that detention center."

"Jim, we have an afternoon off. What do you want to do?"

"Terry, I'd better get back to the hotel. I've got some telephone calls to make. Maybe we can meet for a late lunch."

"Sure thing."

Chapter 15

"Hey, you two. Got a break between classes?"

They hung up their coats and came into the living room where Caroline sat on the sofa reading.

"Yes, we do." James smiled at his mom. "We really do need to study. We won't make any noise. You don't have to leave."

"Caroline, have you heard from Daddy?"

"No, Lynn, not for several days. Emmajean's trial started this week on Monday. I'm guessing he's tied up with the trial and those can last for days. I expect he's tired when he reaches his hotel room."

"Lynn, if we haven't heard anything that would be a good thing. If something bad happened, Dad would've let us know."

"I guess so." Lynn looked at the floor.

The telephone rang. All three looked at it. Caroline rose and crossed the room. "Hello."

It was Jimmy. "How are you and how is the trial going?"

"Pretty much in Emmajean's favor, we think."

"I'm glad for that. But I'm sorry Emmajean has to stay at the detention center for the length of the trial."

"How are the kids?"

"They're doing fine. They both decided to enroll for summer quarter."

"When will they be home from classes?

She looked toward the kids and smiled. "They are here now. A break between classes and they both intend to stay here and study."

"Would they have time to speak to me a minute?

"Sure, hold on." She turned toward Lynn and James. "He wants to talk to both of you. Who's first?"

James indicated that Lynn should be first. "Daddy! I'm so glad you called. We had just talked about you and wondered what was going on down there."

"Things are going good for Emmajean. You staying busy with school? Are you keeping up with everything?"

"Yes, I'm keeping up with all my classes."

"Okay. I'll let you get to your studying."

"I'm so glad you called. Here's James."

"Dad, so glad you called. I guess you're worn out sitting in the courtroom day after day. How is the trial going for Emmajean?"

"We think things are going her way. The trial may go to the jury tomorrow."

"That's great."

"Is your mom still there?"

"Sure, here she is." James held the telephone toward Caroline. "He wants to talk to you again."

~ ~ ~

"I'm here, Jimmy."

"Caroline I know you can't really say much with the kids there with you. I wanted you to know I'm missing you. We've been in the courtroom for nearly two weeks—last week they picked the jury and the trial started this week."

"I miss you, Jimmy. That trial will surely be over soon."

Caroline spoke and her voice made his heart pound louder. "It's so good to hear your voice, Caroline. I'm hoping we'll get a verdict from the jury tomorrow. There's no way to know for sure."

"I hope so for you and of course for Emmajean."

"With or without a verdict tomorrow I'm coming to Knoxville for the weekend. If the jury says guilty, Emmajean will go back to the detention center, and I don't know when I'll be able to see her again. Of course, if the jury finds her not guilty, I'm bringing her home with me."

"Jimmy, either guilty or not guilty, you're probably worn out. We could come to Newton for the weekend."

"That makes sense. If y'all can come to Newton it would be good. I'm about wiped out." They continued to talk, falling into a comfortable rhythm.

Although Emmajean's fate weighed on him, talking with Caroline helped Jim to relax and the muscles in his shoulders to loosen. They finally said good-bye. Jim had needed that time with Caroline even if it was only on the telephone. And he'd see her and the kids this weekend at home. His sleep tonight would be much better than the restless night he'd spent tossing and turning last night.

~ ~ ~

The next morning after the judge took his seat and rapped his gavel he spoke to Mr. Cox. "Are you ready for your closing arguments?"

"Yes, Your Honor."

"Proceed."

Emmajean's lawyer carried a few loose papers with him as he approached the jury. He laid a hand on the railing separating him from the jury box, the hand holding the papers hung limp at his side. He leaned in toward the jurors and made eye contact with each of them in turn before he spoke.

"Your Honor, may I request that the court reporter read to this court the last paragraph the prosecutor spoke before you recessed court yesterday?"

"Of course." He turned to the court reporter whose fingers had stilled on her machine. "Please find and read the last paragraph the prosecutor spoke before adjournment yesterday."

The court reporter found the paragraph and spoke clearly: *"You cannot dismiss the facts you've heard here in this trial. Put all the facts together you've heard from witnesses and the only verdict you can come up with is guilty. Guilty! Guilty of possession of an illegal substance with intent to distribute."*

"Thank you. Let me say that last sentence once more: *'Guilty of possession of an illegal substance with intent to distribute.'* Gentlemen of the jury the prosecutor himself is not certain of the charges in this trial."

"The defendant, Miss Emmajean Callaway, is charged with *aiding* the act of possession with intent to sell an illegal substance, which is a misdemeanor. Aiding! You have heard the questions the prosecutor and I have asked the witnesses and you have heard their answers. Please remember, this case you're hearing concerns only Miss Callaway. Not her roommate, not her customer-friend, just Miss Callaway.

"You heard the prosecutor continually harass Miss Callaway with questions about the house she lived in with her customer-friend. You heard him ask if she had seen about ninety pounds of marijuana in his bedroom. She continued to answer him saying she had not ever been in her friend's bedroom, and she had not seen *any* marijuana. The prosecutor mentioning the amount of marijuana—ninety pounds—lets us think that is how much the police found in his bedroom.

"If marijuana is found in a residence to which more than one person has access, the prosecutor would have to comply with the law of constructive possession. What I've just said describes the case brought against Miss Callaway: she and her friend had access to the house they both lived in.

"The law of constructive possession requires the prosecutor to prove specific elements before a defendant can be convicted. In the case of Miss Callaway this law would require the prosecutor to first prove that Miss Callaway had knowledge of the marijuana's presence. She did not know about the marijuana's presence. You heard her testify under oath that she had *never* been in her friend's bedroom. Detective Hamilton testified under oath that his men searched the entire house and only found the marijuana in her friend's bedroom.

"Secondly under the law of constructive possession, the prosecutor would have to prove that Miss Callaway had knowledge that the substance was marijuana. What substance? Miss Callaway testified she had never seen any marijuana in the house.

"Thirdly, under the law of constructive possession, the prosecutor would have to prove that Miss Callaway had dominion and control over the marijuana. Again, what marijuana? Miss Callaway did not have knowledge of marijuana being in the house. The state must prove that the defendant was aware of the character of the substance to prove that the defendant acted with knowledge. "The prosecutor"—Mr. Cox waved his hand toward the prosecutor—"has shown no proof that would satisfy the three parts of the law of constructive possession. The prosecutor has not presented any evidence or testimony to prove Miss Callaway guilty. Under these circumstances, I urge you to find Miss Callaway not guilty of the charges against her." Mr. Cox took his seat.

The judge turned toward the jury. "I remind you in deciding your verdict it is important that you follow the law spelled out in those instructions I read to you. There are no other laws that apply to this case. Even if you do not like the laws they must be applied, you must use them. For nearly two centuries we have lived by the constitution and the law. No juror has the right to violate rules we all share. Any time during your deliberations if you have a question concerning this case you may give a note to the bailiff who will bring it to me.

"Bailiff, please escort the jury to the jury conference room." The bailiff motioned for them to rise and follow him as they left the room. When the jury box emptied, the judge rapped his gavel again. "This court is adjourned awaiting a verdict from the jury. All parties involved in this case will be informed when that verdict is reached and at that time court will be reconvened." He left the courtroom through a door on the opposite side of the courtroom, across from the jury box.

Jim and Terry hung around the courthouse for a while hoping for a quick verdict. When none came they went to their hotel, staying close to their room telephones.

"Terry, will the jury deliberate over the weekend?"

"Not usually."

"So, if we don't get word that they reached a verdict by five o'clock that'll mean that trial business is pretty much over until next week. Right?"

"That's right."

Jim stood at the window while he worked on his decision. "Would it be safe then for me to leave after five o'clock and go home?"

"I think so. Didn't know you were considering going home for the weekend. You want me to go or stay here?"

Jim hadn't thought about that. "Why don't you stay here. You can call me if anything happens I need to know about. I won't check out of the hotel, just keep this same room because I will be coming back late Sunday."

"Okay, then I'll stay close by the telephone and let you know immediately when I hear anything."

~ ~ ~

When he pulled into his driveway the house was lit up like a spend-the-night party. Light shown from windows in almost every room. His *family* had arrived from Knoxville. His family—is that what he should be calling them?

By the time he was lifting his suitcase out of the trunk, Lynn was beside him. He set the luggage on the ground and grabbed her. "Lynn! It's been so long." He pushed her away at arms' length, then they hugged again.

He carried his suitcase as they walked toward the house. There Jim saw Caroline and James. His happiness at seeing them all nearly made his chest burst open. When he and Lynn reached the wide porch, James took the suitcase and set it inside in the foyer. Jim and James shook hands and Jim gave his son a "man" hug—slapping his back.

Then there was Caroline. She had given him time with his children first but fidgeted for her turn. Still careful about their show of affection in their children's presence, Jim gave Caroline a shoulder hug and a kiss on her cheek. Walking into the house, Jim left his arm across her shoulders and she placed her arm around his waist. Jim saw Lynn notice Caroline's move, but his daughter didn't seem disturbed about it. A while later they all sat in the living room, Lynn seated on the sofa close beside her daddy.

They listened as Jim relayed all the information about Emmajean's trial. He didn't try to hide his anguish as he told them about Emmajean being led from the courtroom at the end of each day. "She has to stay in a women's detention center somewhere around Atlanta till the trial is over."

"And it's almost over now, right, Dad?" James said.

"All over except the verdict. Terry stayed down there so if anything happens he can call me. He looked at Lynn. "You know, I think your Aunt Emmajean and Terry have a thing going on between them."

Lynn looked puzzled. "What kind of thing, Daddy?"

"Oh, you know, I think they like each other. He's sure been a great support for Emmajean. She looks so much better than the first time I saw her in Atlanta, and she smiles more. She had let all this drug mess put her way down. Terry and I being there has been a good support for her."

Jim became aware that Caroline did not enter the discussion about Emmajean. He'd really made a big mistake in his homecoming. He should be talking about them and not about his experiences surrounding Emmajean in Atlanta.

"Well, now, what's this I hear about you two taking classes during summer quarter?" He glanced at Caroline who gave him a slight smile.

"Dad, we're both taking just two classes. That's really a light load but it will help down the road if we face a hard quarter. You know, then we could take fewer hours," James said.

Jim turned toward Caroline. "And how does Mom feel about this?"

"Just fine. We didn't want to bother you in Atlanta so I told them okay."

"I would have agreed with you."

"Daddy, how long can you stay here this time?"

"Don't know for sure, Lynn. I hope till late Sunday. All the trial information has been turned over to the jury. Terry said they wouldn't be deliberating over the weekend." He'd done it again. Talking about the trial. He had allowed the trial and Emmajean to swallow him and that was uppermost in his mind. For the rest of the weekend, he'd have to be careful not to bring up the trial unless one of them asked.

"Hey, about some hot chocolate, Dad? I know it's summer but I can always drink some hot chocolate."

"Sure, James." James looked at his mother and she nodded.

"Come on Lynn, let's go fix some."

Left alone with Caroline in the living room, Jim could feel the heat between them. "Jimmy, I'm so glad to see you. I guess the last two weeks have crowded your mind, leaving no room for anything else."

"No, that's not true. Just two nights ago I dreamed you came to me in my hotel in Atlanta. You were coming down the hall, dressed in a white nightgown, and you had a glow about you. When you walked into my room I wanted you there. Then the dream stopped. I think of you every day."

She joined him on the sofa, took his hands, and kissed his cheek. He took one of her hands and brought it to his lips. Just a simple kiss on the back of her hand, but her heart lurched and her stomach dropped. She laid her head on his chest and heard the rapid thumps of his heart.

"You'd better slide over a little before the kids return from the kitchen."

Their timing was great, for coming into the living room the kids brought a tray of mugs full of hot chocolate. James put the tray on the coffee table and passed out the mugs. Lynn took a seat on the sofa on the other side of her daddy.

It was already past their bedtime. Jim made the first move toward the upstairs. "Here, I'll take your luggage upstairs, Dad." Jim followed him. Caroline and Lynn cleaned up the hot chocolate tray with empty mugs.

"Good night, ladies." James stood at the top of the stairway, looking toward the kitchen.

Lynn came from the kitchen and started upstairs. She yelled, "Good night, James." Caroline locked the door and turned out the lights before climbing up the stairs. "Good night, James."

The three of them made their way to their bedrooms. However, Caroline took a detour to Jim's bedroom. His door stood open and she took that as an invitation to enter. "Jimmy." He looked up to find her sitting on the side of his bed. "You seem to be coiled inside, ready to fall to pieces if that verdict is guilty."

"Terry and I think Emmajean has a good chance of getting not guilty. But we don't need to waste time talking about things in Atlanta." The bedroom door was not closed but Caroline stood and walked toward Jim. She slid her hands inside his sport coat and reached around him, laying her head once again on his chest. Jim wrapped his arms around her, and pulled her close. They stayed that way for several moments before parting. "I've missed you. Oh, how I've missed you." He leaned down and found her lips that eagerly took his.

Jim knew this was a mistake. Either one of the kids could stick their heads into his room, especially Lynn. He didn't want her to find his door closed and come in to find them in his bedroom. How did he get to this place?

You got to this place because of what you did by Caney Creek.

He heard the clear words directed at him.

You've made your journey from there to here. Now what?

Jim eased out of the kiss and the embrace. He held Caroline by her shoulders and gently pushed her to arms' length. "We can't."

"Why not?"

"Caroline, the kids are just down the hall. They feel free to roam this house and Lynn could stick her head in the door just to talk to me. I haven't spent much time with her lately."

Caroline spoke precise words without raising her voice. "Jimmy, did you hear what you just said? Did you? You're correct. You haven't spent much time with your daughter lately. You haven't spent much time with your son either. Or with me. For many weeks you've only telephoned a few times. You're spending more time in Atlanta than here or in Knoxville."

"Caroline, I'm in Atlanta to support Emmajean. You know that."

"Yes, I know that."

"Does that bother you?"

"Yes, it does." The volume of her voice rose. "You're putting Emmajean ahead of your mill and your family."

"Emmajean *is* my family."

"Yes, she is. But we're your family also—Lynn, James, and me. But you've had her at the top of your priority list for several months. You're thinking more about your sister than about your two children and me." Now her voice raised as she stepped away from Jim. "You're putting her first. How do you think Lynn, your daughter, feels about that? And James looked forward to building a relationship with you—what about that? Like that's going to happen. And never mind me. I've waited years for a relationship with you but you always have a reason to prevent that—either it's Emmajean, Atlanta, Arthur's son, or when the trial is over. It's never *Us*."

She turned to leave his bedroom. Jim caught hold of her arm before she left. She glared daggers at him. "Turn me loose."

"I will turn you loose if you'll stay and calm down."

"Why should I stay?"

"Caroline, I love you. Be reasonable. All those things you mentioned *are* standing between us."

"Sometimes love is not enough. If you're in love with someone you act upon it, you put them first. But, no, you've put Emmajean first. Emmajean this, Emmajean that. If you wait till the trial stuff ends, you'll help Arthur with his troubles, and get yourself busy with the mill. Then, maybe you'll give me some time and start talking about marriage. By then it might be too late."

"Caroline, you can't mean that."

"Yes, I do mean it." She jerked her arm from Jim's grip. "When we were young I was impatient. I had to have what I wanted when I wanted it. As I matured I became a more patient person. I've been quite patient with you since Christmas. But you've put me on the shelf. You've just about pushed my patience too far." She stamped her foot, wheeled around, and traipsed out of the room.

Chapter 16

"Caroline . . . ." But he was talking to his open bedroom door. He closed his door, lacking energy to do anything else. He stretched out on his bed, heeled one shoe and then the other and let them fall to the floor. What Caroline said replayed in his mind. She was right. But he couldn't be two places at the same time. He couldn't, and he'd decided to be there for Emmajean. Encourage her through a tough time. Why did Caroline react that way? Why can't she understand?

A soft knock sounded on his door. "Come in." When the door opened, Lynn's face appeared as she looked at her daddy.

She spoke almost in a whisper. "Daddy, is everything okay? I heard some loud talking and then two thumps on the floor. Is anything wrong?"

"The two thumps on the floor came when I let my shoes drop to the floor."

"Who was talking so loud?"

"Caroline and I were discussing something, and our voices got a little out of control."

"Discussing what? It sounded like an argument."

"It's nothing for you to worry about."

"Are you sure, Daddy? I wouldn't want you and Caroline to get into a fuss."

"Do you and Caroline get along with each other?"

"Yes and James and I do too."

"That's good. I'm glad for that."

"Uh, all we need is a daddy and we'd have a real family."

Listen to her words.

He pushed the pillows up against the headboard, and scooted up to sit against them. He'd heard those words but nobody else was in the room with them. "Lynn, are you doing okay living in Caroline's home? Everything working out good enough for you?"

"Oh, yes, it's much better than living in the dorm."

"That's good."

"Well, I better get back to my room now that I know everything's all right in here."

"Good night. You have nothing to worry about with me."

She started to the door and turned around. "Good night, Daddy."

~ ~ ~

The next morning Jim padded into the kitchen wearing his socks, blue jeans, and a T shirt emblazoned with a large, orange T in the middle of his chest. Lynn had bought it for him at Christmas. Jim went to the counter to pour a glass of milk and sat at the kitchen table. Where was everybody?

James and Lynn came into the kitchen next. "Where's breakfast? Mom usually gets breakfast on the table. Have you seen her, Dad?"

"Nope. Good Morning."

"Good Morning, Daddy." Lynn came over and gave Jim a peck on the cheek.

Jim looked over the situation. No cook, no breakfast. "Of the three of us who's the best cook?" James and Lynn pointed to Jim.

He set down his glass of milk and sauntered over to the refrigerator. He began pulling things out and setting them on the counter. Shortly he had bacon sizzling and eggs scrambling. He set the orange juice and three small glasses on the table. The toast popped up from the toaster. He laid the bread on a small plate, pulled out some butter from the fridge, and handed them to Lynn who put them on the table.

"What kind of jelly or jam do y'all want?" "Any kind." They both answered together then looked at each other.

"Dad, where's Mom?"

"I don't know. I haven't seen or heard from her this morning. Sleeping in, I guess." He put the cooked bacon on some paper towels, pushed the scrambled eggs from the skillet into a bowl, and handed the bowl to James for him to put on the table.

He looked at Lynn and James. "Milk for you two?" When they nodded he grabbed two glasses from a cabinet, the milk from the fridge, and put them on the table. Jim followed that with assorted jellies then placed the bacon on a plate, carried the plate to the table, and sat. They all helped themselves, telling Jim what a good cook he was.

"Oh, I see you started without me." Caroline stood at the refrigerator fully dressed.

"There's plenty of food here, Mom. Sit down and I'll get you a plate. Want milk?"

"No, James, thank you. Juice will be fine." James handed her a small glass from a cabinet and the juice from the refrigerator then returned to his chair. Caroline dragged an extra chair to the table and sat near Lynn.

"We thought you might be sleeping in. Daddy said he hadn't seen you and James and I hadn't seen you. Are you feeling all right this morning?"

"Yes, Lynn. Thanks for asking."

Caroline didn't glance in Jim's direction. He got her unspoken message loud and clear. Their argument last night still stood between them. How long does a woman hold a grudge? Caroline looked as if she would have her feelings of resentment toward him for a very long time. He'd tried to apologize last night. What else could he do?

Lynn looked her daddy straight in the eyes and tilted her head toward Caroline. Jim got that unspoken message also. With her look Lynn had meant Jim should say something to Caroline.

"Good morning, Caroline."

"Good morning." Not a glance toward Jim. Boy, he was in the dog house and he wasn't even married. He saw James look at Lynn and they both lifted their shoulders. They didn't know what to do. Lynn, of course, had to know a little something after she'd come in his room last night and asked about the loud voices she'd heard.

"What's on the agenda for today? Anybody got plans— separately or for us all?" Jim said.

Caroline, having finished her juice, pushed her chair away from the table. She went to the sink to rinse the glass. "I have no plans." She left the room, and Jim could hear her climbing the stairs.

"Dad, you'd better do something. Quick. When Mom gets that quiet it means trouble. You need to follow her."

"James, I think not this morning. Your mom and I had a discussion last night that turned into a disagreement. I'll give both of us some time for that disagreement to simmer down."

"You don't know her like I do. She doesn't simmer down fast," James said.

"Daddy, please keep peace in the house. You and Caroline need to come to an agreement on whatever y'all were discussing last night."

"Kids, thank you for all the advice. Remember I've known her from way back. I think things will be okay—eventually."

"But Daddy, maybe you'd better not wait for eventually. Not this time. We've all found each other and it's no time for arguments."

Jim looked at James and thought about what he had said. "Y'all think you can clean up the mess I made fixing breakfast?"

They both nodded. They looked at Jim with a go-fix-everything expression.

~ ~ ~

Caroline heard the soft tap on her door. She stayed silent. The next tap was a little louder. "Who is it?"

"Jimmy. May I come in?"

Caroline approached her side of the door as if on cat's paws. "I don't think that would be a good idea." She laid her hand flat against the door.

Jim didn't hear any movement from inside the room. "Caroline, please open the door. I'd like to talk to you."

"I think you talked last night all you need to talk." Unshed tears stung her eyes. Since Christmas she'd never thought she'd refuse Jimmy anything.

"Caroline, please open the door. I apologize for our arguing last night. I'd like to see you and apologize to you."

The bedroom door eased open, then stopped. Jim took the opportunity to push the door open, and entered the room. Caroline stood by the bed and an opened suitcase. She sorted through her clothes putting them in the luggage in a precise manner.

"Caroline, what are doing?"

"You're pretty smart. What does it look like I'm doing? I'm packing to leave."

"It looks like your body is leaning sideways from that heavy chip you have on your shoulder."

She twirled toward him. "Jimmy, how can you say that to me?" She felt the tears begin to trail across her cheeks.

"Aw, Caroline, I've made you cry. I don't feel worthy to kiss the bottoms of your shoes." He covered the space between them in three strides. "All of that talk last night from me was careless and I've hurt you. I'm so sorry."

Caroline determined she would not let him in her room and here he was standing in front of her so close she could feel his breath in her hair. Further, she determined she would not cry in his presence and now here she had. She took the last step needed to touch him. She put her arms around his waist and her cheek against his chest. He encircled her with his arms. They both held on tightly to the other as if being rescued from an angry storm.

"Jimmy, I acted like high school last night. I shouldn't have said all those things."

"Caroline, I apologize. I shouldn't have allowed us to argue. But before I could cram down my feelings you hurried out of my room. I had a restless night."

"So did I." She raised her head from his chest, her tears leaving a soggy place on his T shirt.

"Let's try to forget last night and do something fun for all four of us."

They heard the telephone downstairs ring. James called from the bottom of the stairway. "Dad, it's for you." Jim and Caroline moved away from one another. "I'll be right there, James." He kissed Caroline lightly on the lips with a promise of more to follow.

Jim trotted down the stairs and took the telephone from James. "Jim here."

"Jim, it's Bert Cox in Atlanta. I wanted to update you on something."

"Something bad?" Caroline had made her way downstairs and stood beside him.

"The jury deliberated till late Friday night. They had a question they wrote on paper and gave to the bailiff before they left the building for the day. The bailiff then delivered the jurors' message to the judge. He summoned the prosecutor and his assistant and me and my assistant to his chambers. The jury's question was if Emmajean carried marijuana in those sacks did that not mean she was in possession of an illegal drug." Mr. Cox kept talking, not giving Jim a chance to jump into the conversation. "So this Monday morning at seven o'clock, we'll all go to the courtroom, except Emmajean, and the jury will be seated.

"As per our discussion in the judge's chambers Friday night, the judge will speak to the jurors and reiterate what I had said in my closing arguments about the law of constructive possession, which requires the prosecutor to prove specific elements before a defendant can be convicted. In the case of your sister this law would require the prosecutor to first prove that Miss Callaway had knowledge of the marijuana's presence. She did not know about the marijuana's presence. Therefore, when she carried the sacks containing marijuana in them she had no knowledge of the drug's presence."

"Bert, the jury heard only one defense witness—Emmajean herself. What if the jury's not convinced by her admission? It's just her word. What if the jury doesn't believe her?"

"I thought of that and early this morning I visited Barry Wagner in his cell. I had to get the prosecutor to go with me. I couldn't talk to his client without him being present. The prosecutor agreed with me that his case against your sister is weak. Anyway, he offered Barry a deal if he would sign a statement that Emmajean never knew what she was doing when delivering for him."

"Did he take it?"

Bert continued talking as if Jim hadn't spoken.

"It was the strangest thing. If two defendants are charged with the same crime, it is common practice for the prosecutor to offer a deal to one of them if he or she agrees to testify *against* the other. But the prosecutor offered the deal if Barry would make a favorable statement about your sister—that she had no knowledge of what she was doing. He took the deal and will get less punishment than if he hadn't taken it. Usually deals are made if one defendant will testify against the other. Here this Barry fellow is testifying *for* Emmajean. I've never seen anything like it in all my years in a courtroom. The judge will read Barry's statement to the jury and that ought to be enough for us to get a quick verdict.

"Just wanted you to know where everything stands."

"Thanks for calling, Bert."

"See you Monday morning."

"Monday morning then."

Jim wasn't surprised when he heard the dial tone. Bert Cox didn't waste any time. When he'd said what he wanted to say that was the end of the call.

When Jim returned the telephone to its cradle, Caroline stood at his elbow. "Was that bad news about your sister?"

Jim knew he had to weigh his words from now on. "No. Just her lawyer giving me some information so I can be kept up to date."

He went into the kitchen where the kids were cleaning up. Caroline followed him. Jim looked at James and Lynn. "Now, what have we come up with that would be fun to do today."

"Daddy, why don't we pack a picnic lunch and go to Buford Park. James has never been there. I'm sure you and Caroline have, but it would be lots of fun anyway."

~ ~ ~

Lynn and Caroline gathered the remains of their picnic, and the guys disposed of in it the trash can nailed to a tree. As Lynn and Caroline packed the basket with things that needed to be returned to the house, James and Jim passed around a football. Caroline enjoyed watching her son and Jimmy spending time together. Soon tiring, they joined the girls on the blanket.

After a short rest, Lynn jumped up, and grabbed James's hand. "Come on, let's go down to see Caney Creek." Caroline and Jim turned toward one another.

"Come on, James. The creek is beautiful and so peaceful." Finally he gave in to her pleading. Holding hands, they ran down the slope to the creek.

Quiet settled around the parents of the young people. Who would speak first? And what would they say? Caroline scooted closer to Jim. "They look happy. We were happy here at Caney Creek a long time ago."

"Yes we were. Just don't forget how young we were. But let's not spend time dwelling on the past."

"Jimmy, our past is what we're made of. I think about it daily."

"But always thinking on the past won't let us forget it. We have to think about the future if we want to live beyond the past."

"Jimmy, do we have a future together?"

"Caroline, let's not get into that here. Lynn planned this for fun time. I have to go to Atlanta tomorrow. Let's keep it light and fun for us all today. Can you do that?"

"Sure. I can act like I'm having fun." She crossed her arms in front of her. "I've had over twenty years of pretending."

"Okay, start your show. The kids have started back from the creek." They watched their children, all smiles, making their way up the slight incline from the creek.

"James, why are you carrying your shoes and why are your pants rolled up?"

"Mom, I know you and Dad have been down to the creek but you really should go take a look."

Lynn stopped laughing enough to talk. "James wanted to wade in the creek. I told him the water would be cold, even if it is summer. But he went anyway. I suppose he's happy now."

Jim tried to cover his smile with a cough. "James, you'd better do what your little sister says next time."

"I guess so. It's so peaceful at the creek. Lynn told me so when she compared our Tennessee River to Caney Creek. She certainly was correct."

Peaceful? Caroline moved the word around in her head. Yes it is a peaceful place. A place shrouded with memories and she was certain Jimmy remembered them also. A lull stilled conversation.

Jim sprang from the blanket. "Everybody seen enough of Buford Park? Ready to head home?"

"Daddy, James and I wanted to ride the swings before we leave. Is that okay?"

"Sure. But not for long. Caroline and I will carry some of our things to the car."

As they packed their car, Jim stole a quick kiss. But Caroline was quicker and wrapped her arms around his neck lengthening the kiss. They broke apart when they heard James and Lynn approach.

"Dad, here's the rest of the things. I left everything picked up."

~ ~ ~

On the drive home, being tired from the lazy afternoon outing at the park, not much conversation passed among them.

While Jim helped Caroline put things away in the kitchen, the kids took their books to the television room to study.

"Jimmy, James and Lynn know just about everything in our past. Why don't you want them to see us kissing or hugging?"

"Caroline, we don't need to talk about those things now."

"Jimmy, why don't we? Why? Give me one good reason."

"It's too soon for them to see any intimacy between us."

"Jimmy, they both know we've been very intimate or James wouldn't be here. So, why is it always 'it's too soon'? What are you waiting for?"

"Caroline." His black eyes looked into the depths of her indigo ones. Thinking of their pasts, he let his mind roll her questions around—like making a snowball then letting it roll down a hillside as it picked up more snow until it became large enough to be a snowman's body. "We have to go slow or everything could collapse around us."

"What do you mean, Jimmy?"

"We don't want any us to be hurt."

"Hurt? What, for instance"

"You and Lynn get along great now but if you and I marry I think she could resent having to share me with you."

"*If we marry*? I thought we'd already settled that. When you want to change that to *when we marry* then I agree with you that we don't have a reason to talk."

She turned to leave the kitchen and started for the stairs. "Now, Caroline, don't leave in a huff." He reached the bottom of the stairway by the time she'd taken the last step and turned toward her bedroom. He'd done it again. Together almost two days and already fussing. He remembered her as being stubborn and sassy. She had perfected them both and he hadn't figured out how to react to her or when to keep his mouth closed.

Chapter 17

Jim tossed around in his mind the way Caroline gave him the cold shoulder when she left his house that morning. She did not have any words for him. How was he supposed to get through to her? Every suggestion he'd made she'd shot it down. He had to find a way very soon to improve their relationship. Did they have a relationship, could they develop a relationship, or was having a relationship with Caroline impossible?

That afternoon he drove to Atlanta. He still had his mind on how to get through to Caroline. Jim shook his head. He must keep his mind on his driving, and deal with problems he had with Caroline later.

When he reached the hotel he told Terry about the jurors' question and the discussion of it as Bert had told him.

"Hot dog! Emmajean's finally getting a break in this trial. Jim, this is the best news I've heard since the trial started."

"You really think so?"

"Yeah, I do. When the judge reads Barry's statement to the jury that will be all she needs. Should be a quick verdict for sure."

"Okay. You've convinced me. I didn't really know whether to be excited after Bert called me."

~ ~ ~

Judge Orr took his seat and nodded toward the bailiff who went to lead the jury into the courtroom. They walked single file to their appointed chairs.

Everyone was in place except Emmajean, as Bert had told Jim she wasn't to be in the room when the jury got their question answered. The judge rapped his gavel and cleared his throat. Turning toward the jury his expression sobered. When he finished giving them the information Bert had used in his closing statement he explained to the jurors that Emmajean was not considered to be in possession of an illegal drug.

He glanced toward the lawyers, then back to the jury. He waved a single sheet of paper in the air. "I have a statement I want to read to you. This is a sworn statement duly executed by authorities and witnesses. This comes from Barry Wagner: 'At no time when I knew Emmajean Callaway did she have knowledge of what she was doing for me. She never saw illegal drugs in the house we shared. She did not look into the sacks she delivered to cars for me.' Signed, Barry Wagner."

The judge handed a copy of Barry's statement to the bailiff. "Return the jurors to their room. You may give them this copy of what I just read." He tapped his gavel once and left the room.

Bert looked back at Jim and Terry, giving them a nod and a slight smile. Jim and Terry stood. "If you think Emmajean's verdict will come soon, should we hang around here?"

"Yeah, I think so. At least a little while." Fifteen minutes passed by when Jim saw the bailiff come into the courtroom and exit through the door used by the judge. Jim elbowed Terry. A big smile slid across Terry's face.

"What?" Jim said.

"He's going to get the judge. The jury's made their decision. Quick."

Within a few minutes the matron jailer escorted Emmajean to her seat. Emmajean glanced toward Jim and Terry and they responded with powerful smiles. The judge appeared, followed by the bailiff. As he took his seat, the judge instructed the bailiff to bring in the jury, and pounded his gavel.

The judge looked over the courtroom. He rapped his gavel again, calling for complete silence. "Chairman of the jury, have you reached a verdict in "Case #176, Emmajean Callaway charged with aiding the act of possession with intent to sell an illegal substance, a misdemeanor?"

"Yes, Your Honor, we have."

The bailiff reached for the piece of paper the chairman of the jury held. He walked to Judge Orr's bench and handed him the paper, which the judge read. He passed the paper back to the bailiff who returned it to the chairman of the jury.

The judge faced the jury. "Please read your verdict." Before the chairman read the verdict the judge swiveled toward the lawyers.

"In the case of the state of Georgia versus Emmajean Callaway charging the defendant with aiding the act of possession with intent to sell an illegal substance, we find the defendant, Emmajean Callaway, not guilty."

The judge turned back toward the jury. "Gentlemen, the court thanks you for your service. You are free to go. This court is adjourned." One last rap of his gavel.

Jim went straight to Emmajean, Terry not far behind. Jim grabbed his little sister in a powerful hug. She smiled and cried at the same time. Then she reached for Terry. Jim watched as he took her in his arms and tried to restrain his desire to hug her as close as possible. Watching the delight of the two of them made Jim think of Caroline. And of Lynn and James. Why couldn't he be as free in his feelings about Caroline as Terry appeared to be about Emmajean?

When Bert reached for Jim's hand he automatically shook it and grinned. But something flipped inside of him and took his breath away. What kind of fool had he been since Christmas when he and Caroline had accidently discovered one another after twenty years apart? No wonder she gave him the silent treatment this morning when she left Newton. He felt like slapping himself. What a gift had been placed in his life—Caroline, James, and Lynn—a family. But a family without a daddy, as Lynn had told him. Nobody but Jim could change that. If he wasn't too late. Will Caroline tell him he's too late?

Emmajean punched her big brother in the arm to get his attention. "Jim, you look like you just saw a ghost. This trial has been awful but, look, we're all still standin'." She took Jim's hand and then Terry's hand. "Let's get out of this place." Then she turned to Terry. "Can I leave here?"

"Yes, you can." Jim watched Terry almost drown in Emmajean's bright blue eyes.

"Well, what are we waitin' on?" Terry nodded toward Bert Cox, hinting that she should thank him.

"Mr. Cox, thank you very much for gettin' me through this trial. I don't know what I would have done without the three of you. Thank you."

Bert shook her hand. "I knew you were innocent all along. We just had to get the jury to agree and they did."

~ ~ ~

Emmajean, Jim, and Terry pushed through the courthouse's tall front doors. Emmajean hesitated and inhaled a long breath. "You know, it's been weeks since I've appreciated a breath of fresh air. It sure feels good."

"It's too early for lunch. Little sister, what do you want to do next?"

"I have a choice, don't I? Nobody pointin' here and pointin' there or pushin' me to line up for meals. Unless they've been behind bars people don't know . . . what's happenin' with Barry?"

"I'm sure Barry will have his own trial starting shortly. You don't have to think any more about him. Ever." Terry took her hand.

"You want to go to the YWCA and start getting your things together? We could do a little before lunch."

"Get my things together for what?" She looked from Terry to Jim.

"Why, to start back to Newton." Jim looked at his sister trying to sense what thoughts twisted around in her mind.

"I'm goin' back to Newton?"

"I assumed you would want to. Where had you planned to go after your trial was finished?"

"I guess I hadn't thought about that. Silly of me, I guess. But goin' back to Newton probably wouldn't work. Before the trial I'd drifted so far from family I'm sure they don't want me within miles of them."

Jim stammered, reaching for the right words to say. "Let's just go on to the YWCA and rest a while then get lunch. We don't have to make any decisions about anything right now."

~ ~ ~

"Holy cow! I can order anythin' from the menu, can't I, Jim?"

"Yes, ma'am."

"After the food I've been eatin' everythin' on this menu will be a great treat."

"Just take your pick."

Emmajean looked at Terry. "What are you goin' to eat?"

"A big, juicy hamburger, but then I'm a hamburger fan anywhere I go."

"Jim?"

"I think I'll have the beef stew."

"Well, that leaves me to decide." She scanned the menu. "I think I'll have a big, juicy hamburger too. How about that?"

Emmajean looked at Terry as if for his approval. "If that works for you that's all that matters."

The waitress came soon with three glasses of water and took their orders.

They stayed quiet while they ate. Emmajean wondered exactly what Terry thought about her. And what Jim expected of her now that the trial had finished. She could ask her brother outright but with Terry, only time would answer that.

Jim finished eating first. "That beef stew was good but not as good as what Lynn makes."

"Lynn can cook?"

"Yeah, your niece is a good cook. But I don't get treated to her food now that she's in Knoxville."

"Lynn's in Knoxville?"

"Lynn attends the University of Tennessee there. Emmajean, we have a lot to catch up on."

"We will. We will."

"When? What are your plans after today?" Jim said.

Emmajean took a sip of her iced tea then looked at her hands on the table. "I didn't make any plans. I've just been livin' from day to day, Jim. For a long time. Definite plans haven't been a part of my life since I left Newton."

Terry took her hand. "Emmajean, you've been alone too long. I hope you decide to return to Newton where you have family . . . and me."

Terry's words warmed her as she held on to his hand. "I guess I could go to Newton for a while. Nobody there will probably remember me."

"Emmejean, the family asks me about you all the time. They've never forgotten you and will be happy to see you."

"Lynn's what now, eighteen?"

"Almost nineteen."

"That how old I was when I left Newton after high school. Boy, I thought I had the world on a string. I was goin' to bust Atlanta wide open, show them what I had and get any job I wanted."

Jim reached across the table and patted her arm. "Things sometimes don't go the way we think they will." He stared at his empty plate. "But, hey, I've got a big house and one of the bedrooms has your name on it. We'll help you pack up your things and you can go to Newton. You can go back with us today."

"I guess so. How can a girl pass up the chance to travel with two handsome men?"

~ ~ ~

When Jim and Emmajean entered his home in Newton she covered her nose. "Phuwee. This pretty house doesn't smell good."

"The house has been empty much of the spring and summer. If it's cool in the morning we could raise some windows and let fresh air in."

"Jim, why has the house been empty?"

"Emmajean, I've been in Atlanta with you much of the time. And I go to Knoxville whenever I can to visit . . . Lynn."

"Oh, that's right. You've been spendin' time with me. Who's been runnin' the mill while you're gone?"

"It's all under control. I've got one of my top men filling in for me."

Emmajean went to pick up her suitcases, and started for the stairway. "Which bedroom, big brother?"

"Ah. Uh, Emmajean, put down your suitcases and let's sit in the living room a while."

"Okay. You're scarin' me. Have I already done somethin' wrong? I told you I wouldn't fit in here in Newton."

"You haven't done anything wrong. Please come to the sofa and sit with me."

Settled on the sofa, Jim looked at the sunken face of his little sister. Emmajean really needed to be taken care of to get back to her old self. Knowing her stubborn streak, he hoped she'd stay with him a long time and not just up and go away again.

Jim took her hand. "A lot has gone on since you left Newton. Do you remember how I got this house?"

"Yeah, when the owner was killed in a car wreck."

"Yes. That was a little over seven years ago. When Lynn was eighteen I moved her into a dormitory at the university in Knoxville. She met a boy she liked and brought him down here around Thanksgiving. He's a nice guy, polite and considerate. He lives in Knoxville with his mom. They invited Lynn and me to visit their home after Christmas, which we did."

"Jim, why are you tellin' me all this?"

"You'll see. Just have patience with me a little longer. I'm sure you remember when Lynn's mother died—Louisa. You were about fourteen then. Back when you were around ten years old, I dated Louisa and also the mill owner's daughter, Caroline." He was trying to get to the bedroom situation.

"Your brother wasn't very good, dating the both of them at the same time. Anyway, down by Caney Creek with Caroline one July Fourth I lost my will power, and gave into her beauty. One time."

Emmajean jumped up from the sofa and took a few steps backward. She put her hands on her hips. "Jim, you shouldn't be tellin' me this."

"I have to tell you or you won't understand my life." He stood and pulled her back to the sofa. "So, Caroline became pregnant but I didn't know it. Her daddy disowned her and on Christmas Day he sent her to her aunt's in Knoxville. I never saw her again. But last Christmas, as I said, Lynn and I visited the boy's home, and learned his mother is Caroline."

"Okay . . . ."

"The boy at UT she liked is Caroline's son, James. Lynn and James are half brother and sister. Caroline and I had to tell them how our past would mess up any romantic future for them. Lynn is now staying in Caroline's home. The three of them sometimes come here to visit, and I go up there every now and then. Now, this is my point. I have five bedrooms upstairs. One, of course, is mine. Caroline, James, and Lynn claim three of them. So you don't have your pick of bedrooms. I'll show you which one is for you."

"Gosh, you sure did lay a lot on me in a few minutes. Is everyone okay with this? My two aunts?"

"Yes, they've become accustomed with the way things are, and they have accepted Caroline and James."

"Wow."

Jim left the sofa and sauntered to the window. "Emmajean, do you understand what I've just told you? I am the father of James and Caroline is his mother. I'm the father of Lynn and Louisa was her mother. Do you understand what I'm saying?"

Emmajean joined him at the window, looking across the front lawn. "Yeah, I do. Big brother, you got a family but you don't live like a family. You goin' to marry Caroline?"

"We've talked about it. The love is still there. We love each other. Even Lynn and James have tried to talk to me about marrying Caroline. I've been dragging my feet. But today when I saw you and Terry at the courthouse hugging one another and looking so happy, I wondered why—why have I not married Caroline yet? James calls me Dad and Lynn can't understand me waiting so long to make us a real family. Caroline and Lynn get along fine."

"Well, you know big brother, I don't understand either. It's not ever' day somebody comes along and then all the pieces fall together. And, boom, there's love and you need to follow your feelings not your mind. Your head can get you in a heap of trouble if your heart's not goin' along with it."

"You know, Emmajean, you make a lot of sense."

"Well, you're not the only Callaway that's smart. I'm not dumb. I look around and I see some married couples who can't keep their eyes and hands off each other. Then I see some who don't even talk much and then it's to argue. If happiness is in reach, I say grab it."

"Emmajean, you haven't even met Caroline and you're encouraging me to marry her."

"Yeah, I am. From what you told me about Lynn and James, they think like I do. What're you waitin' on?"

Jim hugged his baby sister. "Thank you, Emmajean. I agree, you're not dumb. James and Lynn are taking some classes at UT this summer. They can only come down on weekends. Would it be okay with you if they all visit this weekend?"

"Hey, this is your house. You make those decisions. I'm probably just passing through for a while."

"No, Emmajean, you can stay here as long as you want to. I hope you will make this your home. This big house certainly has room for you."

"I don't know, Jim, maybe. I like Terry a lot. Do you think he might like me if I stay around here?"

"From the hugging I saw in the courtroom, I'd say absolutely. I hope you'll take better care of yourself here. Lynn and Caroline would be glad to help you put a glisten to your hair. And we need to get you in the habit of eating well. You've become so skinny a good wind would blow you away. No more talk about you leaving." Jim put his arm around his sister's shoulder and they made their way upstairs to find Emmajean's bedroom.

~ ~ ~

Late afternoon the following Friday Emmajean puttered around in the kitchen when she heard a lot of voices coming from the front of the house.

"Emmajean, come in here. There're some folks here I want you to meet."

She wanted to meet Caroline and her son, but she dreaded it too. She almost wished Jim hadn't told her all that he had. She walked toward the foyer. Jim made the introductions and everyone went into the living room.

Emmajean had never seen a woman as beautiful as Caroline. Wow. No wonder Jim was still in love with her. And James was without a doubt Jim's son. James had the same black hair and dark eyes as Jim. They both stood about six feet or maybe a little more.

"Lynn, I'm your long-lost aunt. I'd like a hug. Would that be okay?

Lynn crossed the room and gave her aunt a hug. "If my daddy loves you, I love you too. I'm glad you're here, and all that mess in Atlanta is in the past."

Emmajean looked toward a smiling Caroline. "Emmajean, we all knew you were innocent."

"Thank you, Caroline. And, James, you're the spittin' image of your dad. Two of the best lookin' men in Sanford County. I'm so glad to meet you and your mom. I really am." Emmajean glanced toward Caroline who still smiled.

"James and I are quite fond of your big brother."

Caroline would be a lot fonder real soon. Emmajean and Jim had gone shopping this week at Goldberg jewelry store. Jim had finally jumped off the fence, making up his mind not to wait any longer to marry Caroline. Emmajean had the best big brother anybody could have. She hadn't seen The Twins in a long, long time. Jim told her they were still in the army and in Korea right now.

"How was the drive down, James?"

"Good, Dad. They finally finished that construction below Maryville, so we didn't have any bumper to bumper, or any starting and stopping."

"Jimmy, we're letting Lynn drive the car some. She does well. Not on this trip of course but around home."

"Good. Good." Jim stood to pat his daughter's shoulder and motioned to James. "Let's get the suitcases out of the car. How much did the ladies load you down with this time?" Laughing at the expense of Caroline and Lynn, they went out to the car.

~ ~ ~

Caroline and the kids had arrived too late to prepare a meal at home. They all went to the Blanchard Hotel dining room for supper. Emmajean had never been there although having grown up in Newton. She'd seen folks going and coming from the Blanchard. It appeared that the customers eating at the Blanchard dressed more casually than in her younger years.

They had ordered a simple, light meal, and just finishing, their conversation picked up. "Anybody made plans for the weekend while y'all are here?" Jim looked toward Caroline. She shrugged her shoulders. Lynn and James did the same.

Jim looked to see if Emmajean had an answer. "I'd like to spend some time at Buford Park. Is it still here?"

Emmajean thought she must have said or done something wrong because a chilly silence fell around the table. It was Caroline who recovered first.

"Yes, the park is still here. Lots of room and the scenery is beautiful."

"But, Mom, we spent time there when we were here before."

"That's true, James, but Emmajean hasn't been recently. I think her idea is a good one. We can pack a picnic basket like we did before and have a wonderful time. Is that okay with you, Jimmy? And you, Lynn?"

They both nodded and Emmajean silently thanked Caroline for making things a little less uncomfortable.

They soon left the Blanchard Hotel for Jim's house. James and Lynn headed to a room in the back of the house and Emmajean shortly heard the sounds of a television set. Should she stay in the living room with her brother and Caroline or consider herself a fifth wheel and make her way to her bedroom?

As if reading her mind, Caroline drew Emmajean into the conversation. She seemed sincere in her attempts to get to know Jim's sister.

James and Lynn came from the television room to the living room. "James and I have some studying to do so we're going on up to get some done before bedtime. Good night, all." Everyone exchanged their farewells and the youngsters went upstairs.

Emmajean turned to Jim. "Jim, do you think Terry might enjoy going to the park with us tomorrow?"

He returned her smile. "Well, he just might. You want to call and ask him?"

Caroline looked toward Emmajean and Jim. "Who is Terry?"

"Terry Fields is the local lawyer who went with me each time I went to Atlanta. He couldn't be actively included in Emmajean's case, but I sure felt more comfortable with him there to explain things to me."

"Would it be okay if I invited him, you think?"

"Sure." Jim and Caroline answered in unison.

"Jim, do you have his telephone number?"

"It's right by the telephone out there in the entrance."

"So, okay, I guess I'll go make a telephone call."

In a few minutes she poked her head back into the living room. "He said yes. He'll be here about mid morning. Will that work?"

Jim planted a big grin on his face. "Great. I'm glad he's going with us."

"Me too." Emmajean said her good nights and drifted upstairs.

~ ~ ~

Jim joined Caroline on the sofa. They exchanged a smile and with her palm against his cheek she gave him a light kiss.

"What? You're not still mad at me?"

"Jimmy, you do try my patience but I love you too much to stay mad at you very long."

They both scooted down, put their heads against the back of the sofa, slid off their shoes, and plopped their feet on the coffee table. The gentle noise of having people around gave way to a peaceful interlude. Jim took one of Caroline's hands and kissed it. He kept her hand in his and laid it across his heart. "Can you feel that?"

"Hmmm." She nodded.

"That's what your nearness does to me. I can't stop it. My heart just jolts away double time when you're around."

Caroline sat up straighter, pulling her legs up on the sofa. She turned toward Jim and gazed into the black depths of his eyes.

"What?" Jim said.

"I just want to look at you. I want to soak in all there is about you and hold onto it while we're apart."

"Me, too."

A loud voice came from upstairs. "Mom, did you bring my economics book? I can't find it."

Caroline turned away from Jim so her voice would drift upstairs to James. "Yes, James. Look in my bedroom. It's lying on the bed."

"Thanks. You're great."

"You're welcome, dear." She turned back to Jim who hadn't moved.

"You *are* great, you know?"

"Really and truly?"

"Yes, Caroline. I think you're growing on me. Back at the mill this week, my mind kept wandering to you and waiting for today when you'd arrive. I love you."

"And I love you. So very much."

"Me, too."

Caroline snuggled up toward Jim. They leaned their foreheads together. His lips found Caroline's, which were searching for his. Their kiss was much more than their New Year's Eve brush of their lips had been in this very living room. Caroline was first to pull back.

"Jimmy, we're sitting in this big room with nothing to prevent anyone from walking in on us."

"I know." He put his hand on the back of her head and pulled her in for another kiss.

"Jimmy, stop this. What's come over you?"

"You. You is what's come over me. The only thing I intend to keep us apart from now on is war or death."

She swatted his shoulder. "Hush that awful talk. No war and no death. At least no death for several decades."

"Besides," Jim said, "there're two steps about half way down the staircase that squeak. We'd have plenty of time to assume a dignified posture."

She dug her fingers into his ribs, and he squirmed. "I'd forgotten about them. You're right. I'll have to remember that from now on."

He wrapped his arms around her and pulled her to him. "This is it. Right here. Right now."

Chapter 18

"This is beautiful." Emmajean looked around Buford Park, taking in the freshness of the foliage, the gentle slope off to one side, and the sound of the slight gurgle of Caney Creek somewhere across the way.

"Ladies, where do you want to pitch the picnic?"

They decided on a spot and spread out the stuff. The picnic was fit for a king and enough for the three guys and three ladies. Jim spoke a short blessing over the food. After they'd filled their paper plates and stuffed themselves they all got comfortable with another glass of iced tea. The warm breeze ruffled the leaves of the white oak tree near them. They mostly had the park to themselves—only a few others roamed around the grounds.

"James, let's go to the swings, want to?"

"Sure, Lynn." And off they went, the youngsters of the crowd.

Jim stood and put his cup in the trash can. "Come on, Caroline, let's go see the creek." He extended his hand to give her a lift from the ground. As they started across the park down toward the creek, Jim looked back at Emmajean and gave her a wink.

"What was that wink for?" Terry said.

"Oh, Jim and I have a little secret."

"You going to tell me?"

"No, Terry, you have to wait like the others to find out about the secret."

"Okay, okay. Hey, we're all alone. What would you like to do?"

"Nothin'. Absolutely nothin'. It's such a treat for me to be able to make decisions for myself since last spring. Sittin' here doin' nothin' allows me to think deep inside of myself."

"Emmajean, what do you think of deep inside?"

"Oh, you know, I never gave much thought to the future before now. I just went about my life kinda like a leaf floating along in a creek. I knew real soon after I got to Atlanta that I didn't have any control over anythin'. I saw that I couldn't change things so I just went along, day by day. But now that I'm here maybe things will get better for me, after all."

"When you feel like you're down, the only way to look is up. Maybe that'll work for you." He took her hand. "Emmajean, I think a lot about you. I like you very much. I'm hoping you'll stay in Newton and we can get to know one another better."

"Really? I like you Terry. You were such a big help to me in Atlanta. When I'd see you in the courtroom, it gave me a boost."

"Emmajean, I'd like to be a big help to you here. Do you think we could see more of each other?" He squeezed her hand.

She returned the squeeze. "I think that could be arranged."

~ ~ ~

"Careful, now. Those rocks don't look too sturdy." Jim took Caroline by the elbow and guided her down to the creek bank where the ground was level. They found a log to sit on, facing the creek.

"Jimmy, you know where we are, don't you?"

"Yeah."

They both watched the running of the peaceful creek as it splashed across small rocks here and there. The sun shining through trees overhanging the creek made ever-moving patterns sparkle on the water. Caroline dipped her feet into the shallow creek water but jerked them out in a flash. "Mercy. That water is cold. I don't remember the water ever being that cold."

"Caroline, you told me we couldn't talk again unless I was ready to say *when* we get married instead of saying *if* we get married." He touched her chin with one finger and turned her face toward his. "I'm ready."

"You're ready to say *when* we get married?"

"Yes." He brushed her lips with his. "Do you want to talk to me now about us?"

Caroline threw her arms around his neck then pulled back making sure he meant what he said. "You mean that, don't you? What changed your mind?"

He took both of her hands. "In the courtroom in Atlanta when they declared Emmajean innocent I witnessed a happiness I wanted. When she and Terry hugged that day I stood in awe of the simple act of pleasure they gave each other and I envied them. I wanted what they had—the simple joy and delight of being together. I wanted something that has been within my reach since Christmas. I needed you. I had to have a *you and me*. I longed for there to be an Us. I loved you twenty years ago and I love you even more today." She opened her mouth to speak and Jim put a finger across her lips. "Just one more thing." He fished into his pants pocket and found the small black box. He went down on one knee in front of her. "Maybe I should have asked James's permission to do this. Caroline, will you marry me? Please?" He opened the box to show her the big diamond solitaire ring nestled in the velvet.

"Yes! Jimmy, I love you. Of course I'll marry you." He slipped the ring onto her finger. "Oh, Jimmy, it's beautiful. Oh, my." She lunged toward him, wrapped her arms around his neck and, him being on one knee, they both went tumbling into the creek. When they hit the water, Caroline shrieked louder than she had when he'd shown her the ring.

They still stood in the creek when the others came to them. "What's all the screaming about . . . Oh, big brother, you really did it now. Did you ask the question before you both fell in the water?"

They all laughed at the two, standing dripping wet in the creek. No one knew exactly what Emmajean meant about the question. They all looked at Caroline and Jim with expectation. "What question, Mom?"

Jim took her arm and guided them both out of the water. James and Terry pulled their square-folded white handkerchiefs from the hip pants pockets and offered them to Jim and Caroline. Jim used to rub his face while Caroline patted her face dry. The laughing continued until they stood on dry ground. Caroline shouted. "Jimmy just asked me to marry him. I said yes!" She held up her left hand to show them the evidence.

Lynn and James went to their parents, Emmajean hugged Caroline and her brother. Terry and James shook Jim's hand.

"Daddy, I was afraid you had waited too long," Lynn said.

"Dad, it took you long enough."

Finally Caroline could reach Jim and she hugged him around his waist, water and all. His elegant, sophisticated Caroline stood with water running off her and leaving her sundress clinging. He'd never seen her in such a state. It didn't seem to bother her that her daily polished image had slipped. Jim wondered whether staying around his family and friends might help her to allow her refined demeanor to loosen a bit.

"Okay, I guess that's the end of the picnic. Sorry we have to cut it short but I sure would like to get out of these wet clothes." Jim looked toward Caroline who still had that smiling radiance around her. "And I'm sure my fiancé would say the same."

~ ~ ~

Emmajean had agreed to attend church with Jim and his family but she didn't feel right. She hadn't been to church since she left Newton after high school graduation. Caroline and Lynn helped her choose what she'd wear. Last night Lynn had given her some of her shampoo to use that would make her hair shine. Then this morning getting ready for church, Caroline and Lynn helped her with her makeup. When all three were ready they started down the stairs.

"Wow! Look at those three beautiful women." They saw James at the foot of the stairs.

Jim and Terry joined him in his assessment of the womenfolks. Terry looked at Emmajean with warmth in his eyes. Just like in the courtroom, Emmajean wanted Terry with her this morning for support. She dreaded the nosy looks from the people when she entered the church.

Later, as they went into the church, Emmajean took Terry's hand. They found a pew with room enough for the six of them. Once seated, Emmajean leaned toward Terry. "That wasn't so bad. Nobody stared at me, which I thought would happen." Terry nodded with a smile and tightened his grip on her hand. She listened to the sermon.

In the car on the way to lunch Emmajean talked nonstop. "Terry, I enjoyed the church service. It's been so long since I've been I really didn't know what to expect. The people welcomed me."

"Of course they did. Maybe we can attend services again."

"That's a good idea, Terry."

They all met at the Blanchard Hotel dining room for lunch. Again, Emmajean was glad nobody gave her any special attention.

"We'll have dessert at home. Lynn helped me to bake a cake last night."

"Caroline, are you sure it will be good?"

"Daddy, I helped her and I'll vouch for Caroline. Her cooking skills are becoming quite good."

~ ~ ~

James came down the stairs with luggage in each hand. "Got everything yet?"

"No, Mom and Lynn have some more stuff. Have you ever traveled with women? I think they brought enough for a week when they knew they were only staying the weekend."

James's words circled in Jim's brain. "No, not lately."

"You'll get used to it after you and Mom marry."

"Yeah, I guess."

"James."

James looked up the stairs. "Yes, Mom."

"We still have some things up here. Come get them when you can, please."

"I'll go see if I can help, James. You take those pieces on to the car."

Jim took the stairs two at a time and bowed before Caroline. "At your service, ma'am."

"Oh, Jimmy, stand up." She swatted him on a shoulder.

"Where's the rest of the stuff?" She laid her hand on his chest.

"No, no, Caroline. None of that right now. I've got to get your things."

"If not now, then when?"

Jim sidestepped her and started for Lynn's bedroom. "Where's your stuff?"

"That would be my bedroom—this way."

He pivoted and started in the other direction toward Caroline's bedroom. He went directly to the pieces of luggage sitting inside the door and began to gather them in his arms and hands. Caroline approached him and he didn't have a defensive move available. She leaned in as best as she could to grab a kiss. It was brief but she got one.

"No fair hitting a man when he's down. Come on, let's get this stuff downstairs."

After James had loaded all their things in the car, he and Lynn jumped in, ready to go to Knoxville. Caroline stayed on the porch with Jim. "Next Wednesday will be July Fourth. Think of me that day."

"I think of you every day but maybe I will a little more on Wednesday." July Fourth would be seared in their minds forever. That was the day they conceived James.

"When are you coming to our house?"

"Soon, I hope. Some things at the mill got a little behind while I was away so I think I'll be busy this coming week. I'll get up there next weekend if I can."

"I don't like it when you use that word."

"What word?"

"That word—*if*."

"Okay, when. That better?"

"Yes. Jimmy, this has been a great weekend. I'm glad I met Emmajean. I can see the strong bond between you two. I'm sorry I got upset when you were spending so much time with her in Atlanta. Forgive me?"

"Sure. I may be crazy, but I'd forgive you for anything."

"Jimmy, you've made me happier than I've been since my parents sent me away to have my baby." She leaned in and gave him a quick peck on the lips. "I love you. I've always loved you."

"I love you, Caroline." He pulled her to him and they kissed good-bye.

James tooted the horn. Jim could hear him and Lynn shout their approval.

Caroline and Jim stepped apart, still holding hands. Jim looked into her sapphire eyes and saw the depths of her love for him. "You'd better go. The kids will get restless. Take care of them and yourself. I'll telephone you—more often."

He took her elbow, and walked her down the porch steps and to the car. "Hey, you two take care of yourselves. Have a good week in school." Jim helped Caroline into the back seat, and shut the door. He stood in the driveway, and watched as James backed out of the driveway. He swallowed the lump in his throat. This long distance relationship would be harder than he imagined.

When he turned to go back inside, he saw Emmajean standing at one of the living room windows. He joined her there.

"How're you doin' Jim?"

"Okay, I guess. That wasn't easy having my new little family drive away."

"That's what I figured."

Chapter 19

Jim wasn't lying when he told Caroline he'd be busy at the mill this week. Bob did a great job in Jim's absence but some things didn't get done. Things that only Jim would know to do or to check on every now and then.

He stood at Peggy's desk. "How have you been, Peggy? Your family doing well? Since I've been in and out of here I've lost track of a few things."

"Mr. Callaway, I've been fine. My family is well. It's good to have you back. But Bob did a good job while you were gone."

"How are the plans going for the July Fourth mill picnic at Buford Park? Everything set up and ready?"

"Yes, sir, I believe so. I've been supervising from afar. I didn't want to hover while the girls put everything in order."

"Do you have anything I need to do right away?"

"I've put your things in stacks on your desk. On top of each stack I've written what it is and what you need to do. That should help you."

"Thank you, Peggy. I couldn't ask for a better secretary."

He entered his office, and shut the door. He saw the stacks of papers on his desk as he approached his chair. After reading all of Peggy's notes Jim swiveled his chair toward the window to look out over four-eleven, the state road that would take him to Caroline. He and Caroline hadn't spoken of a wedding date. How long would they both be satisfied with their arrangement, visiting on weekends? They needed to talk about this. Maybe he'd talk to Emmajean and see what she thinks.

Two hours later, Jim buzzed Peggy on the intercom.

"Yes, sir?"

"When you have time, come in here and we'll go over some of these things."

"Yes, sir, right away."

When the mill closed for the day and Jim drove home, he felt like he'd put in a full day's work. Not a day's work on the loading dock where he first worked for Caroline's father. Back then he would be physically tired. Since he'd inherited the mill, he went home tired in the mind.

He parked his car in his driveway, gathered his things and went inside. "Hmmm! Something smells good in here."

Emmajean rounded the corner from the kitchen. "Does it really smell good? I hope it will be. I thought I'd cook supper. When you're here by yourself, do you cook?"

"Yes, I can cook some. Enough so Lynn and I haven't ever gone hungry. I'm surprised you can cook. "

"I had to eat somethin' in Atlanta so I learned by trial and error. But much of the time, I'd eat at the diner when my shift ended. But, Jim, soon you really need to make a run for the grocery store."

"We'll go one evening this week."

After his sister had put the meal on the table, Jim prayed a short blessing on the food. "Hey, this meatloaf is really good."

"Thank you. So you admit I'm not dumb and I can cook?"

"Absolutely."

They ate in silence for a while. "Emmajean can I bother you with a question?"

"You could never bother me. Ask away."

"You helped me pick out Caroline's engagement ring maybe you can help me again where she's concerned. This past weekend was a whirlwind trip and we didn't even talk about a wedding date. What's your opinion on that?"

"If it was me I wouldn't see any point to waitin' to get married. But, now, Caroline and I are different. She may want to plan a big weddin' with all the flowers and stuff like that. Does she go to church?"

"Yes. I've been to the church with them. It's a large church to me."

"This is somethin' y'all better talk about together. If Caroline wants a church weddin', you'd better plan on waitin' a while."

Jim drank some iced tea. "Why's that?"

"Mercy, Jim. A girl takes a long time when they plan a church wedding."

"How long?"

She swallowed her mouthful of mashed potatoes. "Let's see." As she counted she stuck up one finger, then two . . .

"I hope that's days you're counting."

"No, it's months." She continued to count. "I'd guess Caroline would take till Christmas at least."

"Christmas! Why, that's . . ." Then it was Jim counting on his fingers. "That's five months away."

"Yeah, that's what I got too."

"Five months."

"Jim, you look a little pale. Did my cooking do that to you or waiting five months?" Emmajean had a big belly laugh, pointing at her brother.

Jim enjoyed seeing her laugh. She'd probably not had many things to laugh about since she left Newton. "Okay, okay, that'll be enough. Five months, huh?"

"I don't know. I wouldn't wait five months to marry if somebody I loved asked me to marry. But that's up to you and Caroline." She continued eating.

"How do things stand with you and Terry?"

"Now you're getting nosy." Jim held up his hands, palms forward.

"Just kiddin' you. He said he likes me a lot and wants us to see more of each other."

"How did you answer him on that?"

"Well, I like him. I told him I did. So, if we continue to get along, I guess we'll see more of each other. Is that okay with you, Jim?"

"Sure. Terry's a good guy. I spent a lot of time with him traveling down and back from Atlanta. I thought I could see a spark starting between you two."

"You know, Jim, when he gave me his grandmother's Bible, I just knew he was somethin' special."

"I bet you did." He pushed his chair back from the table, and stretched his legs. "Now, you may really call me nosy but here goes. When I dated Caroline twenty years ago, she invited me to her parents' home for their Christmas party. I'm sure she wasn't ashamed of me, but she did help me to speak my words better before we went to the party. She said there'd be many of the town's upper crust citizens there and she wanted them to accept me. Terry is a lawyer and he probably associates with the families of other lawyers. Now I'm just wondering if maybe you might want to work a little on your talking."

"What's wrong with my talkin'?"

"Well, you're doing what we all did growing up on the farm. Instead of saying talking you say talkin'. Do you hear the difference? Shirley Ann still talks like we did on the farm. Her husband has a car dealership and I guess her way of talking works for them. My point is that if you're going to spend time with Terry you might want to notice the way you say some of your words. That's just a suggestion, or course."

"Don't you think Terry would tell me if he wants me to change?"

"He might. He might not. We men sometimes have to step lightly where women are concerned. He wouldn't want to hurt your feelings. You took the suggestion from me but you might not if that same suggestion came from Terry."

Emmajean pushed back from the table and carried a few things to the kitchen sink. She turned back toward the table. "You're serious, you really are."

"Well, yeah, I guess I am. It didn't hurt me to change so it won't hurt you if you want to try it. But only if it's your decision. Don't change anything just because I mentioned it."

"I'll think about it." She gathered more things from the table. Jim stood and helped. She washed the dishes, and he dried and put them away.

Jim had never put in a dishwasher in his kitchen when it was just him and Lynn. When they cleaned up the kitchen, like he and Emmajean were doing, it made for some good times to talk. He might have to reconsider that after he married Caroline. He was sure she'd want a dishwasher. Maybe a cook and housekeeper too. He'd better make a list of things they had to talk about.

~ ~ ~

"Emmajean, you sure you'll be okay here by yourself for the weekend while I'm in Knoxville?"

"I sure will. After stayin'. . . oh, staying in those jails, I'll be fine here. Uh, Jim, would it be okay if I invited Terry over for supper tomorrow night. We've bought all this food and I'm sure I can fix somethin'. . . oops, something good."

Jim smiled and kissed his baby sister on the cheek. "Of course it would be okay. That's a good plan. When he telephones tonight be sure to invite him." He saw the relief on her face. "Did you think I wouldn't like the idea? This is your house now as much as it is mine. You can invite your company here any time."

Backing out of his driveway he waved to Emmajean who stood on the front porch. She waved back, a big smile on her face. She'd always been stubborn but Jim thought he could see more self confidence in her since the trial had finished.

~ ~ ~

"You're a good cook, Emmajean. That was delicious." They had finished their meal but still sat at the table across from one another.

"I'm glad you liked supper." She stood and began to clear the table.

"Here, let me help."

"Terry, you don't have to help with women's work."

"This is not all women's work. I dirtied dishes too, so I'll help clean them."

They talked while they did the dishes. Terry pretty much knew all there was to know about Emmajean, considering the trial and all the time he had spent with her brother. But his life was unknown to her, so he started the conversation about his family. "Emmajean, I'd like you to meet my parents some time."

"Where do they live?"

"Have you heard of the Tri-Cities?"

"No."

"The Tri-Cities of Tennessee are Johnson City, Kingsport, and Bristol in the uppermost, eastern tip of the state. There are two Bristols. One in Tennessee and one in Virginia. I never saw it but the word is that the border between Bristol, Tennessee and Bristol, Virginia is a line right down the main street of town."

"I'd say that would be confu. . . confusing, wouldn't you?"

"Maybe but I think everybody up there is used to it now. Anyway, my family lives in Johnson City. That's where I grew up. I went to college there in Johnson City at East Tennessee State University. Then I went to law school in Knoxville at the University of Tennessee."

"That's where my niece, Lynn, goes to school." Emmajean laughed a nervous giggle. "But you met Lynn, you know where she goes to school. Do you have brothers and sisters?"

"No, none of either one."

"Gee, I almost feel sorry for you—you didn't have anybody to fight with while you were grow, uh, growing up."

"I guess you're right. You sure did. You and Jim appear very close. Are you that close with your other brothers and sisters?"

"Well, see, I left here after high school. Before I left we all got along but I haven't seen Shirley Ann since I got back. My two brothers are in the army in Korea."

"Yeah, Jim told me about them. We had a lot of time together while your stuff in Atlanta was going on."

"You did, huh? I guess Jim told you everythin' uh, everything you wanted to know about me."

"I pretty much needed to know a lot about you for me to be of any use to Jim while you were getting through that mess down there. I like everything I know about you. Nothing I don't like." He hung the dishtowel over the handle on the oven as Emmajean wiped the sink clean. They walked to the living room, and sat on the sofa.

"So, I guess you know my parents are dead."

"Yes. You really have nothing to tell me that would surprise me."

"I don't know if I like that. You know all about me and I just know a little about you."

"We'll remedy that soon."

"Remedy?"

"Yes, we'll fix that soon when I take you to meet my parents." Emmajean loved the smile he gave her. He moved a little closer to her, and put his arm across the back of the sofa.

"Oh, maybe someday. Do you want to watch television? There's one in a room in the back of the house."

"If you do, we will. I'm fine right here."

"Okay. What would you like to do?" Emmajean knew immediately she had said the wrong thing. Why couldn't she have left things as they were? Terry moved closer to her.

"I'd like to kiss you. May I?"

"You're asking my permission to kiss me?"

"Yes."

"I've been kissed but nobody ever asked me for my permission first." She looked at Terry's face. He was serious. And he was waiting for her answer. How should she answer? Oh, she wanted him to kiss her, but she guessed she shouldn't sound too eager. Emmajean smiled and nodded.

Terry met her lips in a soft, brief kiss, then pulled back to look at her. She wanted more but what was she supposed to do about that? She'd never spent time with a lawyer and didn't know what he expected of her. She reverted to the old Emmajean. "I liked that. You got another one?" They both laughed at how simple she'd made the situation. They shared more kisses, each one longer than the last.

Finally, Terry pulled away. "Wow, that was great, Emmajean."

"It takes a good partner to be a good kisser." There was that simple wisdom of Emmajean's again.

"Would you like to go outside and walk around, perhaps go back to the creek?"

"The creek at the park?"

"Well, it's the same creek but it winds around the back of Jim's property. Want to go see?"

"Sure."

They went out the kitchen door, and walked hand in hand to the edge of the creek. It wasn't as wide here but still it was a pleasant creek, just like it was at the park. Emmajean reached down, and picked up a tiny stone from the edge of the water. The creek had traveled over the little rock for so long than its surface had become smooth all the way around.

"Pretty." Emmajean moved the stone around in her hand. Terry folded her hand over the rock, and kissed her fingers. What was she supposed to do now? Before she could think about anything very long, Terry put his arms around her, and brought her closer. She put her arms around his waist. He was taller than she but not very much.

They stayed there for several moments. Terry ran his hand through her auburn hair, pulling it behind her ear. Then he whispered to her. "Emmajean, I think I'm falling in love with you." He kissed her again before she could say anything. When he pulled away, Emmajean saw the pleasure on his face. She knew he could see the surprise on her's.

"Oh, I've misspoken. I shouldn't have said that this soon." He dropped his head but then felt her hand against his cheek urging him to look at her.

"I liked hearing what you said. You would be easy to fall in love with, Terry. But you're a city guy and I came off the farm. I might not fit in with your friends or family."

"I don't think there's a chance of that. But, okay, I'll slow down. It won't be easy to do when I look into your dazzling blue eyes, and touch your auburn hair. Where'd you get that beautiful hair anyway?"

"From my momma they tell me."

"I thank your momma from the bottom of my heart."

She pushed him away and turned for the house. Terry came alongside her, resting his arm around her shoulders. "This has been the most interesting and enjoyable evening I've spent in a long time . . . no, I've ever spent." He looked at his watch. "I'd better go now."

"Okay, I'll walk with you to your car."

"No, let's go inside through the kitchen door. I want to lock up the house before I leave."

"You do?"

"Yes, I want to make sure you're safe and sound in this big house."

They went into the kitchen. Terry locked the door, and started for the front of the house. "Do you know if all the windows are locked?"

"No. You want to check them too?"

"Yes, you wait right here." He sprinted up the stairs, and soon returned. "All the windows upstairs are locked."

Emmajean watched Terry as he checked all the windows downstairs. When he went through the front door she followed. "No, I don't want to leave you outside. I want to make sure you're all safe and sound before I leave." He guided her back into the foyer, and held her to him for one last kiss.

"Wow, we're gett . . . getting good at this."

"Good night, Emmajean." He gave her a peck on the cheek.

"Good night, Terry. Talk to you tomorrow?"

"You bet. I'll pick you up to go to church. Okay?"

"Yes."

Chapter 20

"Jimmy, I'm glad you came on up this evening. If you waited till tomorrow half the day would have been gone by the time you got here."

They sat at the breakfast table in Caroline's kitchen. "I wanted to make every minute count so I could be with all of you." He grinned at her across the table. "Thanks for saving me some supper. It's great—who cooked, you or Lynn?"

"It's too late in the evening to get into an argument. Let's just say we both did. Maybe more Lynn as I looked over her shoulder."

"No argument from me." He reached for her hand and held it while she watched him eat.

After they'd done a light straightening of the kitchen, Jim checked his watch. "I guess it's past your bedtime. The kids were already gone to bed when I got here. Should we call it a night?"

"Jimmy! You think I could go to sleep knowing you are in the house? No, we'll not call it a night yet. Unless you're tired by your trip and want to."

They sat on the sofa. "It *was* tiring driving after a day's work. I sure wish they would four-lane that four-eleven highway like they're doing some places across the state. Then it would be quicker and safer to drive between Newton and Knoxville."

"Did you have a hard week at work—were things as behind as you thought they were?"

"Pretty much. But Peggy had kept things well organized while I was out. She made it easier for me to get back into things." He turned toward Caroline. "Enough about me. Tell me about your week. Yours and the kids."

"Oh, they went to classes, and I waited till you'd get here." She leaned in and he obliged her with a soft kiss to her cheek. "Is that the best you can do after a whole week of not being together?"

"Don't get me started, it's too late in the evening for that. But I *can* do better. Come here." Caroline moved closer and Jim wrapped his arms around her. "All week I just wanted to hold you, like this." Then he kissed her for real. A kiss that said this is how it will be for us until we get old and gray. "That's what I want for the next fifty years, Caroline."

"I'll be happy to oblige you." They settled in for another kiss.

"I think we'd better call it a day, don't you?"

"No, Jimmy, I don't, not really."

Jim rose from the sofa and offered her a hand to pull her up. They locked up, turned out the lights, and started upstairs. They arrived at Jim's bedroom first. How was he going to keep her from entering? He'd have to put his foot down and mean it. They stopped at his door. He pushed her hair behind an ear and took one last taste of her love to last him till morning. "Good night, Caroline."

"I can't come in your bedroom with you?"

"No. As much as I would like that, no. We'll talk more tomorrow."

She lowered her eyes and pulled her bottom lip with her teeth. Oh, no, she's going to pout. What did he do wrong this time?

"Please, Jimmy."

Oh, how tempting. "No. Please go on to bed. See you in the morning. Remember, the first one to the kitchen has to fix breakfast. I want you well rested for that chore."

She began to swat him on the shoulder just as he ducked into his bedroom and closed the door. He knew Caroline would hear, but he locked the door.

~ ~ ~

As Jim pulled on his blue jeans the next morning he wondered who got to the kitchen first. He had heard rattling around down there for a while. He pulled a T shirt over his head, combed his hand through his hair, and slipped into some tennis shoes as he headed toward his door. At the foot of the stairs he heard the commotion and giggling coming from the kitchen.

When he rounded the corner into the kitchen, he was mildly surprised. Lynn and James, still in their pajamas, moved from stove to table, she giggling and he chuckling. "Hey, what's so funny this early in the day?"

James looked up. "Uh oh, we've been caught. Dad, what are you doing up so early?"

Lynn gave Jim a peck on the cheek. "Daddy, we thought we would fix breakfast to surprise you and Caroline. Is she up yet?"

"Don't know." He looked over the spread they'd already put on the table. "How long have y'all been down here to get together such a big breakfast?"

"Good morning, everybody. I see I'm successful in not being the first one down here this morning. Who is the breakfast cook today?"

"We are." Lynn and James answered in unison and that got their laughing started again.

"What a treat, don't you think so, Jimmy?"

He nodded while he watched her grace and beauty even at such an early hour. "A treat. Yeah. Everything ready to eat?"

James motioned them toward the table. "Have a seat."

Jim prayed a blessing before they started passing plates.

~ ~ ~

Caroline looked around the table as they ate their bacon, eggs, and fluffy biscuits. Her family. Well, almost legal now. "Jimmy, thank you for always saying a blessing when we eat. I'm afraid I've neglected doing that and even when I remember, I pray a silent prayer."

"God hears those prayers too."

"Yes, I'm sure He does." Caroline looked toward the kids. "So, what is planned for today? Is there anything around Knoxville that is as much fun as Buford Park in Newton? James and Lynn started laughing again. "You mean as much fun as you two falling into the creek?" James said.

"Oh, James, I suppose that was a funny site to behold. And I'm sure you'll never let us forget, will you?"

Lynn looked at her daddy and then Caroline. "Nope. We'll remind you the rest of your lives."

"That's a long time, Lynn." Jim tried in vain to wipe the smile off his face. "Try to give us a break every now and then."

Caroline took Jim's hand. "Jimmy, I guess we can afford to give them a laugh now and then."

"Okay, we'll just all be careful whenever we're around the creek from now on. But what do y'all want to do today? James, you and Lynn got something planned or you going to hang around us old folks?"

"We're going to the library on campus to do a little research for one of Lynn's classes. Then we'll probably stop at Krystal's for lunch. I really started something when I introduced Lynn to those little hamburgers last fall. Mom, want us to bring y'all some?"

Jim looked toward Caroline who shook her head, and Jim answered for them both. "No, thank you, we'll probably come up with some plans of our own."

~ ~ ~

Both Caroline and Jim had showered and dressed for the day. Caroline came downstairs to join Jim in the living room. "Jimmy, you have Caney Creek behind your house. Well, I have the Tennessee River out back. Want to walk and take a look?"

Jim jumped up from the sofa to join her. "Sure. Let's go stretch our legs." Crossing the back yard, the farther they walked the louder the river sounded. They stopped well before the water's edge, and sat on a comfortable bench Caroline had placed there for just watching the water and dreaming. The bench sat underneath a good sized white oak tree, which gave welcomed shade.

"That's a little bigger than Caney Creek for sure."

"Yes. Sometimes I pretend it is Caney Creek and in my thoughts you seem near."

When would be a good time to talk with Caroline about a wedding date? He wondered if he should do it here and decided he should. The kids wouldn't interrupt. Jim put his arm around Caroline's shoulders and pulled her close. They sat without talking for a while, just watching the river splash along.

"Caroline?"

"What?"

"Have you made any wedding plans?" Jim waited.

"Oh, some."

"Can you share them with me?"

"Sure. I planned to do that this weekend." She pulled her legs up on the bench and turned toward him. "Well, first we have to decide where we'll get married—Knoxville or Newton. Then we'll need to choose a location—in a church or at home. I'll probably ask Lynn to be my maid of honor and you'll have to choose your best man. As to any other attendants, we'll need to talk about that later."

Jim wondered how much later she was thinking. "Have you decided when this wedding will take place?" Jim held his breath while he waited for her answer.

"No. We need to decide that together."

"Good. I wondered if you would include me in your planning."

"Of course, Jimmy, we'll both be making decisions about our wedding." She punched his arm. "You're just kidding, aren't you?"

"Yeah I was, about including me. But really we need to decide when."

"It will take a while to get everything arranged. Jimmy, how would you like to have a Christmas wedding?"

"Christmas? Now you're the one who's kidding, right?"

"No, I'm not kidding."

"Caroline, that's five months away."

"Yes. I think we can get all the things done by then."

Jim removed his arm from her shoulders and put his elbows on his knees, his hands under his chin. He looked toward the river.

"Jimmy, what's wrong?"

He straightened. "I was thinking sooner than Christmas."

James and Lynn appeared behind the bench. Their parents hadn't heard them walking across the lawn above the roar of the river.

"Ooops. I think we came at the wrong time, James."

"James. Lynn. We're making some decisions. Come around and help us."

"Daddy, have you been eating pickles?"

"No, Lynn, why?"

"You look so sour. Are y'all having an argument?"

"I think your daddy is trying not to. That right, Dad?"

"James, we're planning some things about our wedding. I think we've butted heads on when it will take place."

"What about tomorrow, Mom?"

Jim was quick to comment. "Yeah, I'll go along with that."

"Oh, Daddy. You and James are so silly. A girl just can't up and get married without some planning. Besides you have to get a license and blood tests. No way tomorrow."

Caroline smiled to Lynn. "Thank you, Lynn, for your support. I guess we'll get back up to the house now. Y'all already had lunch, right?"

"Yes, Mom, we had Lynn's favorite—those wonderful Krystals."

James walked beside his mom and Lynn and Jim followed. Lynn took her time walking up to the house so they could be farther behind. "Daddy, may I give you a suggestion?" Jim nodded. "You and Caroline are getting married. It's not going to be just you, now. You've made all your own decisions for many years but you must remember that now it's *we* not *I*. Things about the wedding have to be planned together."

"Come on, slowpokes." James shouted as he stood at the back door.

"We're coming, we're coming." Lynn looked up at her daddy. "Daddy, please remember what I just said."

"How come you know things like that?"

"I'm a woman. That's the way we think." His little girl calling herself a woman—is that real or was she joking? He'd have to admit she was grown, maybe not a woman yet. But he'd keep that to himself.

~ ~ ~

The sun had settled and dusk surrounded them on the porch swing. Jim and Caroline held hands while he barely pushed the swing with one foot. "Caroline, I have a suggestion about our wedding date. May I tell you?"

"Sure. What is it?"

"Let me finish before you butt in. Next week you get your blood test and I'll get mine. The next time we're together we can go to the courthouse and get the license. Then we can get married but not tell anybody. You could go on and plan the wedding like you want and have it when you want. In the meantime we could be together legally."

"You finished?" Caroline clipped her words.

"Yeah."

She turned in the swing and looked Jim in the eye. "You're serious, aren't you?" He nodded. "You really are serious with this suggestion of yours."

"You don't like my suggestion?"

"No, Jimmy. That would be like teenagers running off to get married. Where did you get such an idea?"

He tightened his grip of her hand. "Caroline, we've been apart for so long. We have an opportunity to reach out and grab happiness together. I want us to be together. You do too. Why do you want to wait till Christmas to be married?"

~ ~ ~

Caroline turned back to her side of the swing but still held Jim's hand. She rolled his words around in her thoughts. Why did she want to wait? Last Christmas when they'd met after twenty years apart, she would have married him that day. What was she thinking, asking Jim to wait five months before they got married? Yes, she wanted them to be together. Did she want a fancy wedding, loving the *idea* of getting married more than getting married? Jim had stopped pushing the swing. He probably waited for her to speak.

Even if she agreed to marry in a few weeks, they had other things to decide. Other things to agree on. Could she live in Newton? Could he live in Knoxville? And what about the children? They couldn't ask Lynn and James to drop out of school at UT.

She faced Jim and looked at him. In his eyes she saw disappointment, fear, anxiety, and love. Especially love. She took his face in her hands and looked into those dark eyes she remembered from their first times together. Jim had grown up with simple ways. Poor, yes, but simple. No longer poor, she could see his longing for simple. Just get married. Why wait five months? Why wait at all? She kissed his lips then drew back. Neither of them said a word. The time to marry was unimportant when compared with growing old together. She needed to tell him.

"Jimmy, I love you." She still held his face in her hands. "I love you more every day. I don't want to disappoint you, ever. When I first saw you last Christmas I would have married you that day." His face relaxed, and a slight smile began to move across his lips. He reached for her, and pulled her against him.

"Caroline, I love you. I don't ever want to disappoint you either."

She could hear the rhythm of his heart as her head pressed against his chest. "Jimmy, you're so good to me. How could I disagree with you or get aggravated with you? I'm sorry if you think I'm hard to get along with. I'll try not to be that way."

Jim kissed the top of her head. "You smell good."

She raised her head. "Jimmy, let's get married—soon. You're right, why wait?" His earlier smile blossomed into full-faced excitement. She had pleased him. Caroline determined that's what she wanted most of all, to please Jimmy.

"You mean that?"

"Yes. Give me about two weeks. I'll need to buy some clothes."

"Two weeks? That would be the twenty-first. I'll be happy to wait two weeks. Where would you like to go for our honeymoon? You name it, wherever you want to go."

"Jimmy, you've probably traveled to more places than I have. I'll leave that up to you."

"*We* will both decide together. Let's be thinking about that. *We* need to talk about some other things, about where we'll live and about the kids. But we don't have to think about that tonight. Let me hold you and let's both get relaxed. Our conversation this morning has shadowed us all day. This evening we will just be. We can enjoy being together without a cloud following us around."

She scooted closer to him to rest her head on his shoulder. He held her to his side, his arm across her shoulders. She reached up and took his hand, holding it beneath her chin. Serenity at last.

Chapter 21

Jim held the receiver to his ear and listened to the ringing. "Hello."

"Bones, it's me. Got some good news to tell you."

"Well, don't make me guess. Tell me."

"Caroline and I set a date this weekend to get married."

"Wow. When?"

"July twenty-first."

"Where is the weddin' going to be?"

"We haven't decided that yet."

"Don't you think you should have decided where when you picked the date?"

"Probably so. We've got a few things to settle yet. You know, her being in Knoxville and me being here. I imagine I'll be on this telephone every day this week talking with Caroline."

"I hope you don't hit any bumps in the road. This long distance thing wouldn't work for me. Of course y'all knew each other before, when you both lived in Newton.

"Yeah. It was like pulling teeth trying to agree on the date. But, you know, Caroline did an about-face and we both agreed. She wanted to wait till Christmas. She made the sacrifice of her wants and we had an agreement."

"I remember her as being rich, spoiled, and selfish. But when we got together when Emmajean came home, she sure seemed to have changed a lot—for the better. Congratulations."

"Thanks, Bones. I just got in from Knoxville so I'm bushed. Tell Callie my good news. I'll talk to you later."

"Callie's sittin' right here and she looks like she knows what we're talkin' about. I'll tell her the details. Bye."

"Bye, Bones."

~ ~ ~

Later that week when Jim returned to his office from lunch he stopped by Peggy's desk to get any messages he might have received while he was out. "Any messages?"

"Yes." She handed him a note. "Mr. Gray telephoned and wants you to call him. Mr. Callaway, you're sure smiling today."

He hadn't told anyone at the mill about getting married but he might as well start with Peggy. "I'm smiling because I'm a happy man. I'm getting married."

"Why, Mr. Callaway, who are you marrying? Is it that Mrs. Hensen you keep calling in Knoxville?"

"Yes it is—Caroline Hensen. Lynn met her son at the university in Knoxville. His mom invited Lynn and me to visit at Christmas last year. We all get along well."

"Well, when?"

"In a couple of weeks."

"My, you do keep a secret well."

"Really no secret but we just set the date." He started toward his office. "Please get Mr. Gray on the telephone for me."

"Yes, Mr. Callaway."

Jim sat at his desk and the intercom buzzed. "Yes, Peggy."

"I have Mr. Gray on the telephone."

"Good. Please put him through."

His telephone rang and Jim picked it up right away. "Bones, how you doing? I didn't talk to you long Sunday night. I'm afraid I forgot to ask how Art's doing."

"Not so good. He missed a couple of times reportin' to his truant officer for his community service on weekends. And he's not been goin' to the AA meetings. I'm ready to drive him there but he won't be home when it's time to go."

"Bones, that's not good."

"Judge Franklin's office called the store today and he told me to bring Art in to see him. He hinted that if what he'd told Art to do wasn't working he'd have to come up with somethin' else. What do you reckon he meant by that?"

"I don't know. When do you go in to see him?"

"Thursday. And he wants us in his courtroom again. I've telephoned Terry and he can be there. Would you like to sit in on it like you did the last time?"

"Yes, if you and Callie want me to. I'm happy to help any way I can. What time is the appointment set for?"

"Two o'clock. Thursday."

"Okay, I'll be there. How are Callie and that beautiful daughter?"

"Jennifer's okay. Callie is like me, just holdin' on by a thread where Art is concerned. Jennifer has never given us a day of trouble."

"Wish I could make it better for y'all with Art."

"I know. You're my best friend in the world."

"Hang in there, now. We made it through the last time with the judge."

"Yeah. I just hope there won't be another time after Thursday."

"How are you going to be sure he'll go?"

"He'll go if I have to sit on him. No, really, he's been goin' to school every day so he'll be at school Thursday, and I'll go to the office and get him from there. Well, I'll let you get back to your work. Thanks, Jim."

"You bet. See you Thursday. Bye."

"Bye, Jim."

Jim took his time replacing the telephone in his cradle. He turned his chair to face four-eleven and watched the traffic. *God, we've all got our burdens in this world. Please give Bones and Callie Your strength in what they're going through. I trust You to guide Art's steps in the way necessary to get him straightened out. Amen.*

Jim turned back to his desk. He thought about calling Caroline then decided to wait till he got home and call her tonight. He might have interruptions at work and he really wanted to talk to her as long as she wanted to talk. At home it was just Emmajean and she usually left him alone when she knew he'd called Caroline.

He wondered what Emmajean was doing. She might be out looking for a job. But Jim had told her she didn't have to go to work now. He encouraged her to wait a while. He wanted her to get rested and begin to eat better. She needed to get back to feeling and looking like her old self before she started working. Emmajean's trial ended but he still had concern for her well being. Finally, Jim turned his attention to his work.

~ ~ ~

Jim listened as the telephone rang, anxious for Caroline to answer.

"Hello."

"Hey. What're you doing? Is this a good time for me to call?"

"Jimmy! Any time is a good time to call me. How was your day?"

"I missed you. Started to call you from work, but I didn't want any interruptions so I waited till I came home."

"I missed you too. Guess what I did today?"

"Went shopping."

"How did you know that?"

"Just a lucky guess. I remember you saying you needed some new things before we got married. Did you come home with lots of bundles?"

"Yes, I did. And one of them held something special that you can't see until our wedding night."

"You just made my heart kick up a notch. Whatever it is it will be beautiful on you."

Caroline and Jim talked for the longest time. About nothing, about everything. He could hear the smiles in her voice. And he smiled just listening to her. A little less than two weeks. But the wait would be worth it to be married to Caroline.

"How are the kids?"

"They are great. Studying a lot. Are you coming up this weekend? We need some time to talk face-to-face. I love hearing you now, but we do need to get together."

"Make a list of what we need to talk about. I plan to come up after work Friday afternoon. I might leave the office a little early. Caroline, put this on your list—where will we live? We've got to get that ironed out. If fact, put it number one on your list. That is, if you agree with me on that."

"Yes, that will be number one. How's Emmajean?"

"Fine. She's getting a little antsy staying around the house all day. She wants to get a job. I guess I'll have to stop insisting she wait a while before going to work. If she doesn't get a job here, I'm afraid she'll up and leave."

"No, Jimmy, she won't leave Newton as long as Terry Fields is there."

"You think so?"

"Yes. You can't see the forest for the trees. Watch how she and Terry look at one another."

"Yeah, I agree. I was just teasing you. Both of them seem to have fallen hard and real quick. Their bond started early on when we went down to Atlanta. I noticed their interest in each other then, and I can see the attraction is stronger now."

"Arthur and Callie doing okay?"

"Bones called me today. Art's broken some of the rules the judge laid out for him, and Judge Franklin's calling them to a meeting in his courtroom."

"Jimmy, I know Arthur is your best friend but please don't get wrapped up with his problems. Help him if you can but you be careful and don't give away all of yourself. If you do, you won't have anything left for you and me."

"I won't let that happen. Not ever again. There will always be a you and me. What's all that noise?"

"Lynn and James just came home from the library. You want to talk to them?"

"Sure, put one of them on."

Jim talked a while with James and a little longer with Lynn because she talked on and on. He could tell she liked living with Caroline and James. And Jim liked that she was probably safer living there.

Finally, Lynn gave the telephone to Caroline. "I guess we'd better hang up. Talk about interruptions. We'll look for you Friday evening."

"I'll be there. Work on your list. Bye."

"Bye, Jimmy."

~ ~ ~

Jim slipped in and sat at the back of the room as he'd done the last time Art had to meet Judge Franklin. The four of them were seated as before at one table facing the judge.

"Let's get into this. Art, the truant officer says you missed some weekends to do your community service. And you've not been going to the AA meetings at all. Am I correct?"

"Yes, sir, you are."

"Explain to me how this happened. You don't want to obey the laws of this court?"

Art looked at his hands clasped on the table top. "I didn't want to pick up trash a couple of weekends and at AA they're just a bunch of losers.

"A bunch of losers, you say." The judge chuckled. "And you think you're better than they are, am I correct?"

Art took a long time to answer. "Well, sir, I drink some but I haven't lost anything like the men who are there."

"Is that right? I disagree with you. You've lost your car because you wrecked it. You lost your driver's license for two months."

Art didn't say anything, and Terry nudged him. "Yes, sir."

Jim was in the back of the room but all he heard Art say was yes, sir. Surely he could do better than that. The judge shuffled some papers on his desk. When he looked toward Art again his face had passion for the boy, yet he looked reticent to say anything to him.

"Art, Mr. and Mrs. Gray, we have a case here that my orders didn't help. But Art needs help, and I must find some for him. He needs help with his drinking, and he needs help to learn respect for those in authority. A program not far from here is set up to help youth like Art. They call it residency rehabilitation. The name of the place is Gateway House. It's located near Nashville. I've already arranged for a place to be ready for Art. How long will he have to stay? That depends on Art. The supervisor there will report to me weekly about Art's progress or lack of progress."

"You're sending me away . . . "

"Young man, you will behave yourself in my courtroom. Counselor, restrain your client from any more disruption."

Callie wept on Bones's shoulder. He put his arm around her. They both looked pretty shaky.

"Mr. Gray if you have family health insurance it should cover the expense of Art staying at Gateway House. Counselor, here's a sheet of directions and what to expect when they get there." He looked toward Arthur. "They will expect you tomorrow. Will you do that?"

Arthur cleared his throat. "Yes, Your Honor."

Jim could hear Callie's weeping from where he sat in the back of the room. His heart hurt for them. All three of them. He couldn't imagine this happening to one of his kids. He had trouble wrapping his mind around this. Bones and Callie had raised two children who were the exact opposite of one another. How does that kind of thing happen?

"I think we're through here. Art the sooner you decide to cooperate with folks, the sooner you'll get back home." Judge Franklin tapped his gavel and left the room. Everyone stood.

Terry passed the sheet of paper to Arthur. Art mumbled to Terry about having to leave home. Terry said a few words to the boy, but put his attention to gathering his few things into his briefcase. Arthur and Callie stood near Art. Arthur read the sheet of paper. Callie dabbed a tissue to her eyes but she couldn't block the flow of tears streaking down her face.

Jim joined them at the front of the room. A somber bunch of folks. Art had stopped grumbling, and sat back in his chair. Jim hugged Callie, then shook Arthur's hand. "Tough meeting. I wish I could help." He turned so Art could hear him. "It looks like Art has worked himself into a corner, and Judge Franklin gave him one out. I hope he'll grab hold of this chance to come around."

Arthur still held the piece of paper and handed it to Jim. "It's not too far to get there. A few hours. We'll try to get an early start."

~ ~ ~

He'd gone through some tough things but this was the worst Arthur had ever experienced. He and Callie rode toward Newton in silence. Overnight Callie had blocked off her tears. She and Arthur had hardly slept. Arthur heard her now swallowing her new tears after leaving their son in that place. The grounds looked neat. The supervisor welcomed them and escorted them to a conference room. He explained the program they ran and asked them if they had any questions. They didn't. He had taken Art from the room to show him where he would stay. Art gave his parents a small wave and walked out the door, but he didn't look back at them.

Now in the car going home Arthur couldn't find words to settle Callie. He needed something to settle himself. They both stared straight out the windshield watching the miles mount up between them and their son.

~ ~ ~

Callie couldn't speak. She could barely breathe without choking. If she spoke certainly the flood gates would open and her weeping would start again. Her heart had never ached this badly before. How could she live each day knowing that her son stayed at a place with other troubled people, some probably more than Art. Her lack of breathing affected her heart. She felt it pound through her brain. Would she pass out? She had to get control of herself. But that was not to be. She remained in this state of adapting to the situation all the way to Newton. Silence in the car spoke loudly. Would Art survive this test Judge Franklin had set before her son?

Chapter 22

He had put his things in his upstairs bedroom and then Jim joined the others in the living room, taking a seat beside Caroline on the sofa. "So, no studying tonight, you two?"

"We've already done some, Daddy. We didn't want to have to be studying all the time you were here." She and James sat in chairs facing the sofa.

"Hey, Dad, Mom told us about your wedding date. That's great."

Jim glanced at Lynn and saw her encouraging smile. "Yeah, we'll all be a happier bunch when we legally become a real family. Caroline and I would like to take a short trip after the wedding. You two be okay here by yourself for a little while? If you'd rather we not leave, tell us."

"Oh, Daddy," Lynn said. "Y'all have to go on a honeymoon. We'll be fine here."

"Dad, I'll watch out for Lynn. Don't let anything here stop your trip. You and Mom go on your honeymoon without worrying about us."

Caroline gave Jim her *I told you so* look. "I knew you'd be okay but Jimmy needed assurance that you would. We haven't decided where we may go but it's on our list."

"What list, Mom?"

Jim laughed out loud. "Your mom has a list of things we have to discuss and *agree* on this weekend. I hope we can do that and get me back to work by Monday morning."

Lynn looked toward Caroline. "What's on your list, Caroline?"

"At the top of the list is where Jimmy and I will live."

The kids exchanged glances. "Good luck, Dad, on that one."

Caroline gave James a stern look with the message to butt out. "My *list* contains things that you both shouldn't bother yourselves about. Jimmy and I must settle some things before we get married. We'll be busy all weekend getting through the things." She checked the time. "Anybody want more cake or ice cream before we call it a day? It's a little warm to offer hot chocolate in July."

Jim patted his waistline. "Not me."

"Me either, Caroline."

"Mom, I agree, no more cake tonight."

Caroline left the sofa, and turned toward the stairway. "Okay then, good night all, I'm going to turn in. Jimmy, you're tired from the trip. You'd better get some rest tonight so you can tackle my list early tomorrow."

With one long stride he grabbed her arm and hugged her. "I won't collapse under your list. But I'll walk you upstairs and turn in too. Good night, kids."

They both said good night, and headed for the television room.

Jim and Caroline locked the door and turned out the lights. Jim put his hand around her waist as they walked upstairs. Caroline turned toward Jim, and they tarried a while outside his bedroom. She put her arms around Jim's neck and smiled like she had just won a prize at the fair. "One more week."

"Yeah. I can't wait to wake up every morning with you beside me." He hugged her close against him. The familiar vanilla scent of her shampoo washed over him as he kissed the top of her head. He stood back a bit, took one finger to lift her chin, and kissed her soft lips. When she began to kiss him back, he almost fell into her trap. He broke away. "One more week, Caroline, and I'll never say no to you again when you want to kiss me."

"I look forward to that. Why did I ever think I could wait till Christmas?"

"I don't know. I'm glad *we* agreed on two weeks. You finished all your shopping?"

"Just about. I've chosen the dress I'll wear at our wedding. Do you have a dark suit to wear?"

"Yeah. I'm okay there. Have you asked Lynn to be your maid of honor?"

"No, I thought we'd do that tomorrow—that's on my list."

That drew a smile from Jim. "One more kiss good night?"

Caroline didn't answer, but pressed her lips against his.

"Good night."

"Good night, Jimmy. I love you more than you can imagine."

"I love you more than that." They both turned toward their bedrooms.

~ ~ ~

The first gray of drawn crept in through Jim's bedroom window. He rolled out of bed as he had planned last night. He wanted to be the first one to the kitchen today. He wanted to be the one to fix breakfast. He pulled on his blue jeans and a T shirt and crept downstairs. He put two skillets on the stovetop. From the refrigerator he took a package of bacon and a bowl of eggs and put them on the counter. He found the Crisco and put a teaspoonful in one skillet and turned on the burner to medium. After the Crisco had melted, he laid several strips of bacon in that skillet.

He found another bowl to crack six eggs into. He set the orange juice container and four small glasses on the table. Back to the stove he turned the bacon slices over. With a fork he stirred the eggs in the bowl then set that bowl aside. He put the milk bottle and four larger glasses on the table. Where did Caroline keep her loaf bread? He found it and put two slices in the toaster but didn't push them down into the toaster. He saw the bacon was almost crisp enough and slid its skillet off the burner.

He put plates and silverware around the table, and added paper napkins. Another dab of Crisco went into the second skillet. When the Crisco melted, he stirred the eggs some more and poured them into the oily skillet. Jim grabbed butter and jellies from the refrigerator. He looked around the kitchen. Almost finished.

Jim went to the bottom of the stairs and hollered. "Breakfast's ready." He heard scurrying above and rushed back to stir the scrambled eggs. James and Lynn came into the kitchen first as he turned off the burners and pushed the bread down into the toaster. When Caroline came around the corner into the kitchen the two pieces of bread popped up. He put the hot slices on a small plate, cut them diagonally, and placed them on the table. He put two more slices of bread into the toaster. Jim looked up at Caroline. Beautiful even first thing in the morning.

He poured orange juice into the small glasses and sweet milk into the four taller glasses. He grabbed the two new pieces of toast and they joined the others on the small plate. He scooped the scrambled eggs into another bowl and set them on the table.

Caroline watched Jim's big production of breakfast. "What is going on in here? I wanted to fix breakfast."

"We did too."

Jim pulled a chair out for Caroline, and the kids found theirs.

"I determined last night I would beat y'all, and I did." He looked over the table. "Have I forgotten anything?"

Caroline looked over the room. "I think not, Jimmy. What a treat."

Jim joined hands with Caroline and Lynn, then James did the same with his mom and Lynn. *Father, thank You for our blessings and this food. Amen.*

They were all delighted with Jim's breakfast. "Daddy, you did a good job."

"Thank you. I can do breakfast pretty good, but I'll let the rest of y'all handle lunch and supper."

They sat around the table after they'd finished. "Well, Caroline and I had better get my messy kitchen cleaned up so we can get to the list."

"Oh, Jimmy, you make it sound so catastrophic. It's just some things we have to get settled."

"James and I will clean up in here. Y'all go on and get dressed and to your list."

Caroline went upstairs first and in a little bit Jim followed.

After everyone had dressed for the day, they sat in the living room.

"Caroline, where're we going to work this morning?"

"I thought maybe it might be pleasant to sit on the bench down by the river."

"Sounds good. Anything I can help you carry?"

"No, thank you."

When they sat on the bench Caroline took Jim's hand. He laid her hand into his other hand so he could put his arm around her on the back of the bench. They watched the river a bit then Caroline began to shuffle through her papers. She struggled with them being blown by the breeze coming off the water. "This might not have been a good idea to work down here."

"Want to go back to the house and spread all that stuff on the dining room table?"

"Yes, that's what we should do."

Having dropped all her things onto the dining table, they both sat, Caroline at the head of the table and Jim on her right. She scattered through the papers until she found her list.

"You know what is number one, right?"

"Where will we live?"

"Yes, where will we live? So, I'll go first with my thoughts on this. Our homes are sixty miles apart. Jimmy, driving here and there is nothing perilous, but if you had to do it every day I'm positive it would soon become a burden on you. What about this: we will live in Newton in your home. As for my home, we could let James and Lynn live here as long as they wanted. But you need to live in Newton, and wherever you live I want to be there too. Forever."

"Those are exactly my thoughts." He leaned over and kissed her lips. "I held my breath when you said you'd go first. I thought you might give me some over-the-top thoughts. I'm so glad our thinking runs the same way for now."

"For always." Caroline took her pencil and put a large X on item number one. "Next, where will the wedding be."

"We should probably figure out how many folks we expect to be there."

"We've already agreed not to have a big wedding. Just family and friends."

"Caroline, it seems you don't have close friends here—just James. We have family and friends in Newton. It would be logical for us to have the wedding in Newton instead of asking them all to drive up here."

"I don't have family and friends in Newton."

"You do, Caroline. You've met mine, and they've accepted you. They've told me how happy they are we finally set a date. My family and friends are yours too. Agreed?"

"I suppose so. They really did act as if they liked me."

"That's because they really do like you. I want to invite my secretary and her husband. You've talked to Peggy on the telephone. She's excited for us. Would inviting her be okay with you?"

"Jimmy, of course. Anyone else at the mill we should invite?"

"No, just associates there, not really what you would call friends. So how many people does that make?"

Caroline began to say the names out loud and count them on her fingers. When she got past ten, she wrote them down then counted them. I get fifteen when I include the teenagers and us. Am I right?"

"You shouldn't count Art. He won't be able to make it."

"Oh, I forgot about that."

"Bones and Callie just took him up to the place yesterday. The trip was awful for them. Bones said Callie was a limp skeleton of a woman when they got back. I wondered how I could do that if it was Lynn."

"Me too with James."

"So, we have fourteen people minus us to invite. That's twelve. Oh, did you count Terry?"

"Of course I did. Emmajean wouldn't show up if he's not there."

"We're getting somewhere now. So, we know how many people will come and we're getting married in Newton. Where do you want the wedding to be? In the church, at my home, or with a judge at the courthouse?"

"Oh, Jimmy, that's not funny." But Caroline laughed anyway. "From those options I think this decision will be easy. With the small number attending, we could fit it nicely into your home."

She put a big X beside that item. "We decided where the wedding will be and who we shall invite. She put another X by the invitation list item.

Jim dragged her list to his side of the table. "We've got the three biggies down and the others don't look too tough."

Jim volunteered Emmajean to talk with Caroline by telephone to coordinate the purchase of flowers and wedding cake. And all the goodies that must be on the table with the cake. "When will you ask Lynn to be your maid of honor?"

"I plan to ask her at dinner tonight. Have you chosen your best man?"

"My best man will be James, of course."

Would dinner at The Regas be a good time for you to talk to James?"

"Sure. Like I said at the creek I probably should have talked to him to get his permission to marry you before I asked you. But I think the way it went gave everyone there so much pleasure I'm glad I did it the way I did."

"Even including us falling in the creek?" She punched his shoulder.

Jim pretended to fight back. They laughed so loud they didn't hear the front door open. "Hey is this for real or just playing? Mom, I don't want to see you and Dad get into a real fight."

"This is just playing. I didn't hear you come in," Caroline said.

"Of course not, y'all were making too much noise," James said."

"Daddy, how's the list coming along?"

"Good, Lynn. We've made good progress today. Have you and James had a good day?" Jim wanted to know where they'd been without being nosy.

"Yes, we did. We caught up on some research we needed to do at the library. We went out while we knew you and Caroline would be working on these things. Now it looks like we'll all four be free to spend time together without interruptions."

"James, y'all grab something for lunch from the kitchen. Jimmy and I'll do the same in a little while."

"Come on, Lynn, let's raid the refrigerator."

Jim watched them leave the room. "We have two good kids."

"Yes, we do. How could we not?"

"I sure wish I could have been around when you raised James."

"I do too. But you didn't know where we were. Don't beat up on yourself for that. We'll have to just make up for the loss of time any way we can. When we're married I hope we'll definitely step beyond the past."

Jim nodded. He didn't want to forget all his past. Louisa would always be a part of his good memories, and he wanted to hold on to them. But his life with Caroline would definitely transcend the ugly parts of their pasts.

The kids came out of the kitchen on their way to the television room. "Mom, the kitchen is all yours." They disappeared into the back of the house.

Jim and Caroline busied themselves in the kitchen making their own lunch. "Caroline, is The Regas open in the evenings? I thought we might go there for dinner."

"It's open but in the evenings you must have a reservation, particularly on Saturdays."

"Is it too late to make a reservation for tonight?"

She spread mayonnaise on her bread but dropped her knife, and went straight toward the telephone. "I'll find out."

When she returned to the kitchen Jim had finished making her sandwich for her. "We have reservations for seven o'clock. Think you can hold out till then for your dinner?"

"If not, I'll just have an early supper before then."

"No, you won't spoil a wonderful meal at The Regas by snacking."

"Who says?"

"I say." Caroline squealed when Jim grabbed her around the waist. He had just taken a bite of his ham sandwich and still had mayonnaise on his lips but she kissed him anyway. She couldn't help herself.

When they settled down, they became aware that James and Lynn stood in the kitchen doorway shaking their heads. "What? You two have never seen anybody have plain old good fun?"

"Yeah, Dad. But I've never seen grown-ups play and make as much noise as you two do."

"Get used to it. After we're married it may get worse."

Lynn and James rolled their eyes and returned to the television room.

"Jimmy, you are incurable."

"And you're my accomplice." He caught her again, this time by an arm and pulled her to him. He hugged her close and spoke into her hair. "I'm looking forward to the next fifty years with you."

"You make me so happy, Jimmy. I plan to be with you all the way."

"I'm counting on that." He laid a hand on the back of her head and bent down searching for her lips. She obliged him and they fell into a kiss that warmed Jim all over. He could feel Caroline shiver against his body and heard her inviting moans.

~ ~ ~

The first time he'd been in Regas Restaurant, when he'd met Caroline for lunch last December, he remembered it as elegant and sophisticated. It was a place for Caroline to be, because that description fit her—elegant and sophisticated. When Caroline told the girl at the reservation desk about calling earlier, she led them to a table nestled in a corner. Jim held out a chair for Caroline and the kids slid onto the banquette.

"Daddy, isn't this about the loveliest restaurant you've seen?"

"Well, yes, it is. I saw it . . ." Caroline pinched his leg under the table to remind him that Lynn or James didn't know they'd been here together.

"You saw it . . . what, Daddy?"

"I think I saw a magazine article about this place."

The waiter came immediately to their table, and laid out their menus and a glass of water for each of them. He left to give them time to look over the selections. "I feel like having a steak. What are y'all ordering?"

Caroline searched the menu for what she wanted. "I think I'll have salmon. Their sauce covering the salmon is delicious." James wanted chicken and Lynn wanted the same. When the waiter returned, Jim gave him the order for all of them and told the waiter to bring four iced teas.

After they'd finished their meal they lingered a while. "Lynn, I'd like you to be my attendant, my maid of honor at our wedding. Would you, please?"

"Oh, Caroline, what an honor to be asked by you. Of course, I will."

Jim cleared his throat and took a sip of his tea. "James, will you be my best man at the wedding?"

"Dad, of course I will. Thank you for asking me."

"We've whittled down almost that entire list, haven't we, Caroline?"

"Except where we will go on our honeymoon, if we take a trip."

"Mom, you'll take a trip," James said. "Lynn and I will be okay at the house. Dad, if you can be gone awhile from your mill, then plan the trip."

"I'm waiting on your mom to decide where she wants to go."

"Daddy, women like surprises some time." Lynn said. "Why don't you plan the trip without telling Caroline? How would that do, Caroline?"

She couldn't refuse the suggestion from Jim's daughter. She looked at Jim. "Can I trust you to do everything needed to make a trip?"

"Thanks for the idea, Lynn. I'll have to think about that," Jim said. "Caroline and I have decided to agree on everything in our relationship."

James chuckled. "Dad, you don't know yet how it will be. living with Mom. If she agrees with you on everything. you must be a magician."

"James, don't make me look bad."

"Thanks, James. I'll have to think about the trip."

They left the restaurant. It was still early evening. "Dad, turn left out of the parking lot. I want to show you the Tennessee Theater."

"Yes, Daddy it's a splendid building inside," Lynn said.

Traffic had dwindled on Gay Street, and they reached the theater in a few minutes. "Wow, look at that marquee," Jim said. "Caroline would you like to take in a movie?"

"I don't think so. We've had a busy day and you have to travel tomorrow back to Newton. Let's just go home. Everybody okay with that?" All consented.

Later at home Jim and Caroline sat on the sofa. "Caroline, did you get your blood test last week?"

"I did, and I have the paper to prove it."

"I did too. I'll need to take your paper home with me, and go to the courthouse to get our marriage license."

"What if they want me to sign something with you?"

"You plan to come down the middle of the week, don't you? I'll wait till then, and we can go together to the courthouse. Then you can check that off your list. Now, about a trip after we're married. I don't want to pick somewhere and surprise you. I'd rather both of us plan our trip together. Is there any place you'd like to go?" He turned on the sofa to face her.

"I've read a lot about Savannah. I've always wanted to go there to see how the streets are laid out in squares, and see the port water. They have historical houses and museums. We could also visit Tybee Island nearby, and walk the pier that stretches into the Atlantic Ocean. There's a historical lighthouse on the island. What do you think?"

He took her by the shoulders and looked into the depths of her indigo eyes. "I think going to Savannah would be a good trip. I'd be interested in seeing the port there. And Tybee Island sounds interesting"

She searched his dark eyes. "Jimmy, you're not just agreeing with me to bypass an argument, are you?"

"Caroline, I'll never lie to you, hurt you, or let anyone else hurt you, and I'll always love you. Believe me?"

As she leaned toward him her kiss almost muted her answer. "Yes, Jimmy."

They broke away from the kiss. Caroline leaned back against the sofa. "Jimmy, I won't ever lie to you either. After twenty years without you, that couldn't possibly happen. I love you."

~ ~ ~

As soon as he arrived at his home, Jim telephoned Bones. "Bones, how are things going? How about Callie? And Art?"

"It sure has been quiet here, even with Jennifer. It's a gloomy place. We miss Art. I've really had to fight to keep Callie's spirits up. I keep tellin' her and myself that this is good for Art. It has to be."

"Have you talked to him since Friday?"

"No, we have to wait two weeks before we can telephone or see him."

"Judge Franklin thought highly of this place. It's bound to be good."

"I hope so. Art's become unmanageable for Callie and me."

"Y'all be here for our wedding on Saturday?"

"We're plannin' on it. Can't wait to see you married again."

"Caroline and I made some decisions over the weekend about things that need to be done. We got everything ironed out pretty good."

"Did you decide on where you'll live?"

"Yeah. Here in my house. And the wedding will be here too."

"Wow. I was waitin' to see if Caroline would come back to Newton. I'm glad y'all agreed on that."

"Well, Bones, I'll let you go. I'm kind of tuckered out and need a good night's sleep. Take care of your girls there, and let me know if I can help."

"Thanks, Jim. Bye."

"Bye."

~ ~ ~

"When are the kids coming down?"

"They had a class tomorrow they couldn't miss but they will leave after it's finished. They should be here before night tomorrow."

"Good."

"Jimmy, I'm getting a little nervous. You?"

"No, not yet. Probably will be Saturday."

Emmajean entered the living room as Jim answered Caroline. "No you won't, Jim. You've been the rock of our family, and handled everything for us. You'll stay calm."

Emmajean and Caroline went over the preparations for the flowers and the cake. They discussed the table where the cake, punch, and other goodies would be. "I've lined up Shirley Ann and Callie for times they will serve the punch. I'll serve the cake, and keep an eye on the table to make sure all the dishes stay full. Anything else you want me to do?"

"Emmajean, what a big help you've already been. Will the cake be delivered or will someone have to go get it?"

"The cake will be delivered and also the flower arrangements and your bouquet. Which car will y'all be tak . . . taking on your trip?"

"Don't answer her, Caroline. She wants to know so they can write on it and mess it all up."

"Then we'll write on both of them."

Jim groaned. "Oh, no."

~ ~ ~

The florist came early Saturday morning and had set their arrangements around the living room in strategic spots to enhance the room for a wedding. The bakery had delivered the wedding cake. Emmajean had supervised placement of the cake on the dining room table, which had been polished to a sheen. She and Jim's sister Shirley Ann helped Callie assemble what was needed to enhance the cake. They laid magnolia leafs around the base of the three tier cake. The bakery had placed a miniature bride and groom as the cake topper.

Arthur had helped Callie to take the punch bowl and cups to the table from the kitchen and then bring in the punch to pour into the ornate bowl. Other dishes on the table held mixed nuts, various pastel-colored tiny square mints, little sandwiches with the bread crusts trimmed away, and a tray of chocolate candy. The candy set off the almost all-white tabletop.

~ ~ ~

Caroline stayed in her upstairs bedroom with Lynn. Her ballerina-length dress made of a cream color silk material swirled around the calves of her legs. She wore a matching loose waist-length jacket open at the front that allowed her elegant dress to be visible.

"Oh, Caroline, you look beautiful. Well, you *are* beautiful but that dress is beautiful on you. Where did you find it?"

"I went to Miller's and found it in their bridal department. When I saw it I had to buy it." She stood in front of a pedestal mirror that tilted at the correct angle so Caroline could see the entire dress. Lynn had helped her fix her hair.

"I think your hair pulled back into the French twist looks so pretty."

"I secured it with a pearl-encrusted comb. Do you think that is too much?"

"No. Absolutely not. It's beautiful. Oh, I keep using that word but you are certainly beautiful and your dress and hair and everything adds to your beauty. Just wait till Daddy sees you."

"How's he doing? Where is he?"

"He and James are in the television room. After the preacher stands at the fireplace, they will go to stand with him. The lady from church will play the wedding march and we will start down the stairs. Are you nervous? Think you can walk down the stairs okay?"

"Yes. And yes I'm a little nervous. You?"

"I'm only nervous for you and Daddy. I hope everything goes well for the ceremony. And, Caroline, I'm so glad you and Daddy decided to get married. He's been by himself for so long. I know he must be even lonelier since I went away to school. Thank you for loving Daddy."

"Why, Lynn, that is so sweet of you." Caroline took Lynn lightly by the shoulders and they had a slight hug. "Thank you for accepting me into your family."

"I'll have to admit that at first, last New Year's Eve, I went along with everything for Daddy's sake. I didn't want to disappoint him. But as I've been around you and watched you and Daddy together, I'm sure y'all both love one another. Your love is real."

"Yes, it is, Lynn. Thank you for being happy for us." She took Lynn's hand and gave it a squeeze.

~ ~ ~

"James, what time is it?"

"Dad, it's almost two o'clock. Now, don't fall apart on me at this hour."

"James, I love your mom. I'm anxious for us to be a real family and after today we will be. Are you and Lynn doing okay with the circumstances your mom and I put on y'all?

"We are. Both of us. Don't worry about us. I'll let you know if anything goes on that you need to know about."

"James, one thing. Is Lynn dating anyone? Do you know if any boys are interested in her?"

"Any guy who sees her would be interested in her. She's such a kind, sweet, pretty girl. But as far as I know she's not seeing anyone. I think she'd share that with me if she was."

"When your mom and I are living in Newton and you and Lynn in Knoxville, the only eyes and ears to help me keep watch over Lynn will be yours."

"I'll take care of Lynn. And I'll let you know if I see any guy coming around. They'll have to get through me to Lynn."

"Thanks, James. And I promise to watch out for your mom for the rest of my life. And we'll never be far away enough that we can't get to you and Lynn if you need us."

"I understand your concern. Thanks."

~ ~ ~

"Is it two o'clock yet?"

They both looked at their watches and then heard the strains of the wedding march drifting up the stairs. "It *is*. Caroline, you ready?"

"Where are my flowers? Can you get them for me, please?"

Lynn picked up Caroline's flowers off the bed and brought them to her. She held her bouquet in both hands slightly below her waist. The white roses with a little greenery and some baby's breath stuck here and there completed the picture. Lynn opened the bedroom door, and walked to the top of the stairway.

Chapter 23

Emmajean had directed that folding chairs filled the living room with space between them for Lynn and Caroline to approach the fire place. They walked slowly down the stairs, both holding to the hand rail until they reached the bottom. Lynn turned to her right and entered the living room. She looked at her daddy and James standing with the preacher. They all smiled but her daddy's smile was the biggest.

Their family and friends turned around to get a glimpse of Lynn and Caroline. Lynn saw the excitement on her aunts' faces. Even the men looked pleasant in spite of having to get dressed up. Then Jim's smile became wider and Lynn knew that he'd seen Caroline enter the room. That moment became all about Caroline and it should have. Lynn felt a lasting happiness fill her as they were about to become a real family.

~ ~ ~

After the preacher pronounced them husband and wife and said Jim could kiss his wife, he and Caroline shared a chaste kiss before their family and friends.

The pianist played louder to usher them toward the other side of the living room. Arthur caught Jim and slapped him on the back over and over. Henry Frank and Terry did the same. Jim wanted to stay by Caroline, but the ladies had her cornered as well.

The photographer posed Jim, Caroline, James, and Lynn for pictures in front of the fireplace. He took pictures of Jim and Caroline, Caroline and Lynn, then of Jim and James. After the picture-taking, Emmajean shooed them toward the dining room. Guests waited to see Jim and Caroline cut the cake. Jim handed Caroline the cake cutter and placed his hand over hers as she prepared for the first cut. Caroline took a white napkin embossed in silver with their names and the date, and laid the cake she cut onto it.

She broke off two pieces of cake, and offered one to Jim, which he picked up. She laid the napkin on the table, and picked up the other piece. "Be nice now, Jimmy." He fed her the cake he held and he did it neatly, no smearing the icing on her mouth.

"You'd better be just as nice, Caroline." She lifted the cake to his lips as he had to hers, and fed him cake. They both laughed, as did those gathered around the table. Caroline handed Jim another napkin to clean up the sugary mess and did the same for herself. They stepped away, and Emmajean stood behind the cake to serve the guests. At the other end of the table Callie poured punch.

While cutting the cake, Emmajean had difficulty pouring punch into the cups. As she lifted the ladle from the punch bowl to the cup her grip didn't appear steady. Emmajean motioned to Shirley Ann to relieve Callie. When all the guests had been served cake, Emmajean went in search of Callie. She found Callie and Arthur in the kitchen. "Callie, are you okay? It looked like you had a hard time serving the punch."

Arthur had his arm around her shoulders. "She was. I noticed her too."

"Oh, y'all, I guess I was just a little nervous. This has been an exciting evening. I'm okay, Emmajean."

"Well, don't be doing any more work tonight. Arthur, you make sure she doesn't tire herself out again."

"I'll stay right with her till we go home."

Emmajean left the kitchen to tend to anything else that might be needed and Callie and Arthur followed her. As she entered the dining room, James was offering a toast to the bridal couple. Terry slipped to her side and put his arm around her waist, which made a tingle run up her spine.

"As the best man, I think I'm supposed to say something here." James cleared his throat, looked around, and lifted his cup. "Mom and Dad, here's to the most deserving couple I know of who should have a happily ever after. I love you both."

Hearing James's words, Jim felt a momentary memory flash flit through his head. He and Louisa had spoken so many times about their happily ever after. He quickly dismissed the thought, and kept his wits about himself.

Lynn stepped next to James and held up her cup. "My turn, now. Caroline and Daddy, I am so happy for you and for us as a family. I love you both."

Bones let loose with a cheer. "Here, here."

~ ~ ~

As everybody milled around, Caroline motioned for Lynn to go upstairs with her. Lynn helped Caroline get dressed for their trip.

They removed all her bridal attire, and Caroline stepped into a pale green suit. The skirt zipped up across her hip, and the short jacket buttoned up the front with same color buttons. Lynn made sure her lapels lay flat and pinned a corsage on the left one. "Take a look."

Caroline turned again to the pedestal mirror. "Where are my gloves?"

"Here." Lynn handed the short, white gloves to Caroline. She tugged them on as she looked around the room.

"What do you need?" Lynn said.

"Where's my purse?"

Lynn handed the white purse to Caroline, and saw a slight tremble in her hands.

"Caroline, why don't you sit for just a moment to gather yourself together. You look a little shaky." Lynn watched Caroline sit and fumble with her purse. "Hey, it's just us. You're really nervous, aren't you?"

"Yes. Yes, Lynn, I am. I thought about your daddy everyday for over twenty years. He and James were my life. But he didn't know where I was. I'm glad he had a short time with your mother. If he hadn't we wouldn't have you with us now. Just thinking about our lives I get a little off kilter. I'm sorry. Thank you for helping me to get hold of myself. Where's your daddy?"

"I think he and James are probably back in the television room getting Daddy ready to go. Can't you just hear James giving Daddy words of wisdom?"

Caroline smiled and seemed to relax at that. That's good. She needs to keep it together till she can be with Daddy in the car. He'd soothe her nerves then. They'll both be happy to leave this houseful of people behind and get to themselves.

"Let me go downstairs to make sure Daddy knows you're about ready. I'll send James up here. I'm sure you want to share some time with him."

"Lynn, you are a mature young lady. Thank you. Yes, send James up."

Caroline stayed seated, but stood when she heard the light tap on the door. It opened and there was James, smiling all over himself. "Mom you look wonderful. Dad's ready to leave when you are. Don't worry about Lynn and me. Go on your trip and enjoy yourselves."

"We will. I left a note in the kitchen at home of all telephone numbers where we can be reached while we're gone. Please promise me you'll get in touch with us if you need us."

"I promise, Mom." He gave her a kiss on the cheek. "You'd better not keep Dad waiting any longer. I love you."

James walked his mom down the stairs and handed her over to Jim. "You two have a great trip." He shook hands with Jim and Lynn hugged Caroline. Then they were out the door only to find everybody in the yard waiting with handfuls of rice. As Jim and Caroline darted for the car, rice peppered them from all directions. When they approached his car Jim had no words for what Bones and the boys had done to the car. Everyone laughed.

Caroline turned back toward the guests and prepared to throw her bouquet. She looked at the girls there, Jim's nieces and also Emmajean. Caroline sent her bouquet into the air with a high arc. Emmajean stretched her six feet height and reached over the smaller girls to catch the flowers and gather them to her chest. All the guys looked toward Terry, laughing and whooping. Terry's face turned a slight crimson.

The photographer snapped pictures as Jim helped Caroline into the passenger seat. Jim ran around the front of the car, and slid under the wheel. As soon as he shut the door, his foot found the gas pedal. He turned the key, pushed the starter button, and off they went. Before they drove out of sight Lynn saw Caroline scoot across the seat as close as she could get to her daddy. Lynn smiled with pleasure.

~ ~ ~

Caroline snuggled next to Jim as they drove south of Newton. "I'm glad we decided to make reservations for tonight in Chattanooga. I can't wait to get you and me alone together."

"Me too. Then tomorrow we can drive on to Savannah and not be rushed."

"How long are you planning to stay away from the mill?"

"I wish I could answer as long as we want to. I'd better not be gone more than two weeks."

"I'm looking forward to every day with you. Jimmy, before and after our wedding, I had time to talk with Lynn. I'm glad I got to know her a little better, just us, one-on-one. She's a mature and lovable young lady."

"Yeah, she is that. Thanks." He tried to concentrate on the road but Caroline's nearness was playing havoc on his focus. "Be careful there, we might have to stop before we get to Chattanooga."

Caroline reluctantly moved away from Jim a few inches. "Yes, sir, I wouldn't want to spoil your trip." They both laughed. "I love you, Jimmy. Don't ever forget that."

"I love you, Caroline."

~ ~ ~

When they arrived at the hotel in Chattanooga they approached the service desk to register. Jim wrote on the ledger "Mr. and Mrs. Jim Callaway," turned it where Caroline could see, and gave her a silly grin.

Getting off the elevator, they followed the bellhop to their room. After the bellhop opened the door, put their luggage inside, and asked if he could be of any other help, Jim tipped him. The bellhop left, closing the door behind him.

Caroline kicked off her high heels, walked to Jim, and slid her arms underneath his jacket, giving him a hug. Her head lingered against his chest. Jim's heart picked up its beat as he returned the hug. Finally Caroline stepped back, searching Jim's ebony eyes. Apparently pleased with what she saw, she pushed his jacket back across his shoulders. He caught it before it hit the floor and tossed it onto a chair while loosening his tie. Caroline pulled his tie from his shirt collar and it joined his jacket.

Jim pulled his shirttail from his pants then turned toward his bride. He undid the three large buttons of her suit jacket with an intake of breath. Caroline wore no blouse. He struggled out of his shirt and pulled her against him. His undershirt and her slip became a barrier between them but even that much brought ecstasy. He had promised he'd never hurt her. He fought to gain self-control.

Jim picked Caroline up, walked to the bed, and placed her down with care.

~ ~ ~

The next morning when Caroline awoke, Jim was sitting up in bed, propped up with pillows against the bed's headboard. He had on blue jeans but no shirt. Caroline smiled and reached her hand to his chest. "How long have you been awake?"

"Long enough to watch you sleep. You're beautiful even in your sleep although you do make a slight snore."

She smacked him lightly against his chest. "I do not snore."

"Yes, you do. Just a little. Your snore is also part of your beauty."

She scurried across the bed to press against him and snatch a kiss.

Jim motioned toward the door. "Control yourself. I'm expecting room service to bring our breakfast any minute."

"I'll behave till after breakfast."

A tap sounded at the door. "That must be our food. He walked to the door barefoot, allowed the young man to roll the cart inside, tipped him, and shut the door. "This morning you shall have breakfast in bed." Caroline sat up, careful to keep the sheet close to her chin.

"Oh, Jimmy, I could get used to this."

"I hope so. I plan to do this every weekend morning."

Chapter 24

On Monday Arthur arrived home after he'd closed the store. "Anybody home?" Silence filled the house. He found a note on the breakfast table from Callie. Or at least he thought it was from Callie. Her handwriting looked awful. He tried to decipher it and made out some words and the number six. He surmised she had written she'd gone on an errand and would return at six o'clock. He held the note up again while worry creased his forehead. Was Callie sick? He remembered that she had a hard time helping at the wedding reception.

Callie did return at six o'clock, stumbling a bit as she came in the kitchen door. Arthur left the table and greeted her with a kiss. "Where'd you go?

"Mrs. Whitson wanted me to help her pick out some flowers over at the garden store. Didn't you see my note?"

"Yeah, I did but it was a little hard to read. Were you in a hurry as you wrote it?"

"I think so. Mrs. Whitson tooted her car horn before I finished the note."

"Where's Jennifer? Will she be eatin' supper with us?"

"She's off studying with her girlfriends. I think she plans to come back in time for supper."

After supper and a little television they turned in for the night. They'd been asleep a while when Callie jumped in her sleep. From her head to her feet she jerked all over, waking them both. "Callie, what is it? Are you all right?"

"Yes. Did you feel that? It woke me. What happened?"

Arthur sat up in bed. "Your whole body jerked. Does that happen during the day?"

"I've noticed a few little twitches. Not enough to worry about."

"Then let's go back to sleep." Arthur lay on his pillow but sleep wouldn't come. Putting together the reception, the note, her slight stumble when she came in, and this jerking enough to wake them, Arthur determined that she needed to see the doctor. He'd mention that to Callie in the morning.

Arthur made the doctor's appointment the next morning, but Callie couldn't get in to see him till Wednesday. In the meantime, Arthur kept a close eye on his wife when he was around, and tried to close the store at five o'clock each day and get home to her.

~ ~ ~

Arthur accompanied Callie to the doctor's office on Wednesday. The doctor had Callie to walk up and back in the hallway. Arthur and the doctor watched her. Back in the examining room, Dr. Wilson told them what he thought. "With what you've told me about your handwriting, your unsteadiness on your feet, and your muscle spasms waking you at night, I think you have Parkinson's disease." Callie reached for Arthur's hand. "I'll give you a prescription that should settle these symptoms down. Come back to see me in a week and let me see how you are." He wrote the prescription and handed it to Callie.

"Doctor Wilson, how long can I live with Parkinson's?"

"Oh, I have patients with Parkinson's I've treated for twenty years." Arthur detected that the doctor tried to sound upbeat for Callie's benefit. "Take this medicine and let's see if you get better. I'll see you in a week. The girl out front will make you an appointment." He left the room.

Callie looked at her hands in her lap holding the prescription paper. "Arthur, what does this mean? Am I going to be crippled?"

"The doctor didn't mention that so, probably not. Let's go." He took Callie's hand and held it until he helped her into the passenger seat. Arthur had someone watching the store so he drove Callie home. She tried the step up into the kitchen, but was unable to do so without Arthur's help.

The medicine Dr. Wilson prescribed didn't help. Things got worse. She started having those jerking muscle spasms all during the day. After a few days, she called the doctor's office and gave a message to the nurse to relay to the doctor.

Later the nurse called the house. "Mrs. Gray, Dr. Wilson said since the medicine he prescribed made your symptoms worse meant that you don't have Parkinson's. He wants you to take two other medicines, which will help your jerking and muscle spasms. He wants you to go to a neurologist who specializes in movement disorders. He knows doctors at Emory and at Birmingham. We'll make you an appointment as soon as we can. I'll let you know."

"Oh. Thank you." Callie couldn't make more words leave her mouth.

When Arthur returned from work Callie still sat by the telephone, her expression blank. "Callie, honey, what are just sittin' there for?"

She pushed a piece of paper toward him where she'd made notes about her conversation with the nurse, and her second call with the appointment.

'So, they're sendin' you to a specialist, is that right? That's great. Birmingham?"

Callie nodded. "Yes, Birmingham. In two weeks."

"I'm glad Dr. Wilson sends his patients on to specialists when he can't help them improve." He didn't smell any food cooking. Callie had probably been sitting by the telephone all day. "Hey let's go get some supper. Are you hungry for a full meal or a hamburger?"

"I'm not really hungry. Could you go pick up something and bring it home for later?"

"I'll do that right now. Where's Jennifer?"

"She's in her room studying."

"Call her if you need anything before I get back, will you?"

"I will."

While Arthur was away, Callie moved to the kitchen table and sat. What was wrong with her? How sick was she really? She straightened her back, moving out of her slumping position. No need to worry about something you don't even know about. *God, I trust you to help the doctor find what's wrong with me. I'm giving my worrying to you. Please take care of us all. Amen.*

Arthur brought their hamburgers home and smiled when he saw Callie sitting at the kitchen table. She determined not to make her health condition a burden to her family. Callie called to Jennifer to join them. After Arthur gave thanks for the food, they enjoyed their meal. Callie tried not to think about her doctor's appointment in Birmingham. The two weeks would fly by. If she could only find peace with Art's separation from the family as easily.

~ ~ ~

When the telephone rang and Jim answered it, he was happy to hear Bones's voice. "How's everybody been doing while I was away? Probably nobody missed me, did they?"

"Uh, everything's goin' fine. Did y'all have a good trip?"

"Yeah, we went to Savannah and Tybee Island. You should see that old lighthouse there. Really interesting. Bones, you sound a little too quiet. You sure everybody's okay?"

"Well, I guess you know me like a book."

"Of course I do, Bones. What's wrong?"

"It's Callie." He explained about seeing Dr. Wilson in Newton and about them scheduled to go to Birmingham later this week.

"Bones, that's tough. How's Callie handling it all?"

"She's puttin' on a good front. I can tell she doesn't want to burden me. But, Jim, she's hurtin'. Her body's hurtin'."

"Wish I could do something to help, Bones. Sounds like something we'll just have to let God take care of."

"That's for sure. Well, I'm glad y'all got back okay and had a good trip. I'll let you know what we find out in Birmingham. Bye."

"Yeah, you be sure to do that. I'll be praying for you both. Bye."

Jim went back to the sofa and sat beside Caroline. "Who was that on the telephone? Didn't sound too good."

"Bones. Sounds like Callie's pretty sick." Jim explained what had happened and about their Birmingham visit coming up this week. "We take our good health for granted much of the time. Callie's hardly ever been sick. Whatever this is it sure has hit all of a sudden." He took Caroline's hand in both of his. "I love you."

Emmajean came into the living room. "Hey, you two lovebirds. You know you have a bedroom upstairs."

"We're just discussing Callie's illness. Did you hear about it while we were gone?" She shook her head. Jim went through the explanation for Emmajean's benefit.

"I finally got all of our things unloaded from the car and put upstairs. How'd you get along while we were gone? Did you get lonely or did that lawyer—what's his name—keep you company?"

"Jim, you crazy thing. Terry—that's his name. Yes he came around some. We took in a movie, went out to eat, and I fixed supper here one night."

"You cooked supper, little sister?"

Emmajean put on an indignant expression. "Yes, I can cook. Well, just about anyone can cook spaghetti and throw a salad together. Terry said he liked it."

Caroline laughed and turned to Emmajean. "I'm not sure I could cook that dinner. Lynn's been helping me learn how to fix some dishes. But now I won't have her to help. Maybe you and I together can keep us from going hungry."

Jim didn't laugh. "Hey, I can't go hungry. I'm a growing boy."

Caroline tossed a pillow at him. "No, you're not."

Emmajean jumped in the conversation. "Hey, y'all, I've been think . . . thinking while y'all went on your trip. You two need your privacy and I think it's time I got myself an apartment and moved out of your way."

"No, Emmajean, stay." Caroline looked at Jim to help her.

Jim had wondered how Caroline would react having Emmajean live with them. He thought sure that Caroline would want her to move and here she'd urged Emmajean to stay. "Little sister, that's what you get when you think too much. There is no earthly reason for you to move out of this house. Look how big it is, how many rooms. There's plenty of room for us and you to have privacy. Forget that idea."

"Jim and Caroline, it's really not the thing to do to have two grown women living in the same house."

Caroline reached for Emmajean's hand. "Who said that?"

"That's what I've always heard."

"Emmajean, please stay here. I've never had a sister and I think of you as my sister. If *two grown women* in this house causes a problem, we'll all sit down and talk about it. Promise you won't be planning to leave?"

"Jim? You agree? I don't want to be in the way and cause any trouble for you and Caroline."

"I agree, baby sister. You stay put. We're all adult enough to talk things out if need be. And let me say here that you don't have to ask our permission to bring Terry or any other boyfriend you want to this house. Now if you bring in some unknown straggler off the streets, we'd have to have a talk." Emmajean threw a pillow at him herself then.

Caroline pelted him with another pillow. "It's two of us against one of you. You'd better behave yourself."

He'd wondered whether Caroline would be content to have Emmajean living here. She seemed to be so today and he hoped that's the way things would remain.

~ ~ ~

Arthur and Callie left early for Birmingham. They'd told Jennifer she was to go to Jim's after school and stay with Emmajean till they returned.

At the appointment with Dr. Markum in Birmingham, Arthur and Callie agreed that she would be the one to converse with the doctor. Arthur assured her that if she wanted his help, all she had to do was turn to him. After looking at all the film Dr. Wilson had sent from Callie's tests, Dr. Markum spoke to them. "I think you have one of two diseases. My strongest suspicion is you have olivopontocerebellar atrophy."

Callie was taking notes and asked him to please spell that, which he did. "My second suspicion is you might have corticobasaliargenglionic degeneration." He spelled that but Callie was unable to get it on her note paper and she handed it to Arthur to complete. He handed her notebook back to her.

Dr. Markum spoke again. "In your films I see evidence that you've had some seizures in the left frontal area of your brain. Continue to take the two medicines that your doctor has you on. We'll do a panel of blood tests while you're here today. These blood tests will check your blood for possible Vitamin B12 deficiency and possible para neoplastic disorder. That second one means that your immune system might be attacking a hidden cancer and also attacking the brain. This would account for the cerebellum shrinkage." Callie and Arthur told him they didn't know Callie's cerebellum was shrinking.

"Yes your cerebellum has shrunk, which affects your balance, and you have more general brain degeneration than normal for someone your age. I want you to come back to see me in a month. I should have the results of all the blood work then and hopefully pinpoint your diagnosis."

~ ~ ~

Driving home, Callie's whole body trembled. "Arthur, I don't know whether to be hopeful or not. What do you think?"

"Callie, I think whatever this is, it's out of our hands. I pray the Lord stands watch over the doctor and us as we go home to wait another month."

"The doctor was young, but seemed very sharp in his field. I like him."

"I agree, Callie. I like him too."

When they returned home that evening they had received a letter from Gateway House. Arthur read it out loud to Callie and Jennifer. "You are invited to attend Family Day with us on Saturday from two o'clock to four o'clock. Any siblings are welcome. During your visit we ask that you refrain from any conversation that has caused you and your son any disagreements or outbursts while he was living with you. We look forward to seeing you on Saturday." Arthur laid the letter aside and smiled at Callie. "Are you up to the trip? We'll have to leave real early and it will probably be dark before we get back."

"Oh, yes, I will be up for the trip this coming Saturday."

"What about you, Jennifer?" Arthur said.

"Yes, I'd like to go with you if you don't mind."

Callie looked at her precious daughter. "Of course we don't mind."

~ ~ ~

At supper on Thursday, Jim talked with Caroline and Emmajean. "Who cooked supper? It sure is good."

Caroline laid a hand on Jim's arm. "Until further notice the cook around here will remain anonymous so just don't ask."

Jim held his hands in front of himself, palms forward. "Okay, okay, I won't ask anymore. When I compliment the meals, just both of you can say thank you."

"Jimmy, how was your day?"

"You know Callie had her appointment today in Birmingham. Bones called at work today and gave me an update. They saw a neurologist who did a good amount of testing. The doctor finally told them he suspected she had one of two things wrong with her. I can't even spell the diseases much less tell you what they are. They go back in a month to get the results of the tests, and find out the doctor's diagnosis. That was a difficult trip for both of them."

"Oh, I hope this doctor can set their mind as ease. At least knowing what's going on is better than wondering."

"Yeah, Emmajean." Jim told them about the upcoming visit to see Art and that even Jennifer plans to go also. "They're anxious to see him but that will be a hard trip also. Bones said he feels like they're living under a cloud."

~ ~ ~

Arthur noticed that the facility and grounds of Gateway House were well kept and clean. They were told to wait in the front room where two sofas and some chairs sat. After a few minutes, Art entered the room and walked directly to them. Jennifer jumped up and hugged his neck. Art patted her back. Arthur stood and offered Art his hand, which Art took. One more to greet—his mother. Callie stood and wrapped her arms around him. He returned her hug without much enthusiasm.

Stilted conversation followed with Art giving one-word answers to their questions. Other visitors in the room could hear their conversation, so Arthur suggested they go outside. They went to their car. All four of them leaned against it, and tried to continue their conversation. "Are they treatin' you okay, son?"

"Yeah, Dad, they are." He turned toward Callie, patted his waistline, and told her they fed him well. "We're not allowed to eat anything between meals so I put it away when I can."

"We might try that at home sometime." Callie smiled to hold back her tears.

After a while a young lady approached them and identified herself as Amy, Art's counselor while he'd be here. "You have a fine son. He's agreeable, most of the time." She shot a smile toward Art as if they were in cahoots about something. "It's about time for our guests to leave now. Say your good-byes and, Art, when your family leaves, come on back inside, please."

"Yes, ma'am." Jennifer's eyebrows rose.

Art looked at his sister. "What?"

"Yes, ma'am? You and your counselor must get along great. That's cool."

"I guess." Art scuffed at the sidewalk with the toe of his tennis shoe."

"Okay son, stay well and keep out of trouble. We'll be back for the next Family Day."

"Thanks for coming, Dad, Mother, and Jennifer." He hugged his sister and then his mother.

Art turned and went inside the building.

~ ~ ~

Darkness enveloped them before they arrived home. It had been a quiet ride. Little conversation had passed among them the entire trip.

After Callie and Arthur turned in for the night, Arthur spoke to Callie. "How did you make the trip today? You didn't mention any problems."

"I made the trip fine, not too many twitches. And I don't think the children even noticed those. It was good to see Art. I do believe I detected some calmness about him I haven't seen in some time. Did you notice it?"

"I did. And he was polite to his sister. That's an improvement."

"So, it was a good day." Arthur put his arm around her and pulled her nearer. She laid her head on Arthur's shoulder. "I pray tomorrow is another good day."

~ ~ ~

The month crept by while they waited for their next trip to Birmingham. Callie had stayed calm during the wait. Arthur wished he could say the same about himself. They arranged for Jennifer to stay after school at Jim's with Emmajean as before, knowing they would be gone for the day.

The young doctor greeted them and sat close to Callie. "Well, I know what you have. You have ataxia, which is degeneration of the brain, primarily in the cerebellum. Your blood work didn't show any other possible cause for your symptoms.

Olivopontocerebellar atrophy—sometimes referred to as OPCA—is the name for what you have. OPCA is a distant cousin to

Parkinson's. It is rare, progressive, and it is serious. We don't know the cause and we have no cure. We can only treat your symptoms.

"You will become disabled in two to five years or up to ten years according to how fast the progression is. For a while you can get around with a cane, then you will need a buggy—a motorized cart. You will eventually become chair-bound and then bed-bound."

Callie had a list of questions and she unfolded her piece of paper. "Why is my brain shrinking?"

"We don't know."

"Are two things going on—the cerebellum shrinkage from OPCA and also seizures in the left temporal area that you told us about earlier? Are the seizures causing my jerking?"

"Probably."

"Is there medicine for the OPCA?"

"No."

"Is the medicine I'm taking only for the jerking? If so, will I take them forever?"

"Yes."

"What is the progression of this disease?"

"If the progression is quick you have two to five years till the end. If the progression is slow you may have up to ten years."

"What developments should I expect along the way?"

"Clumsiness in walking, gait."

"When I'm totally disabled will I become more susceptible to something that I can't fight off that will kill me?"

"Stay active. We'll try to fight off bed sores, pneumonia."

"Did something I did or didn't do cause this?"

"No."

"Is it hereditary? Can I pass this on to my children and grandchildren?"

"No."

"Will I have good days and bad days?"

"Maybe. Emotional and physical fatigue will cause bad periods."

"Is it safe for me to drive?"

"No."

"My stamina is low and fatigue high on occasions—is this caused by OPCA?

"Maybe."

Arthur spoke up. "Doctor, will she keep her mind?"

"Probably."

Callie and Arthur left the appointment, and had lunch in the building without words. What could they say?

On their drive home when they'd barely left Birmingham Callie spoke. "Arthur, will you stay with me?"

"Of course I'll stay with you. What kind of question is that? You're my wife. Yes, I'll stay with you and help you with everything we may be facing."

"What *I'm* facing."

"No, Callie, what we're both facing. Remember—through sickness and in health. This is one of those times and I'll be with you."

Chapter 25

Jim had told Emmajean and Caroline what Arthur relayed to him about Callie's appointment with the doctor in Birmingham.

"Poor Callie. She's never said a bad word about anybody. Why did this happen to her?"

"Emmajean, don't question things like this. God knows what He's doing. He'll bring something good from this. The Bible says so."

"Jimmy, what did Arthur say about Callie's state of mind?"

"Caroline, he said she was coming around. She was a wreck coming back from Birmingham Thursday. But Bones said she seems to have a good outlook about it all."

When the doorbell rang, Emmajean hurried to the door. "Terry! Come on in. We're just sitti . . . sitting around, talking. Join us."

"Hey Caroline, Jim. I don't want to interrupt anything."

Caroline smiled at Terry. "Not at all, Terry. Sit with us if y'all have time."

"Whatever Emmajean wants to do. We're going out for supper." Terry looked at Emmajean. "Are you hungry? Want to go now?"

"Yeah, let's go now, and leave these newlyweds alone."

After they left Caroline spoke. "They are a cute couple. And a couple they're becoming. It's beginning to look a little more permanent every time I see them together."

"You think so? Has Emmajean shared anything with you I need to know about?"

"Not really but I'm sure she cares for him."

Jim moved across the sofa to be nearer to Caroline. He took her in his arms, and hugged her for long time. When they relaxed against the back of the sofa, Jim let out a sigh.

"Jimmy, was that a good sigh or a bad sigh?"

"A good sigh. Since Christmas . . . James and Lynn are doing fine in all ways, we got Emmajean through her trouble and trial in Atlanta, and brought her back to Newton. She's taking care of herself, thanks to you, and she has a boyfriend. Art's in a good place to get the help he needs. Callie's not in good shape but she's holding onto God's peace, and look at us. Here we are, we're an Us. No more I, I, I, but always Us. Eight months ago we didn't even know where each other lived, and look how we've turned out."

"Yes, Jimmy, I finally have my happily ever after with you."

Jim leaned over and kissed her. "I want to share that happily ever after with you for the rest of my life." Caroline returned his kiss as they snuggled down into the corner of the sofa.

Books by Jo Huddleston

Nonfiction

Amen and Good Morning, God: A Book of Morning Prayers
Amen and Good Night, God: A Book of Evening Prayers
His Awesome Majesty: Praising God's Greatness

Fiction

THE CANEY CREEK SERIES
That Summer
Beyond the Past

Other Books from Sword of the Spirit Publishing

2008
All the Voices of the Wind by Donald James Parker
The Bulldog Compact by Donald James Parker
Reforming the Potter's Clay by Donald James Parker
All the Stillness of the Wind by Donald James Parker
All the Fury of the Wind by Donald James Parker
More Than Dust in the Wind by Donald James Parker
Angels of Interstate 29 by Donald James Parker

2009
Love Waits by Donald James Parker
Homeless Like Me by Donald James Parker

2010
Against the Twilight by Donald James Parker
Finding My Heavenly Father by Jeff Reuter
Never Without Hope by Michelle Sutton
Reaching the Next Generation of Kids for Christ by Robert C. Heath

2011
Silver Wind by Donald James Parker
He's So In Love With You by Robert C. Heath
Their Separate Ways by Michelle Sutton
Silver Wind Pow-wow by Donald James Parker
The 21st Century Delusion by Daniel Narvaez
Hush, Little Baby by Deborah M. Piccurelli

2012
Retroshock by David W. Murray
Destiny of Angels by Eric Myers
It's Not About Her by Michelle Sutton
The Legacy of Deer Run by Elaine Marie Cooper
Decision to Love by Michelle Sutton
The American Manifesto by Steven Flanders
It's Not About Me by Michelle Sutton
It's Not About Him by Michelle Sutton
Will the Real Christianity Please Stand Up by Donald Parker
Amazing Love by K. Dawn Byrd
That Summer by Jo Huddleston
The Unexpected Bar Mitzvah by Donald James Parker